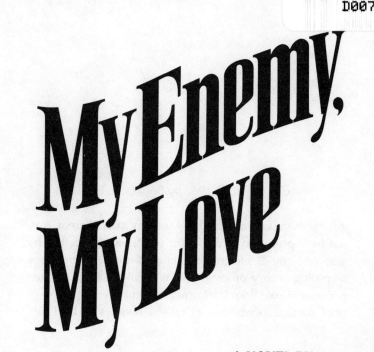

My Enemy, My Love

A NOVEL BY

Susan Evans McCloud

Bookcraft
Salt Lake City, Utah

Library of Congress Catalog Card Number: 80-53391
ISBN 0-88494-414-X

2nd Printing, 1981

Lithographed in the United States of America
PUBLISHERS PRESS
Salt Lake City, Utah

To Sarah Briggs
—And to my own little Sarah,
Morag

Acknowledgments

Special thanks to Daniel Briggs, arms consultant, and to Dr. Jack Johnson, medical consultant.

The Hope of Love

1

"Aim low," the voice in the darkness shouted. "The more we kill, the better. It'll save us runnin' 'em out of someplace else."

The voice belonged to the man on the big black horse that moved with lightning sureness among the men; a swift, dark shadow that towered above the rest.

"Hell, yes," an eager voice growled in reply. "You can never convince a Mormon he's beaten. Not till you put a bullet between his eyes."

The hunters scattered and spread along the fence line, the tall stallion moving from place to place, his rider shouting encouragement to the others.

The shadows inside the fence line crouched and stumbled, avoiding the mounted riders with their guns. The men inside the fence were so many vermin — worthless as far as the gunmen were concerned. Harassing them, picking them off like this one by one, was sport to those who had left their farms and families and joined the Missouri Militia for just this cause. Some of the shots went true, and a crouching figure would fall now and then and lie still in the stubbled fields.

One of the men that Sarah saw fall was her father. She cried out at the sight, but resisted the urge to run, foolhardy, into the line of the mobbers' fire. Martin and her brother, Myles, were the first to reach his body and drag him back to safety, but Sarah was the first to bend over him and look into his face. It frightened her to see the pain-drawn features and the still, pale brow. She threw herself against him, relieved to feel the movement of his chest.

"It's only his leg, Sarah, he ought to be all right," her brother said.

She rose and let Myles take him to Doctor Parkins, not knowing then that the doctor couldn't help, that he lay more seriously wounded than her father. Martin took her hand and pulled her with him, and she saw for the first time the rifle he clutched in his other hand.

He crouched behind a hollowed, rotting wood stump, and she crouched with him, watching with amazement as he braced the gun and aimed into the darkness.

"Three shots left," he muttered between clenched teeth. "All for him."

Martin leveled the rifle and fired. The black horse whinnied and shied as the bullet sang past his head. Luke Morgan, astride the horse, cursed under his breath. He liked it better when the Mormons didn't fight back. It was probably some fool kid taking shots at him! Most of the men knew better than that by now. Martin's next shot chewed up the dust at the horse's feet; Luke bent low over the saddle and the black horse dissolved into shadow.

Martin threw the gun down in disgust at his feet.

"All for a few head of cattle and an acre of corn." His voice sounded bitter, and his eyes were burning with rage.

Sarah shuddered. DeWitt had been ringed with mob forces for weeks now, and violence was breaking out more often than before. The Mormon citizens were safe enough if they stayed to their houses. If they attempted to round up their stock or harvest their fields, the mobbers' bullets were always there to stop them.

Martin took Sarah's arm and guided her back toward the small cluster of buildings. "It won't be long now," he said, "and the mobbers 'll have it all."

She knew what he spoke was true. Most of the families had already packed the meager things that could fit into carts and wagons. What was left — what the mobbers hadn't already destroyed — would simply be left behind.

"How long will it take us to walk to Far West?" she asked the young man who moved broodily beside her.

"Long enough, with Morgan and Ashley at our backs."

"But what real place is there for us in Far West?" Sarah pressed him. "And how long will it be before the mobbers come again? *Then* who will take us in? *Then* where will we go?"

Martin paused and looked carefully at the girl beside him. Her blue eyes were wide with a pain he hated to see. Her wheat-gold hair was tangled and uncombed, and a smudge of dirt streaked along her high-boned cheek. She had never looked more appealing to him before.

"It doesn't matter, Sarah," he said, his voice growing gentle. "We have each other and—"

"It does matter!" she insisted. "I don't want to keep running. I want a home."

He sighed, knowing how little assurance he had to offer. She turned from him and walked on a few steps alone. *We're hated and hunted,* she thought, *with nowhere to belong, and no right to plan and hope —and dream.*

The bullet whined past her cheek and tore into the fence post, leaving a high, shrill ringing in her head. Martin was beside her in a moment, urging her across the few last, open yards before they would reach the protection of barns and houses. Sarah struggled and turned from him as she ran, twisting to look back across her shoulder at the looming statue of a horse and man, standing black against the night, watching them.

She turned and fled then, matching her stride to Martin's, though her breath came in deep gulps that hurt her throat. She could outrace the still man on the horse, but not her fears. They fled with her, swifter than her feet. And the thought came, cruel and unbidden to her mind: *What do other girls who are sixteen dream about?* Perhaps for them there was romance and laughter and love. Sarah's dreams were filled with the terror of burning houses, the lewd and evil faces of angry men, and the image of a tall and ruthless rider, sitting a horse as black and as cold as night. Would her dreams ever be free of those terrors again?

2

The late October sunlight filtered pale and wan through the leafless trees, and there was a bitter bite to the air as General Lucas reined in his horse before the small group of men approaching the camp. A great murmur of excitement swept through Lucas's hundreds of men, his guard. Colonel Hinkle approached the general.

"These are the prisoners I agreed to deliver up."

Very simple. Very final. The general's stallion pawed the packed earth, his rider reined his head sharply to the left, and the prisoners were marched into the camp.

Immediately they were surrounded by several hundred savage-looking soldiers who let out a yell that would have curdled the blood of the bravest man alive. Jacob was a raw recruit under General Samuel D. Lucas. He was new and young, and to him the men sounded like wolves and bloodhounds set loose upon their prey. The hairs on his neck stood straight, and an aching fear began to gnaw at his innards. He fought his way through the thick, seething mass of bodies till he could get a look at the prisoners.

They were still a fair distance off, but he could see they weren't cowed or frightened. The soldiers had now begun to rage —mocking and cursing and threatening the men—but the prisoners stood unruffled; proud and straight. An unexpected admiration rose in Jacob's throat for the stark courage they displayed in the midst of that seething, shrieking hell. The hatred thickened the air and soured his nostrils, and turned the faces of the men close to him into grotesque shapes that made him shudder. He pushed his way back to the outside of the crowd, but the screaming of those thousand voices roared through his head, along with the churning thoughts that jostled there.

So this is the Mormon prophet, Joseph Smith! He is totally different from anything I had expected. In fact, things are just about as turned around and confused as a man could find!

It was true Jacob had joined the militia with reluctance, spurred by an uneasy sense of duty and the irritating realization that it was expected of him. His uncle, Luke Morgan, a fiery leader of the troops from Clay County, had been out here in the thick of things for weeks now. Jacob had no first-hand experience, only reports; the scattered tales and rumors he had picked up as he made his solitary way toward this rendezvous at the city of Far West.

This was a new town, Far West, built by the Mormons only two, three years ago. As Jacob approached that morning, he thought the Mormons couldn't have picked a prettier site. Spread across the rolling, grassy prairie, the place seemed cradled and protected by scattered groves of fine oak and walnut, laced with countless streams and cold-water springs. He had stopped his horse and listened to the soothing music of the water, closing his eyes to take in the serenity of the place; and he hadn't known that it was the last moment of peace, of simple contentment, he would have for a long time.

Jacob walked to the far edge of the camp and the ugly voices faded. He sat on a squat white oak stump and looked off into the shadows, trying to ignore the sense of evil that seemed to cling about the place, like a grey, murky mist, foul and distasteful. One thought crept into his consciousness, sharp and uncomfortable: *What am I doing here?* And he fought down the fear and loneliness which rose with the thought, like a bitter bile in his throat.

He remembered as he had left home how his mother put her hands on his shoulders and looked him straight in the eye. She had a way of doing that which could absolutely stop a man cold.

"Jacob," she had said, and her eyes had never looked so deep, so blue before. "This is work that has to be done. I know the Mormons are troublemakers and have to be stopped. But you remember, Jake, they're people — just people like you and me. And I don't want my son doing anything his mother would be ashamed of."

Jacob rose, stiff and chilled, drawn now toward one of the many fires that dotted the camp. He moved close to the yellow blaze, so that the skin on his cold face tingled with the warmth. The men standing near him were only shadows, and he chose to ignore them rather than face them down. A spattering of brittle rain blew against him, and he kicked at the charred edges of the fire where the wind had disturbed them into little whirls and eddies. It was too cold to sleep outside, but how could he go inside

7

one of the tents and sleep, his body warm against the bodies of those men he had heard and seen today?

He took his saddle and blankets and walked back to the white oak stump, his eyes searching to pick out the shape or features of that one man among the many men he passed. Would the prisoners sleep in a tent tonight? Jacob wondered. The rain was coming hard now. He knelt and spread his blankets and tried not to think of the long, dark hours ahead.

Jacob opened his eyes the next morning and saw him. The man couldn't have been five feet away. There was the same height and large frame, the fine-chiseled head and noble carriage — something striking and dignified and pleasant about him that made the men near him seem common and dull in comparison. He turned now and moved away with the rest, and Jacob rose quickly, remembering that this was no ordinary day, that no ordinary things would be happening.

A small group of soldiers were approaching and Jacob called out to them.

"Where are they taking him?" he asked, nodding in the direction of the men who were walking away.

"Takin' who, boy?" asked a lean, grisly man with a white scar that zigzagged across his cheek and ran into the corner of a thin, hard mouth where it puckered the skin into a sardonic grin, revealing broken, blackened teeth and wide gaps where some teeth were missing.

"Joseph Smith and the others," Jacob answered. The man looked in the direction of Jacob's gaze, then spat and chuckled and rubbed the grey stubble on his chin before replying.

"That ain't Joe Smith, boy, that's his brother, Hyrum. Jest brought him in this morning. Him and that Lyman fella. Yep, we're roundin' up all the ring-leaders. They're ours now." He grinned, and the twisted mouth moved and twitched grotesquely.

"Then where's Joseph Smith?" Jacob pressed.

"Hell, boy, if you'd get yer britches on you could come with us and see for yourself."

Jacob went. He followed the men to the center of camp and stood around the fires, trying to eat the hot breakfast they handed him. But something was churning in his stomach and the thought of food repulsed him. He sipped the steaming coffee and watched, and waited.

The morning wore away and the men grew restive. Some drifted off in small groups, organizing half-hearted games and target shoots. But their hearts weren't in it. They were keyed up for something far different, and they would not long be held at bay.

Jacob listened to their talk, their boasting banter, and learned more than he wanted to know. The details of the massacre at Haun's Mill two days before were facts Jacob had been largely ignorant of. He listened now as Comstock and some of his men recounted in lurid detail their deeds of torture and rape, taking courage from one another and seeming to delight in the suffering and destruction they had caused. Jacob soon turned away in disgust, wondering what kind of force, what spirit could make mobs out of ordinary troops, wondering what part his own Uncle Luke had played in those nightmarish events.

That Luke had been involved in such exploits Jacob had little doubt. He had seen the look in his uncle's face when he rode off to fight the Mormons; the restless excitement, the unnatural gleam of eagerness in his eyes. Jacob hadn't found Luke among the troops yet, and he was glad of it. He sensed that a confrontation now could be extremely uncomfortable, even dangerous. What would he do if Luke pressed him into activities in which he had no desire to take part?

General Lucas came out now and began speaking to the men, but Jacob was too far away to hear what he was saying. There was an immediate tension in the air, men jostling one another to get closer to the general. Suddenly a loud shout went up from the group near the front, spreading like wildfire through the masses until hundreds and hundreds of voices had picked up the cry. Men jumped up and down in their eagerness, clapping one another on the back, loading their pistols, checking their powder horns, whistling and laughing; reminding Jacob of a swarm of schoolboys granted an unexpected holiday after a long, boring morning in school. But their eyes, when he looked into their faces, were glazed with that same frenzied desire, cold and intense, he had seen in his uncle's eyes.

"What's going on? Where are we heading?" Jacob asked the man next to him. He was being carried along now with the press of the eager crowd. The man didn't seem to hear, and Jacob grabbed his arm and shook him, demanding a reply. He finally looked up and grinned good-naturedly.

"Boy, didn't ya hear the general? We're under orders to search the city for hidden arms."

"Hidden arms? But what about the militia? What are they going to be doing, sitting on their hands watching us?"

The men near him laughed, amused by Jacob's ignorance.

"Jest where've you been, son?" one of them inquired. "Colonel Hinkle marched the militia out of Far West and disarmed them. They won't be causin' any more trouble now."

"Hinkle—isn't he the man who brought in Joseph Smith and the others yesterday?"

"That's right, that's right! Yer startin' to catch on."

Someone thumped Jacob on the back and the men laughed. One of them drew up close to Jacob, his unshaven cheeks bristling with black hairs, his breath sour with last night's whiskey.

"Boy, you're in for more fun than you ever dreamed of b'fore. Stick close to old Sy, kid. Sy knows the ropes, yes, sir. I'll make sure ya have a good time."

Jacob saddled his horse and prepared his weapons. This wasn't an order he relished, but he was beginning to see why it had been given. He mounted and, keeping as clear of the man called "Sy" as he could, rode with the rest of the troops into Far West.

Jacob hadn't known what to expect when he rode off to fight the Mormons. But in all his imaginings he had never begun to envision this kind of madness. This wasn't rousting out the rebels and restoring the peace, nor the orderly searching for weapons and hidden arms. This was out-and-out thievery, thoughtless destruction—and worse.

It seemed the men around him had gone mad. On every side he could see them, driving helpless women and children from their

10

homes, then dragging out and carrying away any property of value they could find. There was wholesale destruction everywhere: cattle shot down for the sport of it, haystacks fired, floors and roofs torn to splinters; everywhere he looked some scene of terror rose before his eyes. The men were free to do as they liked, with no restrictions, no restraints. And all in the name of law, in the name of order and peace.

As he watched, Jacob saw three brawny men drag a young girl out of a house and across the yard, and her screams sent shudders along his spine. He drove his horse through the hordes before him, then finally tethered the beast and worked his way more quickly on foot. But when he reached the spot, the men and the girl had disappeared and it was impossible for him to trace where they had taken her.

It seemed a huge, roaring nightmare, and everything within Jacob recoiled. Three of the mob had tied a man to a post outside his house and were whipping him unmercifully. Jacob, sick with the pent-up anger and horror inside him, turned and somehow found his horse, and began to work his way out of the thick of the city.

A sound, small and incongruous, caught his attention, and he looked down to see a child standing near the street; a boy six, maybe seven years old, and he had been crying. When he saw Jacob on the tall horse the child bolted and would have run, but Jacob reached down and caught him by the belt and lifted him up beside him on the horse. The boy was trembling and the tears were smudged and streaked on his cheeks, but he faced Jacob bravely enough.

"What are you doing out here all alone?" Jacob asked, working to make his voice sound gentle and kind.

The boy hesitated.

"I'm not going to hurt you, lad," Jacob added softly, ruffling the boy's thick hair in a friendly manner.

"I was playin' with Tom Schaeffer," the boy began, and his voice was a rasping whisper. "Then suddenly there were men everywhere, and guns and fire, and we hid in the barn, but then the barn began to burn, and Tom ran home, only I can't remember how to find the way . . ." The voice had fallen to little more than a whimper, and the boy rubbed his eyes angrily with a dirty fist.

"Then we'll ride around until you do," Jacob offered, careful to sound calm and unconcerned himself. "Sit tall now and look about, lad—see if you can recognize some landmark you remember."

The boy obeyed, sitting straight in the saddle in front of Jacob, leaning forward in an eager manner, though he trembled still and his thin legs gripping the broad back of the horse twitched nervously now and then. They rode for what seemed like a long time, crisscrossing the streets; some choked with noise and people, others deserted and deathly still, where fear was their only companion. Then suddenly the boy jerked and pointed.

"That tree on the left," he said. "That's the one! Turn there and we're almost home."

He twisted in the saddle and grinned at Jacob, his features flooded with relief and joy.

"I know the way now, I know the way!"

Home, when they reached it, was one of two dozen or so poor, makeshift cabins. They were no larger, Jacob figured, than twelve to fifteen feet square. Some he could see had no chimneys, and the one that opened at their approach had only a dirt floor. An old man stepped out, shaded his eyes, and squinted up at the riders, though the sun was pale and distant in the autumn sky, with little warmth in it.

"It's about time you showed up, Heber." He spoke to the boy, and his voice was deep and mellow. "Your mother's beside herself with worry. Go to her quickly, boy—quick now," and he pulled the youngster down, giving him a gentle shove to start him on his way.

Heber was moving before his feet touched the ground, but he turned and sought Jacob's gaze and smiled a bright, grateful smile. Jacob nodded in acknowledgment and lifted his hand in a brief farewell. The old man rested his arm lightly on the pommel of Jacob's saddle and looked up at him, his patient old eyes studying Jacob carefully before he spoke.

"I thank you for saving the boy," he said simply. "I don't know what his mother'd have done without him. She's already lost his older brother, and her husband as well."

"Lost them?" Jacob repeated, stupidly.

"To the mobs," the man replied, as though stating a simple fact to an uneducated child.

Jacob didn't answer. There was nothing he could think to say that would sound right after such a statement. After a little while the man went on, as though he hadn't even noticed the awkward silence.

"We come from DeWitt, back in Carroll County. Only been here two weeks, a little more." A smile, sad and slow, crept over his features, and he shook his head slightly. "That's why the boy didn't know his way. DeWitt was a fine town. Heber's daddy owned one of the fairest farms there, and part interest in the grist mill, too."

"What happened?" Jacob asked, and his voice was so low that he wondered if the old man had heard him. But it didn't matter, for he went right on talking anyway.

"Same old story," the man replied, with his gentle smile. "The mob demanded we leave our lands by the first of October. When we didn't they beseiged the town—shot the place up a little, killed our stock, blockaded us in."

He paused, and stroked the horse's neck absently.

"The long and short of it is, son, that we left in the end— walked fifty miles across the prairie, our homes burning behind us, and little more than the clothes we wore to show for our time and trouble there."

He paused again, as though tired suddenly of his own tale. "Ah, well," he added, "we had it better than most and shouldn't be complaining."

But his eyes, belying his words, grew deep and warm, and his voice took on a harder note.

"Though Austin, Ashley, Morgan and their boys—they're mean as the devil and twice as heartless. They did their work well, son. Yes, they did their work well."

His voice seemed to fade, and his hand slipped off the horse's neck and hung limp at his side, and Jacob wondered exactly what it was he had lost to Austin, Ashley, Morgan and the boys.

"Morgan?" he said, his voice a question. "Luke Morgan?"

"The same," the old man answered. "As godless a creature as ever I've come across, and I've seen a mighty lot in my time, son."

A figure stepped into the doorway of the cabin, a woman, and she called out something to the man. But Jacob didn't hear. He was still hearing the old man's words, feeling the strange, new sense of shame they drew from him.

What if he spoke out now, spoke to the man calmly and said, *That's my uncle you're talking about, old man. He dawdled me on his knee as a kid—taught me to fish and whittle and ride—joked and sang songs and made my mother laugh. That's my uncle who burned your houses and killed your men and abused your women—that's my uncle.*

"I'd best be going in, son," the old man said gently. "And you'd best be gettin' off the streets yourself. Some of them could come along any time, you know. You're not safe out here alone."

Jacob stared at him, amazed and unbelieving, and he spoke without being able to help himself.

"But you don't understand, I'm one of them—I'm one of Lucas's men!"

The old man's face turned dark for a moment, and Jacob could see his body go hard and tense. Then he relaxed and his eyes grew kind and tired again, and he patted Jacob's leg, outstretched in the high stirrup.

"You're not one of them, son. You're not one of them."

Then he turned and walked toward the cabin, and he didn't look back, and the woman closed the door behind him. And Jacob was left alone with only himself and the echo of the old man's words.

3

Sarah patted the moist lumps of dough, shaping them into uniform loaves, or trying to. But the fire was nearly ready and she had to hurry, and she wasn't much good at this kind of thing, even under the best of circumstances.

She pushed a lock of hair back from her forehead and paused, looking around her. A twinge of pain caught inside, as it always did when she let herself stop and remember — stop and feel. A tiny cabin with a dirt floor and a make-shift fireplace. Chinks in the walls and a homemade broom propped in the corner. A wooden table and a few chairs. Oil lamps and quilts, odds and ends of dishes and pottery — so little, so little of what had been before!

"You're dreaming again, Sarah." It was her mother at the door, carrying the heavy washtubs and the cakes of lye soap. Her voice was neither kind nor condemning but pleasant and practical, stating a fact. "The fire's ready."

"I know, mother." She bent again to her task, attacking the stubborn dough with frustrated vigor.

"What's worth doing is worth doing well," her mother said at her elbow, and she took the dough from Sarah and showed her for the hundredth time how to pull and knead and shape the dough properly.

"Will there be meat for supper today?" Sarah asked.

"Perhaps a little cheese," her mother answered. "And corn and bread in plenty. Enough's as good as a feast."

And with that she dismissed the matter, leaving Sarah with her bread dough, going back outside to her laundry. But Sarah was churning inwardly and fighting the burning tears which seemed to come to her eyes so quickly, so unwanted, during these past few weeks.

She finished her work in silence, not conscious of any difference, any lack. Before this time she had always sung at her work or, with a book propped before her, learned verses to recite to her father in the evenings — such a certain way to win his approval, his coveted pride. But now nothing was the same.

Myles burst in the narrow door, seeming to fill the little room with his sparkle and energy. He snatched a scrap of dough and popped it into his mouth.

"Sarah's at the baking today. That's sure to mean burnt bread for supper."

His eyes were teasing and he ducked as Sarah swung at him with the heavy rolling pin. She couldn't help laughing at the faces he made from across the room.

"Well?" she demanded, anxious to know if he carried any news.

"Well, what?" he countered, and she felt he was stalling, not teasing this time.

"It's very dull and quiet out there," he told her. "Nothing much going on."

"No mobbers lurking around the corners?"

"Why should there be? They got what they came for, didn't they? Brother Joseph and the others. No one's much interested in the small stuff left behind. Besides, what have we got for the mobbers to take—here, in these miserable huts? There were others in the city, I'm sure, with more for them to take."

Sarah fingered her faded calico, worn thin in places, and smiled a sad smile.

"I'm sure you're right. They took everything we had in DeWitt. But that didn't keep me from hiding like a scared rabbit the whole time they were here."

He smiled back at her tenderly.

"You're like the princess hidden in the woodcutter's cottage, Sarah; poverty protecting your virtue. They'll never hurt you here."

"I miss him, Myles," she said suddenly. "It's different, somehow, without the Prophet. Do you think he'll be all right?"

Myles shrugged. What could he answer? It was three days now since Lucas and General Wilson had marched Joseph Smith and the other brethren out of Far West. They were headed for Independence, and heaven only knew what would happen to them there. In a mock court-martial their enemies had sentenced them to be shot—right here at the public square in Far West. But General Doniphan and others had protested against what he called "cold-blooded murder," and so the Prophet had been spared—this time.

"At least the worst hasn't happened yet," she said softly. "Not really."

"Yes," Myles agreed reluctantly, "we're all safe and alive, though I hate to see how father drags that lame leg of his around, as if he has to apologize for it or something."

"You know how he feels, how hard it is for him, Myles. He can't stand not carrying his share of the load, not feeling like a whole man."

"I know, but it's made him pull back into himself and wither up, like the leg. He doesn't seem angry or bitter; he just isn't really there anymore."

Sarah thought fleetingly of that first day of trouble in DeWitt when her father, her gentle, sensitive father, had been wounded by a mobber's bullet. The bullet had gone deep and festered, and the only doctor who could remove it lay sick with a head wound and fever himself.

"I think mother's the same way," Myles was continuing, "so capable and practical, but more remote than ever, keeping her sorrows and sufferings to herself."

"She must take refuge in work," Sarah replied, sighing. "I wish I could." She wiped the flour from her hands along her already dusty apron and walked over to where Myles stood. She took his hand lightly in hers and smiled up at him.

"But then I have you," she said, her voice warm. And . . ." she hesitated slightly, "and Martin."

She felt his muscles tense, and his eyes, which were smiling down at her, darkened.

"Myles," she said uncertainly. "Myles, what is it?"

"Sarah, that's what I came to tell you. I've been to see Brother Eastman. Tomorrow a group of men is leaving to go back to Ray and Carroll counties. They're needed, you know, to help the feeble and poor, the widows—all those who weren't ready to leave before, who need help, who . . ." His voice trailed off and Sarah interrupted him impatiently.

"Yes," she said, "I know. But that couldn't concern you. That couldn't possibly concern you."

He shifted his eyes and looked away from her. "They're desperately short of men, Sarah," he said quietly. "There aren't enough who can leave their own families and go back. They want . . . well, they've asked me and Martin to go back with the group."

The cabin was suddenly stifling, in spite of the cold drafts that played along the floor and numbed Sarah's feet even through the thick woolen stockings she wore. Suddenly she felt as though she couldn't breathe, and she pushed open the creaking door and ran out into the brisk air, which still carried the smell of gunpowder and blackened wood. Myles followed, and when he touched her arm she turned on him, hurt and trembling.

"I suppose they think we can spare you? Father has a useless leg, but he's alive, isn't he? We have seven people to feed, but mother is strong and capable, and there's food to go around. Very little, but there is food."

"Sarah, please!" Myles entreated, but she only took a deep breath and plunged on.

"We have clothes and blankets and a wagon; everything a family could possibly need. I suppose they consider you surplus! And what difference does it make if they take our surplus from us?"

Her voice was beginning to shake now, and hot tears were filling her eyes.

"Sarah," Myles tried to explain, "no one's trying to hurt you. It's just that they need us. They need us desperately."

Sarah bolted then and ran, not even seeing where she was going. She couldn't bear listening to Myles and his logical explanations! She wondered suddenly what Emily would think. Emily had been her best friend since she could remember, and had loved her brother Myles ever since she was a child. Emily wouldn't be docile and understanding, Sarah knew.

Tomorrow the boys would leave her, both at once, and she would be alone. Her mother didn't count and her father had deserted her; and now they were taking Martin. No one seemed to know, or care, that she couldn't exist without him. Tomorrow she must say good-bye. How was she going to do it?

As it was their good-bye came sooner and with a sweetness Sarah had not anticipated. It was well into the evening, with the children settled, her parents already in bed. Sarah hated the nights here; the crowded, undignified lack of privacy. Bone tired as she was, her spirit wasn't settled enough to curl up with her body at the foot of the thin straw mattress, seeking sleep.

Sarah heard a sound outside and hesitated. Then suddenly Myles was there, with the door only ajar to avoid the noisy creaks of the warped wood. He put his finger to his lips, and his blue eyes were sparkling, spilling over with fun. How often he was like that! No matter what was happening, his eyes seemed always warm and vital and gay. He grabbed her shawl from the hook by the door, then took her hand and pulled her out beside him into the frosty night.

It was a black night; Sarah couldn't find the moon. The stars, far above, looked hazy and dull. She sought Myles's face but couldn't make out his features in the dark.

"Come with me," he whispered. Then, grasping her small hand tightly in his own, he turned and began running softly down the dirt lane and into the stubbled field, and it was all Sarah could do to keep her balance while following him over the humped and uneven ground. She stumbled and protested once or twice, but he didn't hear, or at least he didn't slow down, and she clung to him, knowing he wouldn't lead her wrong. At last he stopped. She was breathless, but Myles was breathing easily. She could see the dark outline of a barn just to her right. It must be Brother Thompson's barn at the end of the long corn field.

"Myles . . ." But he put his finger over her lips.

"There's someone in the barn wants to see you," he said, and she could hear the delight in his voice, even though it was only a whisper. "Someone wants to say good-bye." He led her to the entrance and pushed back the heavy door.

She entered the dim, dusty barn as the door closed noiselessly behind her. For a moment or two she could make out nothing, then she saw him; only a vague, bulky outline somewhere ahead. She moved and, hearing her, Martin turned, and the candle he had been shielding with his hand cast a wavering circle of light around him.

She ran to him with a cry, burying her head against his shoulder. He held her close and soothed her and stroked her long golden hair, cold now from the night.

"I'm so glad you sent for me, Martin," Sarah whispered, and her voice, even to her own ears, sounded tense with emotion. "I don't think I could have stood it without — without —"

"Without this," he said softly. "I know."

Then suddenly his hands were warm on her face, his lips close to her own, and he kissed her with a tenderness and a passion that engulfed her. She felt herself responding to him, apart from thought or will, so that she wound her arms about his neck and kissed him in return, hungrily, not wanting this strange new ecstasy to end.

When at last, reluctantly, they drew apart, she laid her head lightly against his cheek, feeling not embarrassed or uncertain after this first intimate moment, but calm and ever more certain of his care for her. And yet there was something different between them now; they could never go back to innocent friendship again.

"Are you afraid to go tomorrow, Martin?" she asked, knowing he would answer her truthfully.

"No, Sarah, I'm not. I feel pretty calm inside. I still think the Lord will take care of us."

"Still? After all that has happened?" she asked, hating to reveal her doubt, yet longing to at the same time.

"Yes, my love," he answered, his breath warm against her hair. "Don't look only at the death and destruction, Sarah. Look at the things the Lord has done for His people. He hasn't forsaken us, Sarah, and He never will; not as long as we don't forsake Him."

"I love you, Martin," she cried, respect and compassion and tenderness mingling with the fierce newness of her love. "I shall never love anyone but you as long as I live."

So they stood, together in the still, dark barn, shivering and cold, but not minding it, unaware of time and place; lost in their own feelings, their own joys and fears. And with the loving and the sharing Sarah grew, and found within herself the dignity and faith she needed to say good-bye to Martin and let him go.

4

When Joseph Smith and some of the prisoners had been removed to Liberty, Jacob was no longer part of the detail assigned to guard them. And from that moment forward it seemed the only thought in Jacob's mind was to obtain an honorable release, and go home. He was lonely and cold. He had seen enough, and his services weren't really needed. It was winter, and by now most of the Mormons were homeless and destitute — frightened and sick. Force was no longer needed to make them leave. Jacob thought he knew the feelings of their hearts. He would have left, too, if it took the last strength in his body.

So he rode with his release paper and his pay in his pocket, his horse's head turned toward home. But he knew there was one last thing he must see to first. It wasn't too much out of his way. It would be worth the trouble. The feeling still gnawed at the pit of his stomach, and he knew there was no way out of it, or around it; it simply had to be done.

Liberty, Missouri, was a dirty little town this time of year. Dirty and cheerless. Jacob found the prison easily enough. A small, pitiful building, rough-hewn limestone, yellow and ugly. He stared at the inscription — *Liberty* — carved crudely on the sign. He was loath to go inside and see the cold dirt floors, the thick rough walls, the chains and indignity.

He didn't stay long. He didn't need to. The jailer took the money, and the ham he had dressed, with a solemn oath that they would be placed in the prisoner's hands. Jacob waited and watched just to be sure, not satisfied until he saw the things delivered into the Prophet's hands.

Joseph Smith sat in a corner, his head bent low over some writing. There were a couple of women in the room, conversing softly with the men. Jacob could *feel* it was all right. It was still there, the dignity and power that had drawn him to the man before.

Jacob turned northeast, back in the direction of Far West. Forty-eight miles. The first long lap of his journey. He was anxious now.

The snows were coming, and winter was beginning to take a real hold upon the land. He rode with a steady pace, and his loneliness fell away from him with each mile he covered.

Just outside of Caldwell County he ran into a small, pitiful group of Mormons. They were camped in a narrow cottonwood bottom, where there was some protection from the driving wind. As he approached their camp Jacob could make out some women moving between the wagons, but no men. He slowed and swerved direction, riding his horse directly into the camp. One of the women climbed into the back of a wagon and disappeared. He heard the thin, hungry wail of a child; a dog barked, and then was stilled.

When he drew up beside the wagons only one woman remained outside, bent over a miserable, smoking fire, stirring something in a pot. She rubbed her eyes, smarting from the smoke and soot, and looked up at Jacob. He saw then that she was young, young and very pretty, with clear violet-blue eyes and a graceful, sculptured face reminding Jacob of pictures of the goddesses from the old Greek legends his mother had read to him when he was a boy. Her hair was the delicate color of corn silk in the sunlight: red and gold and soft, pale yellow scattered and twined carelessly together.

She pushed the hair back now from over her forehead and made a small, uneasy sound. Jacob realized that he was staring at her and dropped his eyes. He dismounted and stood beside her, and she moved back, away from him, and bent again to stir the big kettle. He hadn't meant to make things so awkward! He started to speak, giving her his name. Then he paused, concerned that she might know the name of Morgan and be frightened of him.

"I'm just passing through," he said finally, "and thought you might need a little help."

"Does it look like we need help?" she replied, not glancing up. Her voice was low and melodic and soft, like her corn-silk hair.

"Well, I didn't see any men about, and I thought someone might be sick or hurt or . . ."

Jacob's voice trailed away; he was frustrated that the girl could confuse him in this way. She looked up then, a smile beginning to play at the corners of her mouth.

"As a matter of fact," she said quite suddenly, "there is someone sick. Sister Walker just had a baby, and there's some kind of a fever on her she can't shake. Her eighth baby! I told her she picked a miserable time to be having an eighth child!" She took a deep breath, then plunged on. "And there's somebody hurt besides. I burned my hand on this wretched fire, because mother's in the wagon taking care of Sister Walker, and the two men we do have are off hunting, and I've never been any good at this kind of thing."

She paused and shook her head at him with a hopeless little gesture, looking so entirely feminine and helpless that Jacob could barely stand the sight.

"Oh, and to complete your information, sir, we're wet and cold, we don't have enough blankets, and we have five adults, ten children — not counting the one newly-born — and myself to feed on this one miserable pot of stew!"

She took another breath and laughed, a lovely laugh, light and lilting; and he laughed with her.

"I'm sorry," she said, "but you asked, and so I decided to tell you." She looked away and shuffled her feet uncomfortably, and Jacob could tell she had surprised herself by her outburst. Now that it was over she was a little embarrassed, a little shy of him.

"Who are you?" she demanded suddenly. "You're not a Mormon."

"Well, I'm not a mobber, either," he replied, looking at her evenly with his deep brown eyes, almost enjoying the way she fidgeted beneath his gaze. "Just say I'm a Missourian passing through, and willing to help."

He reached for her hand, holding it firmly in his own, carefully examining the ugly burn spread over the white palm.

"Oh, it's all right," she protested, struggling to free her hand. "You don't have to bother —"

But he had already reached into his saddlebag and was drawing something out. Sarah watched, fascinated, as he spread the thick, musty-smelling salve over her skin, then bandaged the hand with a tidiness and skill rivaling even her mother's. She studied him as he bent over his work. His thick brown hair was close enough for her to touch, his broad brow was knit in concentration. She was painfully aware of his touch, of the bigness of him beside her.

He was very large and solid, muscular of build, but he had

easy, graceful movements; as though he was at home with his own size, not awkward as so many big men seemed. His hands were big, too, but they moved with the gentleness of a woman's. Sarah loved the warm feel of them against her own.

"There, that ought to do it," he said, and he turned from her, putting his materials away.

"It feels much better. Thank you," Sarah said. He twisted his head to look at her, smiling.

"Would you like to stay for supper, what there is of it?" she asked, indicating the kettle over the fire.

"I'd like to," he replied. His voice sounded casual and even, not betraying the interest he felt. "But only if you'll let me contribute my part."

He reached behind his saddle and drew out two plump hares that had been dangling out of sight. "Cottontails," he said, grinning like a boy. "They're dressed and skinned, all ready to go. I planned on roasting them for my own supper anyway."

"That's not necessary," Sarah began, but he walked over and lowered the meat into the steaming kettle.

"That makes six adults for dinner, ten children and yourself. What's your name, or shall I just call you Miss in-between?"

"My name is Sarah," she replied, mustering what dignity she could, knowing he was having fun with her.

"Sarah," he smiled. "It fits you. It's a lovely name." Sarah looked away, turning suddenly hot at his gaze.

"Did you know this wagon joist is about to give out?" he asked her, as he bent down beside the wheel.

She wanted to tell him that if Myles and Martin had been here there wouldn't be any repairing wanting done. She wanted to explain that her father hadn't the strength any more, and that he and Brother Walker had their hands full scouting for food and water and mobbers, cutting wood and caring for the stock, and performing the thousand other tasks they were responsible for. But she couldn't bring herself to complain again, so she answered simply.

"We fell back from the others yesterday so Sister Walker could have the baby. We're hoping it holds a few more days till we catch up."

"Well, it won't. But I can fix it before that stew's ready," he said, and without giving her time to answer him yes or no he bent to the task.

When her father and Brother Walker trailed into camp, weary and empty-handed, they found the young stranger working beneath the wagon, Sarah's mother frying up hot oat cakes, and unexpected meat in the soup. They all ate hungrily, but the atmosphere was strained. Sarah knew the men resented the stranger for his strength and skill, for the self-sufficiency he was no more to blame for than they were to blame for their lameness and poverty.

Jacob sensed it, too, knowing how painful it was for them to have a stranger see them reduced to this pitiable state. He excused himself as soon as the meal was over, thanking the girl's mother warmly, quickly tucking what was left of his money into her salt box, out of sight. They said good-bye to him kindly enough, with a dignity that pulled at his heartstrings.

It was cold. Even with the late afternoon sunlight, it was cold. Jacob shivered to think what the night would be like. The girl, Sarah, walked him to his horse. They went in silence, and he was aware of the smooth, graceful movement of her figure beside him.

He turned to say good-bye and she smiled at him — openly, sweetly. And there was a light in her face which reminded him suddenly of the light he had seen in the eyes of her Mormon prophet, Joseph Smith. Courage — was it courage he read in the deep steady gaze with which she met his own? No, it was that something different — something more . . . tantalizing and elusive, which he couldn't define or grasp. A peace, a kind of assurance — in spite of the snow which had begun to fall, in spite of the cold and the want, and the long, uncertain road ahead. He pulled the quilt, deep and fluffy, from his saddlebag and held it out to her.

"It's for you. My mother made it."

Sarah shook her head and pushed it away, tears beginning to gather in her blue eyes.

"She would want you to have it. She'd admire you, and like you, too."

He took her hands gently in his own, wrapping her arms around the softness of the quilt.

"Please take it, Sarah, for me."

She couldn't answer him, but she held tightly to the quilt. He mounted his horse slowly, hating to have to go, hating to leave her standing there.

"Have a safe journey," she told him. "I'll take good care of this," and she buried her face in the blanket so he wouldn't see the tears that would betray her.

He turned and rode away from her, deeply shaken. She watched him go, through the snow that was coming thickly now, wondering why his kindness had touched her so deeply, wondering why he had made her feel so sorry for herself. She stood until his broad back disappeared into the grey storm ahead, trying to decide what it was that had drawn her so powerfully toward the man.

5

The Mississippi, even dull and grey with the winter, was one of the loveliest rivers Sarah had ever seen. They reached the banks scant days before Christmas and decided to rest there before ferrying over to the Illinois side, as many of the Saints were doing. On the other side of the river the citizens of Quincy were proving sympathetic toward the Mormons, opening up their homes and helping them find work. Sarah longed for the sight of a friendly face and wondered if she would ever overcome the fear of strangers, the caution which caused one to listen to strange noises and turn, startled, at the sound of footsteps from behind.

But here they were, with the end in sight — whatever the end might be — and Christmas upon them, and Sarah was determined that, for a day at least, there should be happiness and gaiety — and gifts.

Sarah tucked the Missourian's quilt around her father's knees where he sat reading, and kissed him gently on the cheek. He looked up at her and smiled, but his eyes were weak and his skin was sagging, and the withered leg was hurting him, she knew. If she hated the mobs for anything, it was for that: fields and farms, stock and houses, were of this world, tangible and corruptible, and they could be obtained again, over and over if necessary. But the destruction of the human spirit — that was a different matter!

She walked outside the camp, her shoes crunching through the thin, brittle layer of old snow. It was colder by the river, so moist that the chill seemed to seep deep into her muscle and bone. She had put the older girls, Ann and Louisa, to scouting for wood this afternoon. Any twig or chunk big enough to burn would do, and now there was quite a pile beside the wagon; and the girls, their cheeks rosy with the fresh air and excitement, were much warmer than they would have been huddled near the wagon all day.

Sarah walked off toward the woods, searching for the pretty partridge berries, ground pine, and fir boughs, and other greens to decorate the wagon for the children. She sang as she walked, her breath frosty in the clear air, and she laughed out loud, realizing that she was excited about Christmas herself.

That evening, after supper, they gathered with the other Saints and sang Christmas carols and favorite hymns, their voices lingering in the night air so that the melody seemed to hang suspended and never cease. Brother Johnson, with his deep, mellow voice, read the Christmas story from Luke. Sarah, who had been watching the people about her, was warmed by their cheerfulness, by their kindness to one another. She didn't hear one bitter word, one self-pitying remark, one complaint. Perhaps they were closer to the Savior here than they ever would be again. Humbled and stripped of all pretense, all earthly display, they leaned toward His understanding and opened their hearts for His help. Perhaps that was why Sarah felt peaceful inside, and happy for the first time in months.

The little ones fell asleep easily, exhausted with the fresh air and the long, busy day. Sarah quietly laid out her presents among the greens and boughs on the old chest. She had bound little sprigs of berries with bright pieces of yarn and tied a poem to every bundle, one for each of the three little girls. As an extra treat, tucked in among the berries, was a big, round piece of horehound candy. The verses were silly and simple, but the children would like them. Sarah was most pleased with the candy, such a rarity these days. She had traded Abigail Swenson her treasured lace handkerchief for the coveted pieces. How they would make the children's faces light up in the morning!

She heard someone beside her and turned, surprised to see her mother standing there. She watched her mother neatly lay out four pairs of knitted stockings, which meant that the largest pair would be for Sarah! She could already feel the soft warmth of them against her skin. It seemed her feet hadn't been warm since the cold weather came!

"Mother, however did you do it? Where did you find the yarn —and the time?"

Her mother smiled one of her rare smiles and picked up one of the stockings, holding it close to the candle for Sarah's inspection.

"See here. Bits and snatches. Pieces I had tucked away, some I traded for. Worked up pretty nicely, if I say so myself."

"They're delightful!" Sarah replied with enthusiasm. Her mother, her practical mother, who was capable of anything! Sarah knew she would treasure the patchwork stockings for years to come.

Her own gift for her mother was safely hidden away until tomorrow. She and Emily had baked pies together that morning, in Sister Simpson's little cabin, and the crust was so light and perfect that she knew her mother would be pleased. She meant to please her mother more, but it always seemed so difficult to do. She didn't have her mother's smooth, quick efficiency. She'd never enjoyed cooking and sewing as her mother did. Sarah would far rather read with her father; sit at his knee and talk long hours, plan and imagine and dream.

Her poem for her father she tucked away behind the rest, then she turned to go to bed and he was there, a dark silhouette beside her.

"This is for you, Sarah," he whispered. "I thought you might like to have it now. By yourself."

He bent and kissed her cheek, and his lips felt thin and cold against her skin. She hugged him, fiercely, and thanked him, grateful for the darkness which hid the fear in her eyes. He held her a moment, tender and soothing, and as he turned to go she asked him the question she had never meant to ask.

"Do you think the boys are safe, father? Do you think they'll come home again?"

He didn't answer for a moment, and she wished now for more light so that she might read the expression on his face.

"The Lord will take care of them, Sarah. Never fear. Myles will come back to us again."

She moved to the end of the wagon with a candle and the book from her father, and wrapped herself in the Missourian's quilt, anxious to examine her gift. She was satisfied with her father's answer until she realized he had said only "Myles will come back to us." She pondered that a moment. What about Martin? Did he mean anything by that reply? Then she decided it was a father's answer. Naturally he was thinking of his own son.

She opened the little volume. It was a copy of Shelley's poetry, her father's copy, back from his schoolboy days. On the cover sheet, in his fine hand, he had copied some verses. The first she recognized as an excerpt from Shelley's *To A Skylark*. The second was a scripture. She read them aloud softly to herself:

> We look before and after,
> And pine for what is not:
> Our sincerest laughter
> With some pain is fraught;
> Our sweetest songs are those
> That tell of saddest thought.

How well her father knew her! She held the sputtering candle closer and read the little verse following, seeing that it was taken from their own scriptures, from the word of the Lord to the Prophet Joseph Smith, for them: "And he who receiveth all things with thankfulness shall be made glorious; and the things of this earth shall be added unto him, even an hundred fold, yea, more."

"He who receiveth all things with thankfulness. . . ." Her eyes filled with tears, and the writing wavered.

She closed her swimming eyes and tried to pray, but Martin's face rose sharply before her closed eyes, so that she opened them again and blinked into the dark. There was too much darkness and distance between her and Martin. How could even love break through?

6

There were more children among them than you would want to count, and each wagon carried at least one sick or injured person. These were the poor and widowed; the last to flee Missouri. They hadn't enough wagons or clothing or food, and for months they had huddled among makeshift shelters, refugees in their own land.

But now, through the efforts of Brigham Young and Bishop Partridge and others of the committee for the removal of the Saints, they were leaving at last. Now, after so much patience and hopelessness there was a future again, and they would have part in it. Others of the Saints, those who had left the state earlier, were crossing the Mississippi River and gathering in Illinois. The Democratic Association of Quincy, one of the more sizeable cities in that state, had held a public meeting pledging support of the dispossessed Mormons and requesting aid for them. There was somewhere to go, and a reason to take hope.

Eliza Goodman smiled as she watched young Martin Walker playing pull sticks and wrestling with the smaller boys. What a godsend he and Myles Chadwick had been. They were young and strong and full of life, and their enthusiasm had done as much for the spirits of the people as their hardy strength had done in relieving physical toils. Handsome boys and kind, they seemed to take courage from one another, so that neither was ever discouraged, and they bubbled over with fun and gallantry and plain, old-fashioned spunk. *Oh, to be young again!* she thought, putting down her knitting and taking up the baby to feed. *Young and unaware, and inexperienced in pain.*

That evening they camped early so the women could wash clothes and the men repair wagons and weapons. They were heading into mob country now, where roaming groups of marauders still terrorized travelers: hard men, restless for trouble since the Mormon wars had dissipated; men who had tasted blood and wanted more, who knew that the governor's extermination order was a perfect pretext.

Myles found Elizabeth Todd trying to drag the heavy wash kettle over the edge of her wagon box.

"I'll take that, young lady," he said cheerily, as he swung it down from the wagon with ease. He pulled out her rocker as well, while she stood with her hands on her hips watching him.

"Now, you sit right there," he told her, positioning the rocking chair in a spot where the weak March sunlight splintered through the trees. She laughed as he gently pushed her into the chair and set it rocking with the toe of his boot.

"And what am I to do, while you take care of my work?" she asked him, laughter bubbling in her voice, delighted with his lively impudence.

"You might read to me if you'd like," he replied quickly. "I don't understand half the words, but I love the sound of your voice."

She laughed outright now and shook her head at his teasing. "I can't read. The books are packed too deeply away."

"Well, sew then, if you must do something to feel useful. I'm content enough to have you just sit there beside me and rock."

He stopped what he was doing and walked back to the wagon with long, easy strides. Elizabeth watched him, appreciating the fluid movements of his lean young body, loving the feeling that came over her when he turned his dancing eyes and looked upon her.

Elizabeth was a widow. A young widow, but with two small children, nevertheless, and a husband a scant seven months in a mob-made grave. She knew that Myles Chadwick, cheerful and kind and helpful by nature, in addition was attracted to her. She could read it in his gaze, which was sometimes lingering enough to make her color rise and her heart beat crazily. Already there had been looks cast in their direction, and raised eyebrows — but Elizabeth craved his warm, happy companionship so much. There had been something spontaneous and natural between them from the first. There was nothing improper about their relationship, nothing wrong, but she felt they were beginning to need one another. That made her uneasy, and she ignored it as best she could.

Myles jumped down from the wagon and brought her the sewing, then turned to unyoke the oxen, whistling lightly under his breath.

"There'll be dancing tonight if the work's done early," she said a little shyly.

"Why, in that case, I'll stop taking my time! In fact, I'll finish here and then go help Widow Wilson and see how old Brother Marlowe's getting along. That is," and he stopped what he was doing to look at her, "if you'll promise me every dance."

She laughed at him, lightly, but dropped her eyes, feeling her skin growing warm under his gaze.

Myles looked at her now, noting how the sun sparked streaks of fire through her brown hair as she bent over her task. Her skin, in spite of wind and weather, glowed like rose-tinged ivory. She was as lovely as any of the young girls Myles had been attracted to, even though she was already twenty-four. And maturity lent her something the young girls didn't have; a kind of gentleness, a graceful way which they seemed ignorant of.

When the shadows grew long and the dusk too grey for the men to see by, they lighted fires and sat together resting. The women nursed their infants, or sewed with fingers too practiced to need much light. Some of the men carved and whittled, or scraped and tanned long strips of the leathery hide that was always in constant demand.

Martin had gathered children to him like flies to honey, for he could whittle little birds and woods animals faster than the eye could see. There was a constant stream of small girls tugging at him, smiling up with a winsomness they were not aware they possessed, hoping to receive one of the tiny treasures. Martin couldn't bear to disappoint any of them — even the boys, who hung back, desiring a somewhat different gift, too awkward to ask. He set the boys to chopping on pieces of their own, then moved among them, instructing and praising, unaware of the adoration in the young eyes that followed his every move.

A strain of music, almost too soft to discern, sifted into the still night air. A voice began singing, and then another, "Sleep, my child, and peace attend thee, all through the night. . . ." The mothers singing a lullaby to their children. More and more voices entered softly in,

> Guardian angels God will send thee,
> All through the night.
> Soft the drowsy hours are creeping,
> Hill and vale in slumber sleeping,
> I my loving vigil keeping,
> All through the night.

Martin crept away, the silvery sounds following him like a spell. The music set a mood of loneliness upon him, a sadness of soul, a sense of not belonging — even here. Myles watched him go and knew what it was. Sarah. How deep the love between them had grown. He sat by the fire, listening to the lovely sounds, feeling vaguely disappointed and let down. Why didn't he long for Emily as Martin longed for Sarah?

From the time he had been old enough to know about such things, Myles had assumed that he and Emily loved each other. Yet the sweet pain, the devotion, the desire to please and protect — he hadn't really known those feelings as Martin knew them. What was he missing out on? Had he and Emily come to take each other too much for granted, already? Was it his fault, perhaps, because he didn't know how to be gallant and romantic?

He sighed. The song did have a sad feel to it. He lay back and soaked it in, not aware that his thoughts were more for gentle, feminine Elizabeth and her two beautiful children, than they were for Emily.

It was too cold the next morning and too early for any man to sit comfortably in a saddle. The leather creaked beneath him, and

Myles's bones were stiff and complaining, too. This was their second day into the territory of the mob marauders, and so far they had seen or heard nothing; all was quiet, perhaps too quiet. But the camp was out of meat and someone must hazard hunting, away from the little ring of protection the group offered. He and Brother Russell had scouted a wide arc around the camp and had spotted nothing; all looked deserted and safe.

He swung down from the horse, his legs feeling numb beneath him. A little warm oatmeal in his stomach, and he would go out again. But this time with Martin, and on foot. Just in case there was someone out there that the animals would alert. He doubted that anyone would be out in weather like this; not if he had a choice. Though really Myles didn't mind the prospect of a long tramp in search of game. It offered diversion from the monotony of the trail; and, besides, anything he did with Martin was bound to be an adventure.

They said good-bye in high spirits to anyone who would listen and kissed the plump, motherly women who had prepared them a lunch. Myles found Elizabeth and, though she wasn't alone, he touched her light hair that the morning breeze had feathered about her face, and kissed the little ones, promising them the rabbit's feet for good luck if any were found.

When they left, the sun was already climbing the sky, dappling through the bare winter branches in great yellow splotches or, caught in the tangled height of some giant tree, diffusing down in thin, gossamer sprays.

Everything crackled with the cold. They walked through the winter woods to the sounds of snapping branches and creaking limbs and dim, eerie cries from the birds which criss-crossed above them too quick, too high to be seen. Only the crows sat their low branches, shining purple and glossy, blinking back at the boys as they passed; and their call, loud and raucous, was the loneliest sound of all.

As the hours wore away the two young men walked deeper into the woods. The morning was fine, and there was prospect of better hunting further in. At last, spotting a deer and catching his trail, they tracked him through the thick, tangled ground growth, over hillocks rough with stones and scattered debris—relentlessly, until they were close enough to begin hoping, to begin imagining what it would be like dragging a big buck into camp. How good the tender, hot venison would taste!

Concentrating, pushing harder now, they approached a little rise behind which the deer had momentarily disappeared. Myles pressed ahead, then stopped suddenly. As Martin reached him they both heard the shot bark out, sharp and grating in the clear air.

"By damn, Zeb, I think you dropped 'im!" They heard the voice, too, and the shouts that accompanied it, so close that they felt shivers along their spines.

"They're right in a little hollow over the rise," Myles whispered. "So close we could reach out and touch them. We've got to get out of here—now! While they're busy with the deer!"

They turned, making their way cautiously down the sloping incline, not hearing the voices this time, as the man named Zeb said softly, "You hear those stones scatterin' — back there below the rise? Might be another deer."

"It ain't another deer," one of his companions responded, but Zeb had his musket primed and was sighting it anxiously. "You're trigger happy, Zeb. Leave it alone."

"Aw, all right, jest one shot for good measure." Zeb aimed his weapon and fired, dead at the spot where he had last heard the faint, scurrying sounds. Then he grabbed Turley's rifle and shot again, this time kicking up dirt and small stones, which skipped and clattered down the slope.

"If there was somethin' out there afore, there ain't now," Zeb said with satisfaction. "Let's go take care of that deer, boys. Make sure old Dudley don't cut out the best parts for hisself."

The boys, at sound of the first shot, had dropped to their bellies and rolled the rest of the way down the rough slope. Myles was on his feet instantly, though crouching still.

"Martin, did they see us? Do you think they were shooting at us? Come on!"

He spoke over his shoulder, not really turning around until he sensed there was no one behind him. Then he spun on his heel, his eyes searching for his companion. It took him a moment to spot

Martin, who hadn't come far from where he had rolled and stopped. He was dragging himself through the dead leaves and grasses, dragging his body along the ground, leaving a long, darkened stain of blood in the crushed and trampled leaves.

Myles was upon him in a moment, kneeling down beside him, gazing with horrified wonder at the thick blood oozing out of Martin's leg, forming a red, sticky pool where he lay. He met Martin's eyes, and the pain he saw there drew away his tattered courage into shivering pools of sympathy and fear.

"We've got to get you out of here," he whispered. "Hold onto me."

"I can stand if you'll help me," Martin responded, already attempting to rise.

Myles supported as much of his friend's young, supple weight as he could, and together they began their slow progress off the path and into the cover which generously closed around them as soon as they entered the trees.

Heading as evenly as he could back in the direction of the camp, Myles moved deeper into the woods, putting distance between them and the men who might be following. But Martin could not go far, and too soon he sunk, moaning, at Myles's feet. Myles half-carried, half-dragged him into a little copse of young elm trees and tangled blackberry bushes. Here he made Martin as comfortable as he could, talking the while to avoid the heavy silences which fell between them like the quiet hand of doom settling in.

Martin said nothing, suffering Myles's pullings and tuggings with patience, his teeth clenched against the pain, his hands knotted in tight fists by his sides. At least here there would be no easy following of their tracks; even the trail of blood merged with the stains of mulched and rotting leaves, the dank darkness of decay in ground that stayed cold and moist beneath the trees all winter, never seeing the sun.

But just to be sure, or perhaps to satisfy the restless curiosity which was nearly as great as his fear, Myles retraced their steps alone, covering the signs of their passing as best he could, moving slowly and listening to the sounds of the silence around him.

Here in the dense forest he was an intruder, swallowed up and ignored by forces much older, much wiser than himself. His enemies could be within arms' reach and he would not know it, and the thought disarmed him so that he found himself pausing every pace or two, searching with his eyes and with his senses, in tense readiness. His mind refused to think beyond the moment; and the need of the moment was protection—safety for himself and Martin. Food and water, care for Martin's wound, escape back to the camp—these came after, and he could not risk trying to deal with them. Enough for now to know that no one was within sight or hearing. Whoever was following—if someone was following—was far behind, perhaps confused, perhaps pursuing a trail that would lead him nowhere. Myles turned back, resisting an impulse to run, and carefully picked his way to the spot where Martin waited.

Back in the little hollow over the rise Zeb Powell and his group cut up their deer, slicing thick, generous steaks to roast over the fire that night. No one followed the noises that Zeb had shot at. But Siras Murdoch, going out for water, saw a trickle of blood leading off into the trees and told Zeb about it.

"Might have been an animal after all. You must'a hit somethin' out there."

"Course I hit somethin'," Zeb growled back at him. "I told yah I heard somethin' an' I did. Zeb knows what he's about, boys, Zeb knows what he's about."

Restless and aroused the men were in a mood for hunting now. Sammy Cook suggested they scout around to see what they could find.

"We might even be lucky and scare up some Mormon stragglers."

They went off in high spirits, and Myles, in his hiding place, heard them crashing past, close enough to startle Martin's eyes open in surprised alarm. Now Myles knew he dare not make the fire he had been considering. He sat down beside Martin, coaxing him to eat some of the cheese and bread they had brought with them. Myles ate none himself. He bantered back and forth with

Martin, keeping his voice encouraging and light. But his mind was with the mobbers, wondering where they were headed and what they would find.

Brother Marlowe saw the riders approaching, but he had no time to warn the others. He could no longer walk. Not that his seventy years had made him that way; it was the bullet lodged in his spine since Crooked River that had made him useless before his time. He sat in a spot of sun near the edge of the wagons, cleaning the rifles other men would use.

Everyone heard the shot ring out, but only a few boys, playing in the dirt beside the wagon with the small wooden marbles Martin had taught them to make, looked up in time to see the old man's body slump and slide and be kicked out of the way by the man who had shot him. There wasn't time for the mothers to gather their little ones and disappear inside the wagons, though a few dropped their tasks and scooped up their babies, moving quietly out of sight of the mounted men.

Finding this group of Mormons was more than Zeb and the boys had hoped for. They rounded up the men, prodding them along with kicks and with sharp jabs from the butt ends of their long rifles, calling out obscenities and threats which made the women shrink closer to the wagons where the strangers couldn't see. John Russell's dog, old and half-blind, settled in a circle at his feet. Lulled by John's whispered assurances, he never felt the bullet that tore into his skull, nor the hands of the little boy who broke through the press of men and fell, crying, against his fur.

"Tell the boy to shut up, or he'll be next," Zeb growled. "Mormon brats are as good dead as left alive to breed more Mormons."

Zeb's boys were itching for mischief now. They rode restlessly around their victims, daring each other on.

"Fine-lookin' bunch of Mormons we got here, don't ya think, boys?"

Zeb's eyes, small and narrow, darted back and forth greedily. "What do you say we do with 'em?"

The answers that spilled out were too horrible to bear listening, and Eliza Goodman, leaning against her wagon out of the men's sight, closed her eyes and prayed that the Lord would not allow the scenes of Far West and Haun's Mill to happen here all over again. Suddenly she remembered Myles and Martin, out hunting alone, and a cold, sick feeling crept over her. What had happened to them? Could they possibly have been brought in prisoners with these beasts?

She crept around the corner of the wagon and looked. The group of Missourians was small, only six men in all—and the two young men were not among them. She watched as her husband, captain of their little company, left the circle and walked toward the leader, the man called Zeb.

"We're only the few you see here," he said, "but we're not as alone as you might think. A larger group is expecting us, and they'd come looking for us if we didn't show up."

His voice carried clear and firm among the men. Only Eliza, who was so much a part of him, could discern the little signs which betrayed how afraid he was.

"We pass through here only, taking nothing, and doing no one harm."

There was silence for a moment, when Eliza could hear the painful beating of her own heart.

"And you expect us to let you go, just like that?"

Zeb's answering question was full of scorn, but Benjamin Goodman, his eyes deep and steady, still held his gaze.

"All right, then, if you're so all-fired anxious about it, go!" Zeb shouted suddenly.

There was no response, not from his men nor the Mormons, and he shouted louder, his eyes growing narrow and mean.

"Get the hell out of here, I said. You've got fifteen minutes before we send you all to hell where all Mormons belong."

Still the men hesitated, not quite sure what was happening, what was expected of them.

"Here. I'll help you get started." Zeb raised his rifle and aimed at Sister Nelson's old milk cow tied to the tongue of her wagon.

"You don't need this kind of baggage slowin' you down."

The ball struck the cow's thin side and she bawled once, her big, liquid eyes moving around in slow amazement before she sank to her knees.

"And you ain't got time for this," Zeb growled, as he tipped a big pot of stew into the fire.

"You're travelin' light, remember, and movin' fast."

His men got the message, and as the Mormons moved now, desperately yoking their oxen and pulling the cumbersome wagons into line, the Missourians harassed them on every side: smashing barrels, spilling the precious beans and flour, dragging out chairs and chests and breaking them into pieces, tripping the men and chasing the women, shooting and destroying.

Somehow the little company began to move, but the nightmare followed them: the mobbers relentlessly driving them on, determined to enjoy the sport as long as they could. Young Sally Simpson got in the way of Sammy Cook and he dragged her up onto his horse and kissed her, and held her there until the others, tiring at last, forced him to let her down. She ran, stumbling, through the path of ruin to the slow-winding wagons, stepping on her own torn gown which lay crumpled at her feet. It had spilled from her mother's old chest the men had hatcheted, and she was too frightened even to stop and pick it up.

Elizabeth stumbled along with the rest, frantic with the fear that choked in her throat, making it difficult to even breathe. She lowered her head and cried into the rising dust: "Please don't take him! Just because I've started to love him, don't let Myles die!"

Zeb and his men watched them go, tired and laughing and pleased with themselves. They had been merciful, after all. Those fool Mormons were lucky to escape with their lives.

This kind of fun worked up an appetite, and the men thought now of the tender venison steaks waiting to be cooked. Back in the quiet forest Myles heard them riding into camp, noisier and bolder than before. He shivered and looked up at the thinning sky, wondering when it would be dark enough and quiet enough for him to attempt sneaking back to the waiting wagons for help.

7

Sarah looked up and saw him. He was crossing the street with Emma, his arm around her waist, his eyes dancing as he bent low and said something for her alone to hear. He looked thinner perhaps, but not haggard; there was the same sprightly energy to his step, the same sparkle in his eye.

Sarah had flatly refused to believe it that morning, nearly two weeks earlier, when Emily had appeared at their wagon and calmly announced, "Brother Joseph's escaped from Liberty Prison. He's here right now, in Quincy, with us!"

"News that good can't possibly be true," Sarah had responded, though her heart gave a little involuntary flutter.

"It's true, Sarah, it's true. Sally Carpenter's seen him, and so have some of the women in our camp." Emily's china-blue eyes sparkled, and she laughed gleefully at Sarah's reluctance to believe.

"Oh, Emily, if it *is* true, then something will happen at last," Sarah had responded. "I know it will. The Prophet will see to that!"

It wasn't as though she didn't like Quincy, Sarah reflected. The people here had been kind to them and she was grateful. It had been weeks now since she had gone to bed hungry. And yet a wagon, cramped and drafty, sitting on somebody's else's land by somebody else's stream wasn't her idea of a home.

"A conference has been called for next week," Emily chirped, interrupting her thoughts. "Did you know that?"

Sarah nodded. "I wonder what they'll decide? There's been so much talk about where to settle."

"Well, I hope it isn't Iowa. I like it here, in Illinois," Emily replied emphatically.

"Brigham Young and Orson Pratt, Elijah Fordham and some of the others are living in Iowa already, Emily," Sarah reminded her. "They're using the barracks rooms for homes in the old abandoned Fort DesMoines."

"I guess that's as good a shelter as anything for families with nowhere to go. But I'm glad it's not me living there." Emily wrinkled her delicate little nose distastefully. "My vote's for Illinois."

"Well, it's time for something to be decided, that's for certain," Sarah agreed, "and Brother Joseph is here to do it, Emily."

Sarah watched Emma and the Prophet disappear inside one of the stores. She loosened her shawl because there was a warm breeze stirring, bringing faint, fresh smells of earth and spring which made her feel light and happy inside. She felt happy! She had thought she would never feel that way again.

She walked down the street smiling at everyone who happened to pass by, humming a little tune under her breath. There was only one thing she needed to make it all complete. People were pouring across the river, several new groups arriving every day. Perhaps one of them . . . perhaps in a few more days when the conference was held . . . perhaps she would look up to see Martin crossing the street toward her, as she had seen the Prophet Joseph do just now. It was possible. Surely it was possible, her heart sang.

Martin didn't come for the conference, though hundreds of newly arrived Saints crowded together to listen to their Prophet and support the resolutions, among them the appointment of Elder Marks to preside over the Church at Commerce, where the Prophet had purchased lands for the Church. Just as Sarah had known they would, things began to happen. But with spring in the air it had been so difficult to be patient! And poverty, Sarah had learned long ago, required great patience.

She marveled at the patience of Joseph Smith, who could begin time and time again with such painstaking care and faith.

Commerce, when Joseph Smith purchased it, consisted of one stone house, three frame houses, and two block houses, set on land thick with trees and bushes and so wet that teams could not pass through; even men on foot had great difficulty traversing it. A sad, unhealthy spot. But in early June Brother Theodore Turley had raised the first of thousands of houses to be built by the Saints there, and somehow families with no food and no money made the seventy-mile trip up river from Quincy into Hancock County, or crossed over from the Iowa side.

Many of them did no more than unpack their baggage and set up tents before they were struck with the deadly malarial fever which raged with such force among people who had been living at survival level too long and had no reserves of strength to combat it.

Patience — patience again as the disease claimed its share, until Brother Joseph rose to rebuke it and heal the sufferers. And those who outlasted the seige rose too, weak and bleary-eyed but grateful to be alive, and willing to start again, with nothing but their own bare hands as a beginning.

Sarah's family had not suffered the devastation of the disease; some illness, yes, but not the full onslaught, being too well doused, perhaps, with her mother's herbs and home recipes. For that Sarah was grateful. Watching those who still struggled for recovery, Sarah knew instinctively that her father could never have survived if he had been stricken with the sickness.

But the Saints had always been survivors; Commerce was now the focal point for them, and the spirit of gathering was there. Homes were being built, summer crops were growing, and the swamp was giving way to a city. And this was, after all, a beautiful spot.

Sarah, walking out alone in the early morning hush, wandered down beside the river she grew to love more every day. Here the Mississippi was over a mile in width and made a graceful horseshoe sweep round its rock-bound shore. Sarah could see across to the long reach of green and wooded bluffs on the Iowa side of the river. She had fallen in love with the setting that first day, knowing her heart could settle easily in such a place.

She leaned against a rock and closed her eyes, letting the soft morning sun caress her skin. Today this place felt more her own than ever. Today she was seventeen, and seventeen was so much more a woman than sixteen had been. She felt that she, like the city, was on the verge of a new beginning, a new life — a fulfillment as beautiful and happy as any dream.

She opened her eyes and turned, so that she gazed not upon the river but over the quiet little city which was growing from the rich, black soil, nestled among the spread of ripening fields. Her eyes sought out the place and rested there; a green, sunny stretch half-way up the hill where the city would climb — a perfect spot for a home.

She drew pictures for herself in her mind, savoring every delightful detail; and in each dream she drew, Martin was there, laughing and teasing and loving Sarah in the strong, quiet way which thrilled her so. On and on her imagination took her until the fabric of her dreams was more real than the frail moment which held her now in check.

A large splash startled Sarah and drew her reluctantly out of her world back into the present one. Two boys were throwing rocks into the river, seeing which could outdistance the other, laughing and splashing and enjoying themselves. Sarah sighed. Suddenly she no longer felt seventeen, but ageless, and forever beyond all innocent, thoughtless joys.

"The beings of the mind are not of clay," Byron had written. Ah, but she felt hers were. Clay like the river clay on which she stood, muddy and cloudy and disintegrating before her eyes.

She turned her back on the river and walked home, slower now, feeling that seventeen was colorless and empty without someone to love.

Her seventeenth birthday was the longest Sarah had ever spent, because Martin didn't come, and the breathless, aching pain of hopeless anticipation burned through her all day, leaving her exhausted when at last the final hours took their turn and spelled out her defeat.

So she shut her heart to all thoughts of him, needing a reprieve from the pain; but she could not shut out her need to know — to look with hard longing into the face of each newcomer, the same old question rising unwanted to her lips no matter how she tried to bite it back. Each day that passed grew longer than the last, and she found herself getting touchy, so that the slightest little annoyance set her nerves on edge.

"You walk around mad as a wet hen," her mother accused her, and she knew it was true, so she tried living each day as it came. But the days were too endless, so she tried each hour, each minute, making it through only the task at hand, never letting herself look beyond.

Then one day someone knocked at the door of their cabin and Sarah opened it; not to Martin or Myles, but to a man who was instantly familiar. Her heart gave one leap of joy, until she looked into his face and something within her froze.

"Brother Goodman, you're here! Where are Myles and Martin? Why aren't they with you? They're all right . . . aren't they?"

Her voice sounded small, and it betrayed too much of the fear inside her, so she stepped aside and let him enter. Even after her mother came in from her baking, flour up to her elbows, and her father, leaving his books open, limped into the room — even after Brother Goodman had worn the details thin going over and over them — even then her heart closed tight around the last fragment of hope and would not admit the truth. She neither spoke nor cried out, but sat stony-faced, staring straight ahead, until their old friend came up beside her and took her small, cold hands in his own.

"Sarah," he said, his voice sounding strange, for she had never heard it pleading before. "Sarah, please forgive me. There was nothing we could do. You must not give up. They may be safe somewhere. Even now they may be working their way home."

She looked at him with unseeing eyes; and when she spoke it was to her father, and her voice was high and bitter.

"You promised, father. You promised!" She turned her blue eyes, hard and accusing upon him. "Christmas eve, remember? You told me. You said the Lord would take care of them!"

"I know what I said," her father answered, and his voice was toneless; not hard like her own, but empty and cold.

"Everything comes to those who wait," her mother said, reaching out to touch her.

"Wait!" Sarah wrenched away from her mother's outstretched hand. "Wait! I've done my share of waiting and suffering, and begging for help. I can't do it anymore, I can't!"

She flung open the door and ran, crying and stumbling, out to where the fields dwindled into raw, uncultivated land which had never felt the plow. Out past the marshes she ran to the wide, whispering river that was her only friend, and she flung herself at its feet and sobbed, consumed with her own anger and fear and pain.

But even the deepest anguish exhausts itself, and when the rooks had tired of circling and the jays of scolding, and she was alone with only the gentle slap of the river waves washing the rocky shore, Sarah had cried herself dry; nothing was left but a dull heavy ache inside.

A cool breeze was blowing up from the river. Wet with tears and perspiration, Sarah shuddered, hugging her arms against her body. She didn't want to go back; she didn't want to see anyone. But what was she to do? She couldn't stay here. In the gathering dusk the river seemed to retreat from her, cold and uncomforting, a secretive stranger now.

She rose and walked home, struggling to be brave for Martin's sake, recalling the words he had spoken when they parted—"I still think the Lord will take care of us." She walked alone in the gathering dusk, remembering all that was noble and true that Martin had told her, repeating the words for comfort in her mind—"The Lord will take care of us." That was all she had to cling to now.

8

Myles rubbed the handful of soot and ashes into the wound, and Martin winced. "It doesn't look good, Martin. Seems twice as swollen as it did yesterday. I'm afraid it's putrefying—looks badly infected. We can't go on like this much longer, you know."

Martin nodded. He knew. He was afraid. At first he hadn't been afraid. He had pushed everything aside, matching wit and courage with Myles. But the pain was wearing him down, and the fever; and he was afraid now.

"You're as hot as an over-fired pistol, Martin. I've got to get some help. I've just got to."

Martin bit into his lip and shook his head.

"No. Not yet. We can't be far, Myles. One more day. Let's see where we are in one more day."

Not far! Not far from what? Three times they had walked almost into the laps of bands of marauders whose paths they crossed. Myles remembered with a cold, gripping chill what he had felt that first night after creeping through the woods in mortal fear each step of the way, feeling his path back to the camp they had left, to arrive at last and find only debris and broken remains scattered spectre-like across the quiet deserted prairie. He had stood in the thick night air and trembled, straining his eyes in the darkness for what was no longer there, standing until he was numb because he couldn't bear stumbling back through the eerie forest and facing Martin again.

How they had managed during these days he didn't know. They took one step at a time: this valley, that gentle slope, now the narrow ravine beyond. They chewed bark and grasses, ate old berries and an occasional fish and what game they could scare up. But every shot they fired was a risk which set their pulses racing; and the woods, taciturn and silent, hid their creatures well.

They moved slowly, resting often, and they were always hungry—one day going without nourishment of any kind. Myles thought often of Brother Hansen's experience when he had gone three weeks in the Missouri woods, hunted and alone, spending four entire days and nights without food. But Brother Hansen wasn't carrying a sick man, a man who could barely walk, a man who needed food desperately in order to survive.

Night was approaching, and the hollow prairie-land wind began moaning through the trees, like some lonely, uneasy spirit which would not rest. Myles fashioned a simple shelter of branches and mulch and boughs and prepared what he had decided would be their last bed outdoors. The skies had been red that morning when he awoke, and now a biting wind, strong and steady, was bearing from the northeast. It would bring wet snow in its wake, Myles feared, or at best heavy rains. And there was one bullet left in Martin's rifle, and none in his.

When at last Martin fell into a fitful, uneven sleep, Myles rose to his knees and prayed as he had never done before, knowing there was one hand only which could lead him now. At last he slept, while the wind rose, fretful and whining as a child, and Martin tossed and moaned and suffered beside him.

The morning broke cold, with leaden skies which somehow held the weight of their heavy burden and did not spill over until mid-morning. Then, suddenly, the rain was there in big, splotchy drops that turned to mush, then to pricking sleet; then back to mush again. Martin couldn't stand for more than five minutes at a time. His leg was swollen, his face was swollen, his eyes were red slits that strained against the murky light.

Fear choked in Myles's throat. Twice since the storm began they had come to houses, and he had gone on. Martin's fever was raging, and Myles wondered how long he would be able to put one foot in front of the other. But something had prompted him, had urged him to keep going.

Now, down below the trees, in a green, misty valley a lone farmhouse stood. As soon as Myles spied it he felt warm inside and knew this was the place he had been looking for. He eased Martin down the slope, searching all the while for signs of life and activity, but the house stood stolid and silent against the storm. Perhaps the rain wasn't such a punishment after all if it kept the farmer safe by his warm fire and out of sight.

Myles slid back the heavy barn door and pushed Martin ahead of him. It was dark and instantly warm inside, smelling of hay and molasses feed; the refuge of the place reached out to them like a caress.

Within minutes they were sunk into the deep straw in the loft overhead. Myles could not stop shivering, but Martin lay silent beside him, white and still. Without wishing to, Myles slept. His tense muscles relaxed and the warmth which had been only a tingling sensation on the surface of his skin began to penetrate into flesh and bone.

The slit of yellow light seared him into immediate alertness. He sat up and reached for his rifle in one sweeping, automatic move before he realized where he was, before he remembered the need to keep still. But the man holding the lantern had seen him, or heard him, or felt him there. The yellow light swept the barn, throwing weird shadows trembling against the walls, skipping along the floor. Now the light rose and stopped there, dangling

Myles's shadow, a hundred times his size, in black relief behind him.

"Who goes there?" the man called, and Myles marked that his voice was deep and rich with authority, neither cold nor afraid nor cruel.

Myles raised his rifle slowly, cocked it deliberately, and held it there a moment before replying.

"I've got a loaded Hawkin aimed square at your head," he said, as evenly as he could.

There was a slight pause before the man replied.

"So you want more than shelter from the rain. Well, what is it you want then?" Before Myles could answer, Martin turned in his sleep, moaning as he did so, and the old boards creaked beneath his weight.

"I see," said the man with the lantern. "Why didn't you tell me you needed that kind of help?"

The light moved then and the man's boots scraped the ladder as he climbed the loft. Myles tightened his grip on the rifle and moved back, sitting upright on his haunches, waiting for the face to appear below him.

Jacob cursed to himself as he climbed the ladder. He felt he was in for trouble, and he didn't relish the idea. He should have stayed inside. The animals were fine, as his mother had told him they would be. But habit is a powerful force, and it had been his habit since he was a boy of twelve to make these nightly rounds, checking to make sure that all was well. At first it had been assurance for his mother, a new widow and not used to being alone. Then it had come to satisfy his own young sense of pride. Now it was nothing but habit.

He peered over the edge of the loft, holding the lantern out at arm's length so that it lit up the features of the young man who faced him wide-eyed and tight-lipped. He wasn't as young as he'd sounded, but with one glance Jacob took in the thin body and worn clothes, the lean, hungry look in his eyes.

"What happened here?" he asked, motioning toward Martin.

Myles hesitated, meeting the stranger's gaze, trying to read the intent behind the eyes.

"He was shot. Accidentally."

"Um . . ." Jacob moved the lantern and tried to hide the shock on his face when he looked at the wounded youth.

"How long ago?" he demanded.

Another pause, and Myles replied more quietly, "Five, six days ago."

"Why hasn't he seen a doctor?" Jacob was growing angry now, taking it out on the quiet young man.

"Have you any idea how serious this is? Where do you live? Why hasn't he had any care?"

There was no reply. But suddenly Jacob didn't need one. He set the lantern down hard so that it tipped and swayed before settling.

"God help us. You're Mormons, aren't you?"

Myles looked into the brown eyes and decided to trust them. He told his tale. Jacob listened, moving between anger, pity, and disgust, wondering what perverse fate it was that kept tangling him up with the Mormons and their troubles. He wanted no part of the boy and his dying companion. He didn't like this reminder of the suffering and cruelty that walked hand in hand with bigotry. He had done his bit and more. He wanted to be left alone to forget it all, if he could.

But there was nothing for it now. As Myles finished his story Jacob's mind was already planning the next steps: food and blankets, dry clothes, something warm to drink, and with the first light a ride over the south knoll to fetch Doctor Hardy. If anyone could handle this kind of a situation Doc Hardy could, though Jacob wondered uneasily how much chance was left. And how was he going to hide all this from his mother? That would be a task. She was much too keen, too sensitive to his moods and routines. She would suspect instantly unless he took great care. He sighed, and waved away Myles's awkward thanks.

"Save your thanks. I haven't done anything yet."

He began to climb down the ladder, then paused.

"They say Mormons are great ones for praying, though." There was almost a hint of merriment in his voice. "So you sit up there and say all the prayers you can think of. We'll be needing every one of them, I'm sure."

The first move was easy enough. It was late when Jacob returned to the house, and his mother was already snuffing out the lamps and preparing for bed. It was simple to wait for her, then quietly gather what he needed and slip back out to the barn. He felt foolish doing it, and it reminded him of the days when he was a young boy sneaking out to the barn with his brother, Ira, to drink corn whiskey and play cards. He remembered the time Uncle Luke had caught them and whipped them both—Jacob the harder, which was only right because he was the older of the two.

After that licking Jacob never sneaked out to drink liquor and play cards again. For all his young years he had borne his responsibility as man of the household seriously, pushing himself to do things he wasn't big enough or strong enough for yet. He watched the men and imitated them, read the Farmers' Almanac late at night, scraped his knuckles, wore blisters on his hands, ruined a few things about the place learning how—but he made it. It had been hard, but he had never considered the possibility of failure. His mother's praise, her quiet faith were a strength to him. But it was his father and what had passed between them which had made Jacob determined to succeed.

He was aware in a quiet, inner way of just how well he had succeeded; he and his mother together. And Ira, he supposed. It was strange, but when he thought of them as a family Ira always stood somewhere near the outskirts, dark and sulking and discontent. Jacob didn't understand the boy. Never had. Ira wasn't much like Jacob, nor their mother, nor their father. If the truth were known, he was more like Luke's son, if Luke had had a boy. But Jacob didn't want to think about that. There was precious little about his Uncle Luke that Jacob could find to like. And Ira seemed to be shaping into the same mould; hard and sarcastic, and ruthless in getting his own way.

Jacob shuddered and pushed open the barn door. In solitary moments like this, Jacob faced the truth and realized that he was beginning to hate Luke Morgan for what he was making of the brother he loved.

Dr. Hardy wasn't home. Though the sun was barely coloring the sky and Jacob had risen so early and risked so much, the doctor was off already, seeing to Pete Funk's chopped foot that had gone to gangrene. Pete lived clear across the valley, and Jacob had no time to track the doctor down. The boy in the barn — his leg was gangrenous, too, and even if the doctor came home and got the message Jacob left, it read: "Come after dark, and come straight to the barn." Could the boy make it until after dark? Jacob wondered.

The doctor didn't come until late, and Jacob, after preparing careful explanations for his mother, was in the barn waiting. He greeted the doctor and thanked him for coming, but he gave no explanations as he led him to the boys, and the doctor asked no questions. He knelt down and examined the ugly wound, still oozing blood droplets and infection.

"What's been done for this?" he demanded, already shaking his head.

"Not much, sir," Myles answered. "Pressure and wood ashes to stop the bleeding — a little cheese mould until the cheese ran out. That's about all."

That and a passel of long, powerful prayers, Jacob wanted to add.

"There's definitely a serious infection here," the doctor said, arching his eyebrows as he probed the wound. "I'm afraid we're in trouble this time, boys."

Jacob helped him set up a make-shift operating table with planks and sacks of grain, and the clean blankets he had brought from the house. Ethan Hardy moved with deft, efficient sureness, and his face was a mask. But behind the mask his angry thoughts were seething.

He had studied under Drake at the College of Philadelphia, the finest teacher and university in the country. He was educated — not merely a step ahead of the midwives, as so many doctors were. Why was there still so little he could do?

He could see the first signs of crepitation in the skin above the wound. It was a nasty wound, and the leg around it was going red and was swollen nearly twice its normal size; and the tissues were showing definite signs of the dreaded gangrene. He checked his thermometer; just as he had feared, the boy's temperature was pushing 103. And he had been suffering like this for days! The boy had been walking on this leg, under conditions that should have killed him long before now. He was too weak to combat the infection. If only the lad had been given proper care! Ethan opened his case and began preparing the instruments he would need.

Martin struggled to keep his eyes from shutting and his mind from drifting away. He felt warm and at peace, vaguely aware that Myles had discovered some kind of shelter with food and blankets and protection from the wind. He liked it here. He didn't have to move his leg now, and the pain had lessened. And the soft grey waves settled down whenever he needed them to, taking away all thought, all fear, all pain. . . .

Ethan Hardy made his tidy incision and drained the vile fluid, probing for the ball further than he wanted to into the fleshy thigh. But in the end he had to leave it there, not willing to mangle the leg for a victory that no longer mattered. He applied extract of collocynth and Dover's powder, which contained opium for the pain, and the singsong phrase kept running through his mind: "purge, blister, and bleed . . . purge, blister, and bleed . . . ," the motto of the frontier doctor. Such a pitiable little to give! It seemed at times that the old redskinned medicine men had more to offer with their bags of magic and rattling bones and old tricks than he carried around in that little black case of his.

He buckled the case and rose, arching his back against the stiffness that wanted to settle there.

"That's about all I can do for now," he said. "I'll be back tomorrow night. He'll be comfortable, at least. Keep him warm, give him fluids if he'll take 'em. Have to build up some strength before he'll have even the bare beginnings of a chance."

Ethan Hardy didn't like to mince words. He had seen too many people hurt that way. He'd found that most men could take the truth given early with dignity, but they fell to pieces when it was handed to them too late, after their hopes and fears had worn them to bits and tatters inside. He didn't like the fevered, almost challenging hope in the eyes of the watching youth. So the doctor was surprised when Myles spoke and said simply, "He may very well die? Is that what you're telling me?"

Doctor Hardy looked up slowly and met the youth's steady gaze. "That's what I'm telling you, son."

Myles nodded. "Thanks, doctor," he said simply, then turned back to his wounded friend.

Ethan Hardy dropped his eyes and gathered his things, feeling awkward, feeling (as he so often did) that he ought to somehow apologize for not being able to do more for the patient.

The sky was black, alive with the shadows of stirring clouds, and the wind carried a thousand voices the doctor wished he couldn't hear. He hated the night. He had since he was a boy. It was the worst part of being a doctor for him, riding alone through the blackness with the voices in his ear. He mounted his horse, then shook Jacob's outstretched hand, so big and warm against his own.

"You be careful — with those two in there, you hear?"

Jacob nodded, and Ethan Hardy felt better for having said it. He turned his horse's head toward the gaping darkness where the pale barn light filtered away, and rode off into the night.

9

"I'll be in the back office, mother, working on the accounts."

Laura Morgan looked up at her son and nodded. "All right, Jacob, but don't stay too late and tire yourself. You've been working very long hours lately."

"Well, there's a lot to be done getting ready for spring planting. And remember, I don't have Ira's help as I usually do."

Laura's grey eyes were keen and piercing as she turned them on her son, and her voice, though soft and womanly, held a note of authority easy to discern.

"That's right, Jacob, I realize all that. But you're gone earlier in the mornings and out later in the nights than I've ever known you to be, and every time I try to find you it seems you've vanished into thin air, with no one about the place quite certain where you've gone."

"Sorry to have concerned you, mother," Jacob replied. "I'll see what I can do about making myself a little less scarce."

He kissed her lightly and left, knowing how uncomfortably close to suspicious she was becoming.

Laura watched him out of the room. She would have liked him to stay and visit with her, but she knew she couldn't press the matter further. The long evenings, with nothing but her sewing and her own thoughts, were often lonely, even now; after ten years she could still miss Matthew sorely. And yet, how like him Jacob was! The older the boy grew the more he took on the characteristics of his father: patient and steady and sure of himself, possessing little humor but with a great deal of sympathy in his nature and a fine sense of fair play. She thought it a pity that the two men had never had the chance to know one another.

Jacob rattled around in the office for a while, opened his ledgers and recorded a few figures. The minutes dragged in the chill, quiet room. His mother never came back here; it had always been considered his personal sanctuary. He lowered the wick on the lamp and quietly let himself out of the side door.

As he walked the distance to the barn, he wondered what it was within himself that sparked this unwelcome sympathy to the Mormons and their cause. Watching the two young refugees these past days, he had felt many of the same emotions he remembered experiencing when he had been near their prophet-leader, Joseph Smith. Was he some kind of an easy sucker for the underdog? He thought of the look in the pretty girl's face when he had handed her his mother's quilt.

He pushed open the barn door, instantly reassuring the two young men he couldn't see, but who he knew were watching him, tense and waiting.

"It's Jacob. I'm alone, and all's well."

He climbed the ladder to the loft and Myles gave him a hand, hoisting him up the last little distance.

Martin wasn't improving. Jacob could see that at a glance, and it gave him a tight, painful feeling inside.

"What did old Doc Hardy do for you today?" he asked, hoping his voice covered up the concern he was feeling.

"Let's see," Martin replied, in the voice that had become so soft one had to lean close and watch his lips carefully to catch the sounds. "It was a tincture of iodine compress today, wasn't it, Myles? Yesterday we had a flaxseed poultice, and the day before that he tried some—"

"He's throwin' the whole kit and caboodle at you, isn't he?" Jacob couldn't help chuckling. "Well, that means he's come to care for you, Martin. He's trying every possibility to make you well."

"None of it can hurt," Myles added. "And perhaps we'll hit upon the magic formula yet."

"Meantime I'm getting fussed to death," Martin protested.

"Ah, you're just wishing the doctor was a certain young lady I know . . ."

They talked on, and the barn walls were thick and sturdy, and none of them heard the single horse draw up before the house and stop. It was a mild night for early April, and the young girl who hastily threw the reins over the post and bounded up the stairs wore only a light cape over her head and shoulders, which she loosened now so that her black curls tumbled out and bounced pertly as she ran. Mrs. Morgan heard her and put down her sewing so that she met her at the door.

"Alice! Whatever brings you out after dark?"

"A pretense, luckily, for I've been restless as a kite in a March wind for days now," Alice answered, and her black eyes, dripping with a fringe of dark lashes, snapped as saucily as her curls. Laura smiled as she watched the girl seat herself on the sofa, spreading her skirts around her with a pretty flourish.

"Father sent a message that the two hands Jacob wanted will be ready tomorrow if he needs them." She paused and Laura nodded. "John was going to ride over, but I insisted," Alice continued. "It's such a little distance, and it gives me a perfect excuse to see that stubborn son of yours."

She raised her voice as she spoke, so the lilt of it was certain to carry, and looked anxiously toward the door, as though she expected someone to appear quite suddenly.

"Well, where is Jacob, anyway? You know, I haven't even seen him for over a week. I've been wondering whatever in the world could be keeping him *that* busy!"

"I'm not just certain," the older woman replied, "but I can assure you it's not another woman, if that's what you've been concerned about. He's in the back room. I'll call him for you."

"I'll go fetch him myself," Alice replied, as she stood and smoothed her skirts about her. "Perhaps he'll be surprised to see me."

Anticipation, like sweet honey, softened her voice. She lowered her eyes, naturally flirtatious even now when it worked to no purpose, and asked Laura softly, "Do you think he's missed me? Just a little?"

"I think so. But he doesn't like to be disturbed when he's doing the accounts. Perhaps I'd better walk down the hall a little way and call him."

"Oh, it will do him good to be taken off his guard."

With that Alice tossed her curls and was gone, leaving Laura to gaze after her, somewhat bewildered. She often felt that way in Alice's presence. She turned and picked up her sewing, wondering how long it would be before the two of them emerged to eat a piece of her apple pie and give her a bit of company.

It was too soon when she heard footsteps returning and looked up to see Alice burst into the room.

"He's not there," she said, almost accusingly. "I looked all around and called, but there's no sight of him."

A strange expression came over Laura's face and she laid down her sewing and rose. Alice, thinking only of her own concerns, didn't notice.

"I saw a light in the barn. Could he be out there? I think I'll go and check."

Alice had bent to pick up her cape when she felt a warm, firm hand placed over her own.

"That's all right, Alice. I'll go to the barn for Jacob. You sit right here and pretty your curls and wait for him."

"But I'd rather go my—"

"I'm going, Alice," the older woman interrupted, and her kind, quiet voice held that firm note which even Alice couldn't ignore.

When the three young men heard the barn door creak open it was too late. "Jacob," Laura called out loudly, not trying to cover the sounds of her approach. "Jacob, come down here instantly."

In the few brief moments he hesitated, Laura covered the distance to the ladder and would have been halfway up if Jacob hadn't started down. She waited for him at the bottom, and when he turned to look at her his face was drained and white.

"What are you hiding up there, Jacob?" she demanded. "Tell me now — we haven't much time."

"There's a young fellow who's been hurt, mother . . ."

"Is he alone?"

"No . . . no, there's another one with him. They were on their way —"

"Mormons, aren't they, Jacob?"

"Yes," he answered, "yes, they're Mormons."

"I thought as much," she responded. "Don't look so surprised, Jacob. You never have been able to fool me for long."

"Since when have you known?"

"Known? Not until this very moment. Suspected — that's another matter. Listen, Jacob, there's no time for talking. On your way back to the house, make up a good reason for being out here. You've had a lot of practice with that lately, so you shouldn't have much trouble."

He raised his eyebrows in an unspoken question.

"Alice Sheppard is here. She's come for you, Jacob, all huffy because you've been neglecting her."

Jacob's eyebrows shot higher, and he whistled under his breath.

"That's right, you've got a lot of explaining to do. Go on now, hurry. I'll take care of things here."

Jacob moved then, without so much as a backward glance, knowing how thoroughly his mother could be trusted. Before he had reached the door she was up the ladder and into the loft. She barely glanced at Myles, who stared at her in wonder, but dropped on her knees beside Martin, clucking like an old mother hen and muttering to herself.

"This is no kind of a bed. . . . What's been done for this boy's fever? . . . How much food has Jacob managed to smuggle up here, anyway?" She smoothed the old quilts and fluffed up the straw, straightening out the lumps and pockets Martin's restless sleeping had formed.

"What this boy needs is some good rich broth and a gallon or two of Grandma Morgan's hot composition tea."

She turned on Myles, her eyes bright and indignant. "I'm afraid that son of mine has taken poor care of you."

Myles, blinking back at her, thought she resembled a bristling little whirlwind, all huffed and rankled. He laughed out loud.

"By Jove, you're right," he assured her emphatically. "If I'd known you were here and available, I'd never have settled for Jacob!"

Laura looked into his sparkling blue eyes and they laughed together, liking each other instantly.

"That's a flimsy, miserable excuse, Jacob Morgan, and you know it."

Alice's voice was petulant, almost scolding, as she turned her snapping little eyes on Jacob.

"Well, it's true, Alice, you know that. You'll just have to believe I'm sorry, that's all."

She paused then and fluttered her thick black lashes over her eyes, and when Jacob drew her toward him she yielded softly to his touch and his kiss. This is what she had come for, after all, and she kissed him back with all the practiced skill she could manage, and with an honest desire as well. Alice liked men, she liked their attentions—and she liked to watch the effects her own flirtations and charms had on them. But Jacob was the one man she couldn't seem to get enough of. She knew she could easily make a fool of herself over Jacob, and she resented him slightly for that.

He put her from him, holding her away, but she melted against him again and whispered something into his ear which made his pulse start throbbing. She kissed him until he drew away again, angry that she should push him beyond himself. But she was smiling at him softly, beguilingly, and she ran her fingers lightly through his hair, so that the aching sensation he felt whenever she touched him returned.

"Don't be angry, Jacob. I'll stop if that's what you want . . . if that's what you really want."

She whispered the last words against his ear, and it was too easy for him to turn his face and kiss those soft, very willing little lips.

When Laura returned from the barn a few minutes later Alice was too satisfied to question her delay. In fact, she was grateful for it, because now she knew how easily, if she wanted it, Jacob could be hers.

Things were different, better, now that Laura Morgan was in command. Jacob could go about his work as before, not starting at every sound, not agonizing over contrived excuses, not backtracking to cover for himself and his secret.

Laura would have liked to remove Martin to the house, where she could provide him with a warm bed, a clean room, and the cheering influence of a home. But here Jacob stood firm. He knew the risk wasn't worth it. If his uncle or any of his cronies should discover the two strangers they would take out their vengeance on his mother, and he didn't want that to happen. He didn't want her to see the ugly side of Luke's nature. He didn't know how well she was acquainted with it already.

Myles willingly helped with the work about the place; grateful, even content after a fashion. Carefully he followed Martin's struggle, helpless before that mysterious force which could eat up life and dissolve the very fabric of existence with such ruthless, impersonal skill. There was nothing Myles could do but stand and watch the cruel and senseless suffering of someone he loved.

"Found him. Now I don't know what in tarnation to do with 'im."

The grip around the back of Myles's neck tightened as the big hand lifted him clear off the ground for a second or two, then set him back again.

"Three bags of grain he was totin', Laura." The big man laughed, a gruff, unkind sound with nothing in it of merriment or warmth. "Enterprisin' thief, I'll say that for 'im. But his greed undid him, yes it did. Couldn't get away quick enough with three bags instead of one—"

"Oh hush, Luke, and let the boy go. He's done no harm and has nothing to answer for to you."

The man looked dazedly from the woman to Myles, but he didn't loosen his hold until she insisted.

"Go on, I said. Let go of the boy."

The man removed his massive hand unwillingly, but he didn't step away, and Myles could feel the braced tension of the big body beside him—this man who had driven his people from place to place, who was part of these people he was beginning to love.

"All right, Laura, you'd better explain this. There's somethin' fishy here."

Laura Morgan took a deep breath as she wondered why her life had to be burdened with this man. She had been puzzling that question for years, especially since her Matthew had been taken. It seemed so unfair to leave the refuse behind and take the cream, the marrow, the good, ripe grain.

She needed time to consider, but she had none; so she did the only thing she could think to do.

"You're such a loon, Luke; you always have been." It helped to start out that way, insulting him. He had always hated to look little in her eyes, and it gave her just the slight upper edge she would be needing now.

"This is my cousin's boy, Clint Jackson. Remember him? You wouldn't. Well, this is his boy, and I'll thank you to stop prowling about the place frightening people and insulting my kin."

It was a good little speech, delivered in a nice, convincing manner. Jacob walked up just in time to hear her, and he was glad he was carrying the broken plow shaft and had something to lean on. He had never before heard his mother lie, and he felt a momentary pang in the realization that it was because of him she had had to do it.

"That right, Jacob? Is this her cousin Clint's kid?" Luke had turned to him, stubbornly wanting reassurance of Laura's story.

Jacob looked at him coldly, and he spoke, though he didn't know it, with the voice of his father — the older brother Luke had always admired and envied.

"When my mother tells you something, Luke, you don't need a second opinion."

"Luke, is it now? Yer gettin' a little bit big for yer britches, don't you think?" His voice held more of complaint than of anger, and since no one else spoke he continued, half-nervously.

"I guess that's true about you, Laura. You always could be trusted. Awright, awright — I'm sorry."

What an embarrassment Luke was, Laura was thinking. She could remember the first time she met him. He had looked a lot like Matthew: big and muscular, thick auburn hair, deep brown eyes. A handsome man, really. But there the resemblance had stopped. When Luke talked there was no warmth to his voice, and he spoke as an uneducated backwoodsman, wearing his ignorance like a badge; while Matthew, who had been schooled in the East, spoke intelligently and correctly, with a rich, kind voice.

"Listen, Luke," she told him, more kindly than before, "it's a simple matter, really. Young Clint here was itching for some place to go and something to see; he's just that age, you know. So he's here to help Jacob with the spring plow. You have my Ira, after all."

"Hell, Laura," Luke interrupted, perturbed now. "I thought you didn't need the boy. I'd 'ave brought him if I'd known. Though, truth is, he's just like my own, Laura, and I don't know what I'd do without him right now, what with the —"

"It's all right, Luke. You keep Ira. But bring him to say hello the next time you come. And don't let him get lazy — or over-proud, either."

"That's like you, Laura, fussin' and worryin' about the finer things a man don't pay no attention to."

Laura resisted a temptation to roll her eyes in desperation.

"I'm his mother, remember. Now, if you had a woman of your own around, it would be another matter."

That pricked Luke into motion, and he began ambling toward the gate, where his horse was tied.

"I don't need no woman about the place. I can shift for myself, Laura, always have."

Jacob brought Luke his horse and handed him the reins. He shrugged his shoulders, mounted heavily, and rode off, twisting back to grin and wave. They watched him safely out of sight, then turned to one another with a quiet triumph in their eyes.

"I guess we've been lucky today," Laura said simply. "I think I'll go in and see about Martin now."

She disappeared inside the barn; they all went their separate ways, busy with their separate thoughts, none of which rested easily on the mind.

"But it can't be possible! He's been better, so much better than before."

"It can happen like that near the end—they appear to rally, then suddenly there's a turn and they fail fast."

Myles looked away from the doctor's bright, piercing eyes, which seemed to hold so little sympathy behind them.

"It's been there all the time, Myles. You just haven't wanted to see it. I knew he wasn't getting better—and so did he." Laura Morgan put her hand on the boy's shoulder, wanting to pull him into her arms and comfort that desolate look out of his face.

Myles dropped to his knees beside Martin and took his cold, limp hand and held it firmly between his own, as though he could transmit some of the blood and life and energy that was his into the motionless form. Laura watched him for a moment, then turned aside. Jacob was just climbing the ladder, but she motioned him back.

"Come," she said, and she took Dr. Hardy's arm. "I think they should be alone."

The doctor, his face an expressionless mask, followed her

without a word, but inside he was bitterly berating himself, knowing it was partly his lack of skill and knowledge that was letting the young man die.

Martin opened his eyes once and smiled at Myles, his face bright with recognition and intelligence, peace and love. That one moment brought a strength that filled Myles's soul, so when Martin's spirit slipped away at last Myles could bear the pain and the parting — and the knowledge that he was now alone.

Much later Jacob came. He carried a light with him and climbed the loft, and his presence brought Myles back to the realization that he, himself, was still alive — that his back was stiff and his fingers were cold, that his stomach wanted food and his throat was dry. Life was still there to contend with, and he rose reluctantly to face it; his body feeling old and weak, his spirit battered and drained.

Jacob was awkward and ill at ease; in fact, he dreaded situations of this kind. But he believed it was his place to be here, not his mother's. So he had come, though he was far from comfortable about it.

"Don't grieve for him, Myles," he tried to comfort. "He's past help now, and past pain, too."

"I'm not really sad for him," Myles replied plainly. "I know where he is and what he's doing. I'm sad for myself, and for the others he left behind."

"Of course," Jacob agreed, "that's only natural."

He paused a moment, almost deciding against it, but in the end he asked the question which was deceivingly less simple than he had believed it to be.

"Myles, just where do you think Martin is, and what do you think he's doing?"

"Oh, that!" He looked at Jacob, and a faint smile began to seep into his tired eyes. "He's in the spirit world with those friends and family he knew before. I suppose he'll see some of the brethren who were killed in DeWitt and Far West. He had a little sister who died as an infant. He'll see her again, I'm sure, and get reacquainted. And, if I know Martin, he won't let much grass grow under his feet before he'll find somebody to preach the gospel to."

Myles's smile spread and became real now, but Jacob's brow was knit in painful consideration.

"You make it sound terribly easy, and very much like it is down here."

"Well, we don't become mysteriously different once we die, Jacob. We have the same thoughts and feelings, the same characteristics. So a lot of things will just naturally be pretty much the same, don't you think?"

"I never really thought about it before."

"Well, you ought to, then. It's something that concerns you much more than the few brief years you'll be spending here."

"A world after this — it's that real to you, is it?"

"Yes, Jacob, it is. I've had too many evidences of its existence to doubt it. What we do here — everything we do here — makes all the difference as to how happy we're going to be, how much we'll know, how much we'll be able to do in that next world."

Jacob was fascinated. Something stirred within him, a questioning that was more need than curiosity, more hunger than he wanted to admit. Spiritual matters had always been a blank wall to him. And he couldn't remember ever caring that much about them. Except once, when his father died. Then his young mind had ached for answers that no one seemed able to give, and he could remember clearly still exactly how he had felt: that someone as strong and good and real as his father couldn't just one day end — just cease to exist.

Well, he wouldn't press Myles now, when he looked so totally exhausted. Anyway, he had promised his mother to coax him down and into the house for something to eat.

"Come on, Myles, mother's got a hot supper ready for you. You wouldn't want to worry her, and you're in need of it, besides."

Myles turned to go, then walked over and stood above Martin's body, looking down. "I don't know how I'm going to face her with this news," he said.

"Martin's mother?" Jacob asked.

Myles looked up and their eyes met, and the pain had returned like a burning flame to Myles's face.

"No, no," he replied softly, "my sister. She loved him . . . they loved each other, you see. I'm sure she's trusting me to bring him back to her. Heaven help me—I'm going to have to break her heart."

Later that night, when the meal was done and all was quiet and dark, Myles sat alone, trying to face a future that lay somewhere beyond his emptiness and pain. It wasn't coming easily, and he rose, pacing the narrow farmhouse porch, longing for a lifting of the burden, for some kind of an escape.

Jacob, seeing Myles restless, gathered courage to approach him and pick up the fabric of the discussion they had earlier begun. They sat together, Jacob posing the questions, Myles answering them, long into the night. The mask of darkness helped, and Jacob asked questions he never would have attempted in broad daylight.

When weariness at last forced them to an end, Myles went to his bed strangely settled in body and mind. It was Jacob who stared at the ceiling and could not sleep, who turned over and over in his mind the things he had heard and the feelings he had experienced that night. It was Jacob who faced down his fears and insecurities, who struggled with the truth as a man would struggle with a powerful stranger who had come to master him. It was Jacob who wrestled with his soul in the darkness alone.

11

They buried Martin when the colors of morning were just beginning to penetrate the dull, sunless sky. Laura had wanted to ignore the risk and place his body in the family cemetery, beside her Matthew and the two small infants who rested there. But Jacob and Myles prevailed, convincing her that this spot would more than satisfy, tucked in a grassy hollow between two towering pine trees who would stand sentinel to the lonely grave.

They covered the open earth as neatly as they could, and Laura read the words of the Twenty-third Psalm: "The Lord is my shepherd, I shall not want . . ." Her soft voice carried in the still morning air, and it all had a feel of unreality about it. *What has any of this to do with Martin?* Myles thought. *Martin, who is gentle and intelligent, warm-hearted and alive!*

They walked back to the house in silence. Even the birds weren't singing, and Myles felt he existed in a huge, black void where song and hope, laughter and happiness would never have place.

Now, with Martin dead, much of the risk was suddenly removed, and Myles could fall more naturally into the role of the cousin from New York. Myles didn't consider leaving. Jacob needed him too much. When the spring planting was in, then Jacob would be able to manage alone; perhaps Myles, too, would be able to manage alone by then.

They were up every morning with the sun, working past the gentle fall of evening until their straining eyes could no longer see, then eating and crawling weary and aching into their beds, only to begin the same cycle over again. Too tired to think or feel, Myles lived in an abeyance of his own life, existing as an unreal person in a world which wasn't his, where he didn't really belong. But then, where did he belong? Not knowing where he was going or what waited ahead, just where did he fit into the pattern of his own life?

Because of Myles, Jacob was able to clear and plant several acres he had never been able to handle before. The hard work and Laura Morgan's excellent meals were good for Myles. He put on flesh, and yet his muscles hardened. He felt better and could work harder than he ever had in his life. The comradeship between the two men grew. Sometimes they talked as they worked, or for a few minutes on the porch in the cool spring nights before going to their beds. Often their talk ran to religion, so that Jacob came to know much more than he had that night in the barn when the first fateful question had been asked.

In spite of the long, tedious hours, the days slipped through their hands like water through a sieve. Somewhere they had to end, and finally the evening came that was Myles's last with the Morgans. He was aware of it, and he tried to savor each moment.

He walked the line of the fields he and Jacob had planted. This was what he wanted in his own life. He closed his eyes and was startled to find Elizabeth's face materialize in his mind, her lips parted in a smile, her eyes shining. Where was Emily? Where were those china-perfect features he had once been so familiar with? It had been too long. He would go back and find her. Or would he? Would he find either one? Did he know what had really happened to any of the people he loved?

He walked out to the grave and sat beneath the pines while he tried to take one last farewell of his friend. Jacob had carved a marker and placed it firmly in the ground. It read:

Martin Owen Walker
born February 11, 1819
died in the spring
of his life
April 21, 1839

Myles stared at the writing and thought about it. Martin wouldn't be happy with him, he knew. He had everything to be grateful for, everything to live for, and he was acting the coward's part. Suddenly he realized that if he died tomorrow, as well he might, and had to face Martin he would have some pretty stiff explaining to do. Martin would want him to be happy; Martin would *expect* him to be happy.

He walked back to the house and found Laura Morgan and tried to say good-bye, but in the end she held him to her briefly, and the tenderness between them didn't need to be expressed.

Myles hadn't seen Jacob all evening, and he couldn't find him now. He would see him in the morning, Myles was sure. Jacob had, with his usual thoroughness, prepared all the supplies he would need, including money in the saddlebags and a horse to go under them; a beautiful sorrel Myles had admired. Jacob insisted that Myles had earned every bit, but how do you repay someone for saving your life and come out earning something extra besides? He went to bed and tried to sleep, not allowing his mind to push him into tomorrow and thoughts of what might lie ahead.

It was late when Laura heard the door creak. She didn't look up. Jacob entered and crossed to the mantel, lighting the tall oil lamp so that a shallow halo of light clung around that corner of the room. He took the lamp and came and stood before his mother, the light trembling between them, eating up the shadows and outlining the fear and unhappiness on her face.

"Mother," he began, "I've been wrestling this thing out, trying to come to grips with the thing."

"You'd better tell me about it," she said quietly.

Laura had always thought uncertainty was harder to face than the truth, but this time she wasn't sure. Jacob said all the words she had been afraid he would say, revealing to her the feelings that tore and divided him. When he had finished she rose and faced him. The look in her eye was as hard as flint.

"That's all well and good, Jacob. Just how far do you think my sympathies go? Giving help to a Mormon is one thing; losing my son to them is quite another."

He made a little movement, but she stopped him.

"Yes, Jacob, I have no illusions. If you ever became a Mormon you would be lost to me." She turned on him, her eyes cold and blazing. "You consider yourself convinced already, don't you Jacob? Well, you're not. You're confused. Many of the things you feel concern Myles and have nothing to do with Mormonism at all. Let him go and in a few days . . . a few weeks . . . the turmoil will subside and you'll be yourself again."

He shook his head slowly, his eyes holding hers.

"No, mother, what you speak of has already happened, and it didn't work."

He told her reluctantly what he had been holding back: of the Mormon prophet in Richmond, the boy in Far West, the girl who took the quilt from him with tears in her eyes. He tried to explain what he couldn't understand himself. In the end he said simply, "It would be extremely dangerous for Myles to travel alone, you know that. Let me go with him, let me see him home and face this thing once and for all."

"What if I should forbid you to go?" she asked.

"Then I should have to go without your blessing, mother. I've already determined to see this thing through. I shall never have peace if I don't."

"Will you come home? Will I ever see you again?"

"On that you have my promise," Jacob answered firmly. "I won't fail you, mother. Be assured of that."

Laura trembled, thinking how similarly he had spoken when he was only a boy of twelve shouldering the responsibilities of a man and refusing to run away. She knew she couldn't stop him and she didn't want to part with anger between them. Somehow she kissed him with dignity and control. But she was afraid, and when he had gone she ran to her room and cried as she hadn't cried since Matthew's death.

Jacob's mind was seething. He couldn't separate or identify his thoughts. He walked until he was weary, then sat on the knoll above his farm, looking down upon everything he loved in the world sleeping peacefully below. And he wished he had never so much as heard the word *Mormon*.

In the morning Myles awoke early and prepared for his journey. In the barn stood two horses saddled and ready for travel.

"I'm riding with you," Jacob announced from out of the shadows.

"That's not necessary, Jacob," he urged. "I can find my way fine by the map you drew. Besides," he continued, as he led the sorrel out of the barn, "I wouldn't want to be responsible for having you caught in your own territory with an unexpected Mormon in tow."

"You don't understand," Jacob replied quietly, tightening the buckle cinch on his saddlebag. "I'm not riding with you a little distance to show you the way. I'm coming along."

Myles was speechless. He turned to Jacob, amazement written all over his face.

"That's impossible," he breathed.

"I have to do it," Jacob responded, trying to be casual.

"Why?" Myles demanded. "I don't understand why, Jacob. What about your mother?"

"Those are two big subjects you've asked about in one breath. I'll try to explain as we ride."

He swung his leg over the saddle, gazing down on Myles from his high perch.

70

"Come on," he grinned, "we're wastin' daylight."

Myles shook his head and grinned back. The sun was barely beginning to lighten the wide expanse of smudgy grey above them. Myles mounted his horse and they rode off together, side by side, neither one looking back but each busy with thoughts of what might lie ahead.

Each was leaving something very precious behind; both were totally unaware of what future fate might hold for them in her hands.

The Change of Love

12

The two young men were crossing the dusty, pot-holed road and walking her way. Not recognizing either one, Ellen Chadwick casually noticed them as she bent over the blue worsted dress applying the hot iron here and there. She wondered if they were here to court Sarah, as so many of the young lads seemed to be doing these days. She sighed and turned to the stove, replacing the warm iron and picking up another red-hot one in its place. They'd get nothing but a cold shoulder and an unkind word for their troubles, she could be sure of that. She'd never seen such a stubborn girl as Sarah.

When strong arms tightened suddenly about her waist and someone kissed her cheek, she was totally bewildered. Even when she turned around it took her a moment or two to realize who it was that still held her, grinning, as big as life. She screamed and hugged him then, and they cried and laughed together, and he swung her clear off her feet in his delight.

Jacob turned away, giving them this moment of privacy, and looked curiously around the room. It was certainly simple, only the basic necessities: a rough log table with benches and stools, a bedstead in the corner with a straw tick, near a steep ladder leading up to a loft. A spinning wheel and a draw loom stood in the opposite corner and, of course, a fireplace with oil lamps on the mantel and a rocking chair placed invitingly nearby.

A rocking chair with a quilt folded over the back — a piece-meal quilt made of bits of scraps. . . His eyes began to focus before his mind did. It was a quilt like a gypsy's, with every color of the rainbow — stripes and solids, plaids and checks — a quilt that had covered his own bed many a time and kept him warm. It couldn't be . . . but it was his mother's quilt he had given to the girl in Missouri those long months ago.

"Mother, I'm sorry I'm late." The sweet, young voice was like a melody. Jacob turned as the girl entered the room, but she wasn't looking his way.

"Em and I found a beautiful batch of wild strawberries. Just look how many I've . . ."

Her voice faltered and the pail fell with a dull thud on the packed earth floor, scattering the precious red fruit. She was in Myles's arms in a moment, murmuring things Jacob couldn't hear. But suddenly she drew away, treading the berries thoughtlessly under her feet.

"Where is he, Myles, where is he?"

It was a cry that made Jacob's blood run chill. Myles's face was drained of color, and he turned to her helplessly.

"No! You didn't come back without him! How could you? I won't believe it, I won't believe it! I won't!"

She was screaming, and her own face was deathly pale. Myles tried to explain, but she wouldn't be quiet long enough to listen.

"Stop it!" her mother demanded, taking her firmly by the wrists. Sarah twisted away and would have run, but she found Jacob blocking the door. His presence was so massive, so unexpected, that it stopped her cold and she stood blinking at him in quiet rage.

"Who are you?" Sarah demanded, her voice shrill with emotion. "What are you doing here?"

"Don't you remember?" he asked gently.

She pushed her hair back from her forehead, struggling to recall, to grasp something out of the past, beyond the pain that made thinking impossible.

"He has as much right to be here as I do," Myles said from behind her. "Fact is, without him I wouldn't be here at all. He saved my life, more times than one."

"And Martin?" Her voice was on fire, with that same note of hysteria. It was Jacob she spoke to, her eyes blazing.

"Why didn't you save Martin, too?"

"Don't be ridiculous," Myles said, almost angrily. "You're being thoughtless and cruel. Jacob and his mother did everything they could to save Martin—risked their own lives and all they had. Because of them Martin died in—"

"I don't want to hear how Martin died!" It was a sob of pure anguish that wrenched Jacob apart with sympathy.

Jacob moved a step toward her, but Sarah backed away, trembling.

"I want Martin to be here! I don't want you. You never could take his place!"

She pushed past Jacob, setting him off balance, and ran out of the door. The silence in the room was awful. No one moved or spoke until finally Sarah's mother sighed and said under her breath, "She doesn't know what she's doing—she's not herself."

"I'm sorry it all came down on your head, Jacob," Myles said. "That's something I hadn't expected."

Jacob walked to the door and looked out, but the girl was not in sight. He turned back to the two unhappy people inside.

"That's all right," he said. "There's no easy, pretty way to break a heart. I'm glad I was here if it helped—if it made things any easier at all."

He walked to the door and looked out again, not wanting Myles and Sarah's mother to read his face. It was strange, this thing that was happening to him. He loved the girl! He had known it the minute he saw her again. There was no struggle, no uncertainty within him; he simply knew. But there was pain; pain at Sarah's suffering, and pain in the memory of the dead youth buried on Jacob's land. An uneasy realization moved within him: *Martin's death has unwittingly opened the way for my own happiness!*

"I think I'd better go for her," Myles insisted. "Father said down by the river—she always goes down there."

"You don't understand, Myles. It has to be me." A small panic was building in Jacob. "Otherwise she'll never accept me. She'll never bridge the gap. I'm the only one who can bring her back."

Myles hesitated. Jacob's words rang true. He looked carefully into the steady brown eyes.

"I don't know . . . you don't understand her . . . you don't . . ."

"I'll be gentle, Myles. You know that. Don't worry, you know I'll do my best."

Jacob wandered the river for several minutes before spying Sarah. She was seated perfectly still on a large, smooth rock. The soft summer dusk seemed to enhance the perfection of her form, and he looked on her beauty with a sense of appreciation more gentle than he had ever known before. He had expected to find her sobbing—angry and indignant still. Her calm bolstered his courage so that he dared to approach.

At first she heard nothing. Then, looking up, she saw him, and her face grew dark.

"What are you doing here? Go away and leave me alone!"

He stopped, not moving forward, yet not going back.

"I suppose Myles sent you? He didn't have the courage to come himself. Well, it won't do any good."

"Are you going to stay out here all night?"

She hadn't expected that question.

"I don't know," she answered curtly. "I haven't decided yet. But I won't go back with you," she added vehemently. "And I don't have to talk to you, either. So go away."

Jacob remained where he was. It was so quiet that they both heard the play of the water along the shore and the low drone of the insects which worried the riverside. She fidgeted on the rock, changing her position and smoothing her skirts and stealing a glance at him. Silence. Silence was his only chance.

"Did you know him?" she asked quite suddenly. "Was he . . . there . . ." she hurried over the word, "long enough for you to know him at all?"

"Yes, I think so," Jacob replied carefully.

"Did you like him?" she demanded bluntly, and he could feel her gaze burning into him.

"I can answer that easily, Sarah. Yes, I liked and admired him very much."

When he said her name a shiver ran over Sarah, so that if she had carried her shawl she would have pulled it around her shoulders tight. She remembered suddenly, incongruously, feeling the same way that time in Missouri when he had said her name.

"Even I could tell," he was saying, "Martin was . . . well . . . he was more than ordinary."

At the sound of Martin's name she drew back, and Jacob knew that move had been a mistake. Careful . . . so carefully he must go!

"I hate you. I hate you for being here," she said, and challenge was evident in her voice. "I hate you for being here in his place."

"I'm sorry. I understand that. I think I would feel very much the same."

What could she say? She paused in frustration, and he filled the silence this time.

"Go ahead and rant at me if it helps you. I won't mind."

"I've done with weeping and wailing," she answered him bitterly. "No one cares or listens, anyway. It won't do any good—it won't bring Martin back."

He had no answer for that, and Sarah was grateful. If it had been Myles he would have lectured her on her lack of endurance and faith.

"It isn't all that simple," she warned him suddenly. "You think you can come out here and talk to me and I'll go back to the house like a good girl and everything will be all right."

"No, Sarah," he protested. "I know better than that. I know . . ."

She didn't want to listen! There was something magnetizing about his voice. She was drawn to him with the same fascination she had felt before; the same need for tenderness, for care. She felt trapped, like a caged wild animal—so frantic she couldn't think, could barely breathe.

"Leave me alone," she cried, sliding from the rock and facing him." I don't need you! All of you think if you're kind that I'll stop loving him. Well, I won't, I won't, not ever! Not as long as I live!"

She ran from him, light and nimble as a young, frightened deer. He stood for a moment with the sound of the insects surrounding him, looking off toward Missouri. Then he gathered up the remnants of himself and walked purposefully in the direction Sarah had gone.

The first days in Nauvoo were busy ones, and Jacob saw little of Sarah. He met Martin's family, who received him warmly, grateful for all he had done for their son. Jacob was impressed by their fortitude, by their peaceful spirit which would allow no bitterness or self-pity to enter in. When they urged him to stay with them, to make his home there, he accepted. He felt it would be better that way.

Living under the same roof with Sarah had proven difficult. Every moment she was there he was painfully aware of her. She had grown quiet and withdrawn, speaking to no one, mechanically performing the tasks required of her but living totally unto herself. And yet there was a strain of conflict, a tension which moved silently with her wherever she went. Jacob felt it; it was like a barrier between them — a barrier he must eventually and purposefully break down.

"Myles, oh, Myles, I had to run over just to see if it was true, to see if you still were here!"

Myles and Jacob were working on the masonry in the lean-to summer kitchen they were building for Myles's mother. Both looked up as Emily came dancing in, her blonde hair falling loose about her shoulders, like a shower of bright sunlight continually shimmering there. Her eyes sought Myles, who stirred uncomfortably under her adoring gaze.

"I'm not about to disappear into thin air, Emily," he promised her with a smile.

"Well, that's what you did before," she reminded him, "and I couldn't bear it, Myles, if that happened again."

"I'm sorry, Emily. I'm here. Things will be all right from now on."

She sighed, in happy, trusting acceptance of his statement.

"This is Jacob?" she asked, her eyes resting on him with a frank interest he could feel.

"I've been hearing a lot about you," she said, but he couldn't read the expression in her face.

80

"Somehow you two haven't met yet," Myles responded, laying down his tools with a sense of unhappy resignation. "Jacob, this is Emily Hutchings. We've been friends since we were children."

Emily giggled a little and glanced meaningfully at Myles, so that Jacob found it difficult to keep a straight face. He had forgotten how ridiculous seventeen-year-old girls could act.

"Emily," Myles continued, "this is my friend, Jacob Morgan. If you're happy to have me here, then it's Jacob you have to thank for it."

There was nothing Jacob wanted less than the enthusiastic gratitude of such a girl. She was staring at him, her blue eyes big and solemn.

"I know it, Myles. I know that. And I *am* grateful, but . . ."

She paused, apparently having difficulty saying what she wanted to say, and both Jacob and Myles looked at her in surprise.

"But what, Emily?" Myles prompted.

"It's just . . . well . . . Jacob *Morgan?* He couldn't be any relation to the mobber, could he? The one with the same name—Morgan? It was Luke Morgan and his men who drove us out of DeWitt. Surely you remember that, don't you, Myles? No, it couldn't be . . . I'm certain there'd be no connection . . ."

Emily grew more uncomfortable with each word she spoke, and she addressed herself to Myles as though Jacob wasn't there. It was a rude thing to do, and Myles was torn between amusement at her discomfort and annoyance at her thoughtlessness.

"As a matter of fact, Miss Hutchings, Luke Morgan is my uncle," Jacob replied.

Emily jumped at Jacob's response and turned scarlet at his steady gaze. Jacob felt almost guilty at how much he was enjoying all this.

"Oh, no," she began. "I'm sorry. I had no idea . . . well, I didn't mean . . . after all, just because he's your uncle surely—"

"Surely what?" Myles questioned her, his own eyes twinkling now with fun. "Surely Jacob won't take you by surprise some night and shoot you all in your beds?"

"Myles!" Emily was sincerely indignant.

"Well, Emily, have a little sense," Myles responded, and Jacob noticed that the tender patience had gone from his voice.

"You can talk to Jacob all you want to later," Myles continued decidedly, "and hear gruesome mob stories to your heart's content."

Emily began to protest, but Myles picked up his trowel and turned away.

"We have work to do now, Emily so leave us alone, else Mother and Sarah will be at me for not having their kitchen ready, and I'll have three angry females after my hide instead of one."

She stood there a moment, uncomfortable and undecided. Jacob, feeling a little contrite, smiled at her before turning to his work. Myles looked up from behind his shoulder and winked at her and said more kindly, "Go on now, that's a girl. You come back tonight. You'll have my undivided attention then."

It was enough to satisfy Emily. She bustled off, happily restored. Jacob chuckled as he bent to his work.

"Funny how it is with women," he said, half musing and thinking of Alice in his arms. "Give them a little physical attention, or even the promise of some, and that's all it takes to make them happy again."

"Huh," Myles replied. "I can see you don't know Sarah. I'm afraid you'll not always find it as easy as you make it sound. Besides, it's not that I'm worried about. It's how quickly Emily picked up on the Morgan name."

"Bad omen, you think?"

"Not really. I just hope it doesn't mean we're in for trouble, Jacob. Some of the Saints will have long memories, I'm sure."

"I'm not concerned, Myles. There's not much they can do to hurt me; I have no stake here. But I wouldn't want to involve you and your family in any problems of that kind."

"Oh, don't worry about us," Myles assured him. "We Chadwicks can hold our own."

They worked a few moments in silence. Myles, usually so jovial and sociable, didn't feel like talking. Emily's visit had upset him more than he had shown. Something wasn't right between them, and he knew it was because of him. Emily was as sweet and devoted to him as ever. But Myles had changed. He wasn't the same person who had left her months ago in Far West. He knew it, and he wished that Emily knew it — wished that she was sensitive to the differences in him. But she wasn't. If anything, she was more moody and petulant and demanding than before.

He walked over to the bucket and took a deep drink. Last night he had finally tracked down where Elizabeth lived. The need to see her was like a pain he could feel. But he was afraid; afraid of what he might discover within himself. He wanted to be fair to Emily. Perhaps they only needed a little more time to get used to each other. He would wait. He would spend this evening with Emily and see what happened. Once he saw Elizabeth, he knew, he instinctively knew, that things between himself and Emily would never be the same again.

The pain was like a dull weight she carried with her; waking or sleeping Sarah was never free from the pain. She began to grow thin and her skin lacked luster. Something was shriveling inside her that she couldn't stop. She sat on her rock by the river feeling at variance with the whole world. With an almost desperate stubbornness she clung to her grief.

Who else remembered Martin, or cared? Certainly not his parents, who had taken the Gentile in as if he could be a replacement for their own son! Her father, her mother, Emily — they were so happy to have Myles home that they didn't even have the decency to mourn Martin's loss. He was already being forgotten, his place filled in. It frightened her and made the dull spot of pain flare up into something awful and consuming.

Sarah slid from the rock and picked up a piece of driftwood that had washed up along the shore, angrily hurling it as far out into the calm, motionless river as she could. She needed something to do! She would go crazy living the same colorless routine, day in and day out, with everyone watching her covertly, trying to mask their sympathy if she caught them looking. She didn't want sympathy. She wanted somebody else to care. And she wanted the pain to go away.

She scrambled back up the rock and lay with her face against the smooth, warmed surface, breathing the smell of damp earth and the sluggish river water, pungent and rich. Jacob's face rose up before her eyes and she forced it away. Those deep, gentle eyes of his haunted her. She would not admit, even to herself, how much she longed for his comfort. She remembered vividly his soothing touch, his quiet strength, his warm, resonant voice that first day she had met him along the Missouri trail.

She stretched and relaxed against the rock. She wouldn't think about Jacob. It was too easy then to want him: his attention, his admiration, his care. It was wrong for her to want him at all! She wanted Martin. She would never want anyone except Martin.

But Martin was dead. And she lay on the rock alone, very much alive, very much in need of someone living to love her in return.

13

"It's me, in the flesh. I'm not a ghost come back from the dead, so don't stare at me that way."

Elizabeth did stare, as a warm, tingling sensation spread through her.

"Yes, it's your voice, and those eyes of yours, teasing still."

She struggled to sound casual, but it wasn't working.

"Oh, Myles, you don't know how happy I am to see you!"

Suddenly he was holding her; a quick, friendly embrace. But when they drew apart they were both trembling, and neither was willing to look the other in the eyes.

All these months Elizabeth had prayed that the Lord would bring Myles safely back. For him to never return—that would almost seem like a punishment to her for loving him. She could never tell him this, never explain just how grateful she was for his safe return. She had forgotten how handsome he was; how golden his hair, how deep the startling blue depths of his eyes. How she loved it when he looked at her the way he was doing now!

"Elizabeth," he said, and her name when he spoke it was like a caress, "I thought I'd remembered how beautiful you are. But my memory didn't do you justice. Unless you've somehow grown still lovelier while I was away."

"I've never known anyone who could talk like you," she scolded him; but she dropped her eyes from before his gaze.

"Were you surprised to find the Saints had settled here, Myles?" Elizabeth asked, as they walked and talked together.

"Pleased is more like it. We knew we were headed for the Mississippi and Quincy. But I was afraid we'd get there and find our journey had only begun; or worse, that there wasn't any 'place' to go to at all."

He stood and stretched and walked, looking about him at the city.

"No, I like it here, Elizabeth. There's a feel to the place."

"I like it, too," she agreed. "It's a beautiful spot. And the Prophet has accomplished so much since he first came here in the spring."

"It's always amazed me what Brother Joseph can inspire people into doing."

Myles paused and sat beside her, closer than he had been before. He could feel the rise and fall of her gentle breathing and smell the delicate fragrance which clung about her. *I ought to leave,* he thought. *I've been here too long as it is. Perhaps she has things she needs to do.* She touched his hand where it rested on the bench between them.

"Thank you for coming, Myles," she said softly. "You don't know what it means to me."

"I think I do," he said, and he rose and stood over her. "I think it means about the same as it does to me."

"Myles, please," Elizabeth protested, her heart like a fluttering bird against her throat. "We musn't —"

"That's right. We won't talk about it now. Not yet."

He strode away from her, then back again, and he had regained the merry sparkle in his eye. "Well, what night next week are you inviting me over for dinner?"

She laughed, and her laughter was music to his ears.

"The children will be anxious to see you," she admitted, as though there were a safe excuse in that. "How would Tuesday be?"

"Tuesday will be just fine, Elizabeth," he replied with such enthusiasm that she couldn't help smiling. They walked to the edge of the yard together.

"I'll expect you at six o'clock," she said.

He nodded, then took her hand.

"By the way," he said, "I'm looking forward to seeing the children, you know that. But it's not for them I'm coming, not at all."

She didn't answer; she couldn't think of anything light and clever to say. She watched him walk down the street, and she was afraid. Myles Chadwick was very young, four years younger than herself. She had been a married woman, she had already borne two children. She knew so much more of living and loving than he did. *I musn't let myself hope that he will come courting me in earnest*, she told herself. *Even if he thinks he is serious, some young girl will come along soon enough and snatch him up. I mustn't let myself love him and be hurt.* But she knew as she watched him disappear down the street that it was already much too late for that.

Nauvoo was a city in the building, raw and unfinished. There was a constant sense of excitement in the air, as though some great wind of destiny blew over the people; lifting and stirring and whispering, giving no one rest. Jacob loved it. Every day there was something different to see. The sounds of axe and hammer and saw filled the air, mingling with the shouts of men and the bawling of beasts. There were new faces everywhere you looked—the faces of gatherers, bright with excitement and hope. Men moved with a briskness and greeted their neighbors with enthusiasm, and everything seemed moving and alive.

Jacob was caught up in it all. He liked what he saw. There were dozens of places for him to lend a hand, to use skills and experience which were so much appreciated here. He loved to see things take shape and change and grow beneath his touch.

One evening late, Jacob set out alone. Darkness had already fallen, pressing the trees and houses in silence against the land.

Jacob walked the city, liking the way Joseph Smith had planned it with tidy blocks and wide lots and a ship canal to run straight down the middle of Main Street. There were dozens of cabins already built, and hundreds more in various stages of completion. Gardens had been planted, and flowers and trees, and, further out, fields that were beginning to ripen in the intense and humid Illinois sun. Even now in the stillness he could hear the echo of men's voices and the ring of hammers as they bit into ripe wood.

He climbed the bluff and the air grew cool. He stood alone with nothing but emptiness around him, wondering what the city would look like after it had mounted the hill. What buildings would rise where he now stood? What fine homes, what shops, what schools? *I want to be here to see it!* he told himself.

He turned to start back down when he saw a figure in the shadows. He stopped a moment and listened, but the person moved on and past him, further up the bluff. He watched as the shadow drifted to where an outcropping of rock jutted out as a blacker shape in the darkness. Jacob followed and listened as the stranger climbed the rock, and he thought he saw the faint, swishing movement of a calico skirt as the slight form moved out of the shadow. He paused a moment in hesitation, then walked purposefully out in front of the rock, not hiding his movements but whistling instead.

Sarah, startled, jumped and moved further back on her rock. Jacob, hearing the sound, began to scramble up beside her.

"Who goes there?" he demanded.

Sarah, not recognizing his voice or seeing his face, was frightened; she didn't reply, but moved further back into the shadows.

"Who goes there, I said?" he demanded again, this time reaching into the shadows and grabbing her arms.

She gasped as he pulled her toward him, and she struggled in his hold. But before she could really protest they saw each other's faces in the moonlight.

"Sarah!" he exclaimed. "What are you doing up here alone in the dark? I thought you haunted the riverside. Have you also taken to wandering the hills?"

It was difficult for her to find her voice. "These aren't hills," she retorted, "and I've just as much right to be here as you have. Why did you grab me that way?"

"Why, what did you expect? I heard a movement on the ledge above me and my hackles rose. I thought it was someone up to no good. Possibly Missouri mobbers sneaking about. There's at least one in town I know of. A chap by the name of Morgan. Claims to be friendly, but . . . I don't buy that, do you?"

He looked at her with such comical mock concern that Sarah couldn't keep from laughing. He smiled and sat down, uninvited, on the rock beside her.

"What are *you* doing here?" she asked him. "You haven't explained that yet."

"Oh, just wandering about the place, getting the feel of things. There's something about Nauvoo that works into your blood. It's amazing what's been done here already. It's going to be quite the place, you know."

"So you like what we've done here, do you?" There was a hint of sarcasm in Sarah's tone. "You like what the Mormons have done so far with a miserable swampland no one else was interested in. That's to be expected."

"What do you mean?" Jacob asked her.

"Gentiles have a way of liking what the Mormons do. So much, in fact, that they eventually decide they'd like to have it for themselves. The easy way, you know — where they just go in and take it after all the work's been done."

"Do you think of me as that kind of Gentile?" he asked her gently. Sarah knew she was being unkind and hurting Jacob. He had nothing in common with men like his Uncle Luke. She knew that, and yet she hurt him, anyway.

"I'm not that kind of a Gentile," he said, "and you know it. I never have been. That's why I'm here."

"Yes!" She turned, pouncing on his words. "Why *are* you here, Jacob?"

"You know why I'm here," he replied, unruffled. "Myles has told you and I have told you enough times already."

"Well, what if I don't believe you?"

"You'd be blind if you didn't believe me, Sarah. But I think you do."

She didn't answer, and Jacob, groping, plunged on.

"Sarah," he said, choosing each word carefully. "You trusted me once, that day in the cottonwood bottom in Missouri. Why can't you trust me now?"

"Everything's different now," she said, and the hurt and the angry defensiveness were returning to her voice.

"I don't think so," Jacob said. "Nothing's really different, Sarah, but you."

"How dare you say that?" she demanded. "Martin is gone now, and there's nothing to look forward to, and I'll never be happy again."

"That's nonsense, Sarah. What do you suppose Martin would think if he heard you talking like that?"

"Don't you dare speak of Martin to me! Who do you think you are, Jacob Morgan? You're cruel! You'll never understand!"

"I'm not cruel, Sarah. And I understand far more than you want to admit. I know Martin would expect you to love him enough that you would make something of your life. He wouldn't want to see you destroy yourself this way."

Sarah began to speak, but he placed his finger firmly against her lips.

"I'm not finished yet," he told her. "And you'll have to hear me out. I know I don't really understand what you're going through, Sarah. No one can do that. But every person has trials and private sorrows that others don't see. That doesn't mean you ought to wear yours on your sleeve like this—like some kind of a badge."

She made an angry movement. "I hate you!" she said, between her teeth.

"I'm tired of hearing that, Sarah," he told her, and his voice was deep and firm. "You don't hate me, and you know it."

He paused and held her eyes with his steady gaze.

"You asked me why I'm here," he said, "and I'm going to tell you. I came, it's true, for the reasons you've already heard. But there's more now, Sarah. I'm staying—"

She moved, but he grasped her shoulders and pulled her closer, against her will.

"I'm staying because I've known, since the first time I saw you again, that I love you, Sarah."

"No!" She struggled against his hold. "Don't say that! It isn't true!"

"You know it's true, and someday you'll have to face it. I love you, Sarah. I want you to know that whenever you're ready, my love will be there."

He drew her gently against him and found her lips in the darkness. There was something in his kiss that Sarah had never felt before; a depth of longing, a boldness, a challenge which engulfed her, so that when he released her she didn't move but sat staring into the depths of his dark eyes. Without saying a word he kissed her again, and this time she drew back and rose and moved away from him.

"Go ahead and run," he said, not stirring from where he sat. "You're running away from yourself, if you do."

His voice was deep and warm, with a sureness Sarah could feel. She retreated a little distance until she stood on the path below the rock, looking up to where he sat.

"It won't do any good to run away. Only cowards do that."

His voice drew her toward him, but her pride forced her back and she moved further down the path.

"You don't know what you're talking about," she said, but her voice sounded small and without conviction.

She turned her back and disappeared down the trail, her silent tears falling as she went.

Jacob sat on the rock looking after her. He couldn't even guess what effect his words may have had. And he wasn't thinking of that. Her presence still lingered—and the sweet taste of her lips against his own. He sat alone, longing for her, unable to deny the depth and strength of his feelings. He knew he would wait and suffer whatever it would take before Sarah would be his.

14

"Here," Jacob said, slipping Sarah's arm through his own, "hold on."

The crowds were dispersing, hundreds of people trying to move all at once, children darting and pushing between their legs. Jacob found an opening and Sarah followed silently until they were through the worst of it and could walk more easily side by side. They had lost the rest of the family; even Myles and Emily, who had been trailing behind.

It was the first time they had been alone together since that night up on the bluff above Nauvoo. Sarah walked quietly, occasionally greeting people passing by. Jacob's mind was excited, on fire with what he had just heard. It was the first time he had listened to Joseph Smith preach. The Prophet had taken things which Jacob had always considered to be mysteries, or mere masses of confusion and contradiction, and explained away the error and unfolded the truth on a level which Jacob could instantly comprehend. No one had ever done that for him before. It was like fitting the pieces of a puzzle into place. He had answers he had never dreamed of obtaining, answers so simple he wondered why he had not discovered them for himself. But it seemed the answers brought new questions, and he couldn't suppress the compulsion inside him to know.

"These keys to the priesthood that Joseph Smith talked about," he said to Sarah, who looked over at him in surprise. "He talked about them coming down from Adam and Noah, from Jesus and His apostles."

"That's right," Sarah replied, curious about what might be coming next.

"If it's so important for the keys to be properly handed down, then how did Joseph Smith get them? He apparently claims to have them, doesn't he?"

"You must have missed that," she said. "He didn't go into it very thoroughly today. The keys were given to Peter, James and John by Christ. So *they* are the ones who restored them to Joseph Smith."

Jacob slowed his walk and studied Sarah intently. "Do you believe that?" he asked. "That those three apostles appeared to him and . . . and gave him that authority?"

"Yes, I do," she answered, watching his expression with interest. "Don't you think it's possible?"

"By watching him, yes. When I'm in his presence and under his influence I think anything would be possible with him."

"That's because he's a prophet of God and you can feel it," Sarah said.

They walked on a moment or two in silence. Jacob was thinking, trying to work these things out in his mind.

"If Joseph Smith really holds this power — correctly, properly, however it ought to be — then he has authority to act for God. In that case, no other religious sect would have that authority."

He looked at Sarah, his eyes bright and questioning. She nodded again.

"That's a mighty powerful claim," he said.

"With powerful implications," she answered him. "And, what's more, it makes sense. There has to be form and order wherever God is concerned. There has to be a best way, a right way — His way of doing things. And if men are really His children, wouldn't He want to communicate with them and direct them? Wouldn't they have a natural claim to the powers He could give them?"

Jacob looked at Sarah sharply, a sudden new respect growing in him. Here was a facet to the girl he had never seen before. He liked it. He liked the clear intelligence he saw in her eyes.

"That puts some new dimensions to religion, Sarah. Makes it much more than simply a moral code for good or bad behavior, with a few hazy mysteries thrown in to harass the mind. It's rather frightening."

"I think it's exciting," Sarah said. She went on to expound on some of the principles she felt he ought to know about, ideas that were new and yet rested easily, naturally on the mind. She watched the changing emotions shifting over his face as she talked, the intense interest that darted in his eyes. Checking herself, she stopped before he was utterly confused with too much at one time.

"Where did you learn all that?" he asked her, fascinated by her knowledge, by the fine grasp her mind seemed to have.

"From reading, from listening to Brother Joseph and the others. But from my father mostly."

"You're a lot like your father, aren't you?" he asked.

"Yes," she admitted. "Too much so, probably. It does a woman little good if she can think and read and recite poetry but can't even make a loaf of bread that's fit to eat."

They laughed together, and Jacob savored a sweet, intense happiness he had never known before. From somewhere Martin's family appeared; Mrs. Walker began talking to Sarah, and the spell of the moment was past. But Jacob noticed that Sarah didn't clam up, or speak bitterly, or turn away; and he clung to that small reassurance, that fleeting sign of hope.

Further back, Myles walked with Emily, stunned by the tirade she was pouring into his ears.

"There's always something more we're expected to do," she was saying, and he didn't like the tight, unbecoming look of irritation on her face. "Mother says Joseph Smith wants to keep everybody poor so they'll be humble. We hardly have roofs over our heads or food to eat, but we're expected to contribute to a temple fund, and care for the poor, and start establishing schools; and now a militia—it never seems to end!"

"These things are important, Emily, as important as food and clothing. You either believe that or you don't. Besides, Brother Joseph would never let anyone suffer while he had breath in his body to help, or room in his own house to care for them—you know that."

"Well, I don't know how he expects us to take care of everybody else when we don't even have enough to take care of ourselves."

Myles didn't answer. *I won't be critical!* he told himself. He was trying to understand. *I can't compare Emily to Elizabeth. That's unfair, it's dangerous besides.*

"Well, Myles, don't you agree?" Emily demanded, interrupting his thoughts. He didn't, but he didn't tell her so. He wasn't telling her much of what he really thought these days.

"You get excited too easily, Emily," was all he said. But he thought to himself of Elizabeth and her quiet peace, and he didn't hear much of what Emily was saying the rest of the way home.

Sarah knew that something was different as soon as he entered the room. He carried himself more straight, and the limp and drag of his leg seemed less pronounced.

"What is it, father?" Sarah questioned, rising to meet him.

"Some of the brethren are starting a school," he said, and the excitement he couldn't control was in his voice. "Nothing very fancy at first, you understand. It'll be held for now at the Shumway house."

"And?" she urged him, her own eyes sparkling.

"And they've asked me to come and teach."

"Oh, father," she cried, hugging him. "That's wonderful! It's an answer to our prayers."

"Yes, it is," he agreed, "yes it is."

"Does mother know?" Sarah asked him.

He nodded. "I told her out in the yard."

"Well, father, they were wise to choose you. There's not a better teacher in all of Nauvoo, I would guess."

"My loyal little Sarah," he said gently. She smiled at him, happier in his happiness than she ever had been at her own.

"There's no real pay," he warned her, "except in commodities."

"Well, that will be a help, won't it? I won't complain."

"Nor I," he smiled. "This is just what I've been needing, Sarah."

"I know."

She said a silent little prayer of thanks and went back to her work while her father continued to the rear of the cabin and sought his books. She wanted desperately to share the news with someone, but she hesitated about telling Emily. Emily had been acting strangely these past few weeks—cross and unhappy, and criticizing everything and everyone, even the Prophet and the Twelve. It was a dangerous course to be taking, and Sarah feared for Emily and where it might lead. She must think of some ways to help her. But she didn't want to go to her now with her news, for fear Emily would find some way to deflate and spoil it. It was too precious for that.

Jacob came to her mind, but she pushed the thought away. *I can't go to him plainly and openly, just like that. He'd consider it a victory over me!* And yet, she found herself longing just to see him! Then she remembered that he was working today draining the Walkers' west field. And the Walkers' field was adjacent to their own—and Myles was working in their field today.

She would ask her mother if she could carry Myles's lunch. It would be simple to arrange a chance meeting with Jacob, where it would be only natural to tell him her news. She was elated. Her fingers trembled as she finished her work in time to be through before lunch.

Much later, alone in the quiet attic room, Sarah leaned back against the chest and remembered with pleasure her encounter with Jacob this afternoon. How warm his eyes had become when he looked up and saw her there! He had seemed so honestly interested in her father's news. What was it he had said?

"It's been a living death for your father, not being able to do the one thing he knows and loves. He'll improve now, you wait and see. He'll be able to find himself again."

She had wanted to hug him on the spot, and she clung to his words, so fervently did she want them to be true. She closed her eyes and relived that moment he had kissed her in the night, and the way his voice had sounded when he said, "I've known since I first saw you again that I love you, Sarah."

She went weak inside at the memory, and that same aching response he could arouse in her stirred with the memories. *Why am I fighting against him?* she asked herself. But she already knew the answer. It wasn't pride, nor even love of Martin. It was fear. Fear of giving, fear of loving—fear of finding happiness and losing it again.

She dropped to her knees beside the bed and poured out her

soul to the one ear which was always open to hear and understand. She wanted to know what she should do; she prayed for an assurance that the decision she was making would be right.

She arose with the feeling of peace she had hungered for for so long. It would be difficult; she wasn't sure how she would do it, but she was through running—she wasn't going to run away any more.

"Well, who is she? It's a simple enough question, Myles. I just want to know who she is."

Simple, Miles thought, as he looked at the determination in Emily's face. *It's more like a keg of powder she's insisting I set fire to!*

"I told you. She's a widow. One of the widows in the wagon train we started from Missouri with."

"So you feel duty-bound to help her?"

Myles was having difficulty controlling himself. "Not exactly. I enjoy helping her. She's very kind and appreciative."

"Well, you must enjoy it. You spend far more time there than you do with me!"

"She needs my help, Emily."

Perversely, Emily was looking her loveliest as she stood there pouting and scowling at Myles. Myles checked an urge to reach out and stroke the slim, silken curve of her cheek.

"Why do you have to go today, right now? I want you to come on the picnic so badly."

"I promised her, Emily. She's expecting me. There will be others at the picnic to keep you occupied."

"I don't want to be with them, I want to be with you."

"I can't do anything about it now, Emily." Myles was frustrated, and a little feeling of guilt began gnawing at him inside.

"That's not true. You're choosing to go there instead of with me! It's what you want to do!"

He looked down at her, sensing this was some kind of a turning point that he was aware of and she was not. She gazed up at him, her blue eyes wet with distress. He felt sorry for her, and tender, and even drawn toward her. But the pull wasn't strong enough. He wanted to be with Elizabeth so much more.

He took the fine, narrow face between his hands. "I'm sorry, Emily. Go and have fun. It wouldn't be any better if I were there. All we seem to do anymore is argue and disagree."

New tears spilled out of the china-blue eyes. "I know it, Myles, and I can't seem to help it. I complain and I'm unhappy . . . and . . . and I don't even know why."

He pulled her to him and she leaned against his shoulder, relaxed and somewhat comforted. She was a simple little thing and would probably be easy to please if he only tried. But she was missing so many qualities that Elizabeth had, and he had never felt with her as he did with Elizabeth.

She raised her unhappy face. Myles could see how much she wanted him to kiss her. He bent his head and kissed her, long and gentle. But he felt dishonest as he did—and he knew that his time was running very short.

Myles's fingers brushed Elizabeth's as he took the glass of cold lemonade from her hand.

"Thanks," he said, downing it in one gulp and holding out his glass for more.

"Do you have any idea, Myles, how much you've done around here in the past few weeks? Let's see, you roofed the cabin and finished the inside walls, and added the little lean-to in back. You bricked in the oven and the well house, chopped wood and built the fence—"

"Sounds pretty impressive, the way you're reciting it all at once. Wasn't much, taken bit by bit."

She smiled, loving him, loving his endearing ways. "Well, at least you're reaching the bottom of the list. There can't be much more left to do."

He looked distressed, though his eyes were dancing. "Then I'll have to start inventing things, I guess. Thanks for the warning."

She laughed; the light, silvery laughter he loved so well. "Oh, Myles, I don't know what to do with you. I really don't."

"Just keep feeding me your apple pies and sweet rolls. That'll keep me coming around, I promise you."

They had purposefully avoided any serious talk between

them, skirting it with a desperate play of levity, but the pressure was beginning to tell on them both.

"Myles," a feminine voice called, and they both looked up from their lemonade, startled at the interruption. It was Catherine Mason, one of the young girls Myles's age. Elizabeth recognized her immediately and struggled against the cold, strangling sensation she felt creeping over her. She busied herself with the cookies and lemonade tray as Myles sauntered over to the fence, but she was listening carefully.

"Hi, Katy. How are things going?" Myles was good at being casual and friendly; he could carry it off very well.

"All right, I guess. I didn't know you and Elizabeth knew each other."

The interest in her voice was unmistakable. Myles nodded.

"A lot of work to be done when there isn't a man around the place."

A matter-of-fact statement. Katy nodded in return.

"I hadn't thought of that. Are you going to be at the big dance next weekend?"

"Hadn't heard there was one," Myles replied.

"Oh, yes, a harvest dance. It's about time, as far as I'm concerned. I've been so bored all summer. Brother Jepson's band is going to play. It ought to be lovely."

Myles offered no response, so Katy went on. "Do you think you'll be going, Myles?"

The audacity of some girls! Elizabeth thought, fighting the feeling of panic the girl's presence induced. Myles, standing beside Katy at the gate, wondered himself at her boldness. Katy was one who knew Emily's possessiveness where he was concerned. He sighed inwardly. Well, he might as well start telling the truth right now. It would be easier than covering his tracks afterward.

"What night did you say that was, Katy?" he asked her.

"Next Friday, in Johnson's field at the north end of town."

"Know the place," he nodded. "But I guess I won't be there."

"You won't be there?" Katy sounded stunned. "Are you sure?"

"I've got other plans that night. Sorry." He turned from the fence, calling back over his shoulder, "Nice seeing you, Katy. Gotta get back to work."

Katy stood by the fence a moment, then continued her walk down the street. Myles came over and stopped very close to Elizabeth.

"What are you going to be doing next Friday night?" she asked him, without looking up from the things she was fussing over.

"Same thing I'll be doing the night before and the night after, and the night after that, I hope."

"Whatever do you mean?" she asked, bewildered.

"I'll be here, doing something—anything—spending the evening with you."

She backed away from him, fighting the feeling of warmth and relief his words had produced.

"You can't mean that . . . you're not thinking, Myles. Friday night will come and you'll want to be there. The fun and music, the dancing, the pretty girls—"

He was beside her in an instant and grabbed her wrist so angrily that it hurt.

"Don't talk like that!" he said. "I don't want to hear you talk that way. I'm not going to that dance to be smothered by a swarm of giddy girls, nor to watch the smooth young bachelors fight over you."

"Myles—"

"No, listen to me, Elizabeth. It's time now. You know our ages don't separate us one bit. I don't belong with those kids my age. I don't know what did it—if it was a combination of you and Martin, or if it's just something inside myself. It doesn't matter, Elizabeth. You're worried because of what others will think, and nothing more."

She shook her head, tears coming to her eyes.

"What is it, then? What are you worried about?"

She wouldn't answer. He pulled her to him fiercely, still holding her wrist so that it ached in his grasp.

"Tell me!" he demanded. "Tell me, Elizabeth."

"I'm afraid . . . I'm so afraid of losing you, Myles."

It came out little more than a whisper, and she hid her eyes from his gaze, in peril now that he knew her deepest fears. So much was revealed to Myles in those few words. For a moment he was overwhelmed in feeling and grasping it all.

"Elizabeth." His own voice was soft and as gentle as he could make it. "Look at me, Elizabeth, please."

She slowly raised her eyes, revealing to him her soul.

"I can't dissolve the whole fear for you, Elizabeth, I just can't! Death—I have no more control over death than your husband, David, had."

He paused because a thought had come to him suddenly. "Elizabeth! What torment you must have gone through when I was lost!"

She nodded, the tears spilling out and streaking her cheeks.

"Listen, Elizabeth, listen!" He held her with both hands now, and his voice was husky with urgency.

"I'll never hurt you, Elizabeth. I give you my solemn word. You must believe me! Say you believe me, Elizabeth."

"I do," she whispered. "I believe you, Myles, I do."

"The only way you can lose me is if you send me away. And I can't guarantee that even that would work."

She was crying now in little sobs, but he kissed her anyway, again and again, until she had to draw back to catch her breath. He knew as he held her, as he kissed her, that she was part of him— a part that fit naturally into place and made him whole.

"There's nothing to be afraid of." Myles's voice was firm with an assurance it had never held before. "You remember that, Elizabeth. I love you. I'll always love you. There's nothing to be afraid of anymore."

15

Sarah saw them coming, but not soon enough to avoid them.

"That's lovely material you're buying, Sarah," Sister Liscom said, running her hand over it appraisingly.

"Dresses for my younger sisters," Sarah explained. "They've worn out what little they had."

"You're fortunate to be able to buy new, my dear." That was Sister White, who had a habit of blinking her eyes, especially when she was nervous. She stood close to Sarah, fluttering her eyelids in that annoying way and dabbing at the corners of her watery eyes now and then with a wrinkled, faded handkerchief.

"Father's teaching at Brother Shumway's school, did you know?" What good to try to explain to them that the dress goods were partial payment for her father's teaching fees?

"Why, no! What a surprise! How wonderful for you all!"

Sarah watched the two women, wondering why she always sensed a feeling of insincerity about everything they did. She picked up her package and turned to go, but suddenly Sister Liscom stood square in her path.

"That's not the only news, Sarah. Aren't you going to tell us the rest?"

"What do you mean?" Sarah questioned, instantly suspicious.

"Now, Sarah, don't be difficult, my dear."

Sarah shuddered and turned away from the wet, blinking eyes. "I really don't know what you mean," she answered the ladies, though she was beginning to get a few ideas.

"Why, your brother. Coming back from the dead the way he did and bringing that stranger with him."

There was just the slightest emphasis in Sister Liscom's voice when she came to the word *stranger*.

"Oh, yes — yes, it was wonderful. We're all very grateful."

"Of course you are, of course you are."

Sister Liscom cleared her throat and Sarah slipped to the other side of the counter and began walking toward the door. But the two ladies stayed so close to her that she could feel their skirts brushing against her own as she walked.

"Now the other young gentleman, Sarah, the one who brought Myles home. What family was he from? I can't seem to recall his name."

I'll bet you can't! Sarah thought angrily. *You're just dying to make me say it!* She hesitated only a moment, and then decided what to do.

"Why, I'm surprised, Sister Liscom, with your memory that you could have forgotten. It's a name you ought to be familiar with." Sarah loved the sugary, dripping sweet quality she was creating with her own voice.

"Whatever do you mean, Sarah?"

"His name is Morgan, Sister Liscom. Jacob Morgan. As a matter of fact, he's a nephew of the mobber, Luke Morgan. Now I'm certain you must remember him."

"Why, of course I remember Luke Morgan. That is something we shall none of us forget!" Sister Liscom was becoming indignant. "But the young one — this . . . Jacob, is it? Surely he's become a member of the Church, hasn't he?"

"Heavens, no. No, he's a dyed-in-the-wool Gentile," Sarah answered cheerily.

"Why, Sarah," Sister White interjected, fluttering her eyes. "I've seen you several times walking about town on his arm. That won't do, you know. That just won't do."

"Oh, I don't know, Sister White. I think it does just fine. I find Jacob Morgan far more intelligent and exciting than any of the young men around here."

Sarah gathered her skirts, dipped around the two startled women, and pushed open the door, flashing them a bright, innocent smile. "Good afternoon, sisters," she called, then skipped down the steps and was gone.

As soon as she was far enough away Sarah laughed out loud. *Perhaps what I did was rude,* she thought, *but I loved every minute of it! It's rude to entertain an unkind interest in other people's affairs, as those two worthy sisters always seem to be doing.*

The September sun was hot, but not sluggish and heavy as the summer sun had been. *How can it be September already? How long has Jacob been here?* She thought about him as she walked, the same pleasure welling up inside her that thoughts of him always brought. She marveled that this man who stirred her feelings carried the same blood in his veins as the evil man on the tall black horse who had haunted her dreams. *How many times have we laughed together?* she wondered. *Worked together, talked about everything from nonsense to matters of life and death? How many times has he helped me and understood me? How many times has he kissed me, as only Jacob is able to kiss?*

Sarah walked the familiar path, but her mind was in a world of its own: remembering, wondering — imagining and pretending all kinds of wonderful things. In everything she imagined and desired Jacob was there. Thoughts of Martin came less often and less painfully now. And as she walked down the road making up fancies in her head, the realization never entered her mind that she was no longer thinking in terms of "how many weeks has it been since Martin died?" but "how many weeks since Jacob came here?"

"Well, will you do it for me, or won't you?" Jacob asked.

"Of course I'll do it; I'd be honored to do it," Myles replied. "It's just that you've taken me by surprise."

"Surprise or not, you don't seem very anxious. What happened to the typical Mormon zeal for baptizing converts? Am I that undesirable a candidate?"

"You know it's not that, Jacob. I just want to make sure you know what you're doing." Myles paused and looked at Jacob. "And that you're doing it for the right reasons."

"You certainly could never be accused of high-pressure proselyting, Myles."

"I'm sorry, Jacob, you're right. I don't want to seem unenthusiastic. In fact . . ." Myles walked over so that he faced Jacob again. "If you want to know the truth, there's nothing I want more than to see you a member of the Church. I want it so badly that I have this fear, you know — that if I face it head on I'll somehow destroy any chance of it coming true."

Jacob nodded slowly. "I understand." He walked over to the fence and leaned on the high rail, gazing across the planted fields that spread out in orderly fashion and zigzagged down to the river shore.

"It's not as though this is something I've always wanted to do.

You'll never know how much I've fought it, Myles."

Myles nodded as the deep brown eyes sought his own.

"But a man reaches a point where he can't run away from himself. I know the principles of Mormonism are true. I believe Joseph Smith is a prophet. The priesthood, eternal progression, the Book of Mormon, the nature of God—I believe it all, Myles, so what choice do I have?"

"What about Sarah?"

"Do you think her influence makes a difference here?"

"I just want to know what you think," Myles replied.

"I can't pretend she's not part of the picture, Myles. But it's deeper than that, more personal; something I have to face, Sarah or no Sarah."

"And your mother, Jacob. What about her?"

Jacob frowned a little and pushed his brown hair off his forehead with an anxious gesture. He looked straight at Myles and his eyes were troubled.

"I'm not certain. All I can do is hope, and pray, she'll understand."

Myles nodded thoughtfully. "Well, we'll cross that bridge when we come to it. The business at hand right now is to get you baptized. Right?"

Myles put his arm around Jacob's shoulder, finding it suddenly difficult to speak.

"I remember that night you found us in the barn. I'd never been more scared in my life."

"You handled it mighty well—threatening me with an empty gun."

They both laughed at the memory of that awful time. "There was a bullet in Martin's gun, but I couldn't reach it," Myles reminded him.

"Some would say it was fate that made you choose my barn to hide in."

"Fate . . . Providence . . . whatever you call it, I know it was," Myles answered quietly. "I'd prayed about it half the night. I knew Martin couldn't make it one day longer. I passed three farms in the rain and sleet, but I didn't stop."

"Why not?"

"I'm not sure. Something made me keep going, though it seemed like a crazy thing to do."

"Then why did you stop at my place?"

"You may not believe this, but as soon as I saw the house a warm feeling came over me, and I knew it was right for me to go there."

Jacob was silent, considering what Myles had said.

"I knew it was right again when you walked into the barn."

"What do you mean?"

"There was some quality in your voice—something warm and kind. I felt from the first that I could trust you."

"I didn't realize that; you never told me before."

"I was afraid you wouldn't understand. I didn't want to do anything to turn you away."

There was more Myles wanted to say, much more, but he couldn't get the words to come.

"Have you told Sarah yet?" he asked instead.

A light came into Jacob's eyes. "No, I think I'll tell her tomorrow night at the dance."

"She'll be pleased. It's what she's been praying for."

"Do you think so?"

Myles grinned. "I know so! You think you made this decision all on your own, Jacob? There have been more people praying you into this Church than you'd want to know."

They laughed together and walked back to the house. Jacob gave some thought to what Myles had said. He didn't know much about prayer, but here with the Mormons he had heard story after story about its power in people's lives. Twice now it had influenced his own without his even knowing it. Perhaps he might learn how to use it himself. Perhaps it might make a difference with his mother.

I may know a lot about Mormonism, he decided, *but I don't know very much about being a Mormon!*

"Why didn't you tell me she was young and beautiful, Myles?" Emily's pale skin was glowing with indignant rage. Myles dropped the bushel basket of potatoes he was carrying and tried to take her hand, but she snatched it out of his grasp.

"Sit down here, Emily, let's talk."

"You'd rather be with her than with me! I knew it all along. It wasn't fair for you to let me think she was just an old widow. Katy says she's as pretty as I am, even if she is older and already has two children."

"Stop it, Emily. It doesn't matter whether she's pretty or not. That's not what makes me enjoy being with her."

"Then you admit it! You see, Myles, you admit it. I don't understand. How could you possibly prefer a woman who's already been married? It doesn't make sense, Myles, it isn't even right!"

"You're right about one thing, Emily, you don't understand. So you may as well stop working yourself up this way."

"Working myself up! I suppose you have nothing to do with it! Are you coming to the dance tomorrow, Myles? Just answer me that. Katy said she bet you wouldn't be there at all."

"Well, good for Katy! My activities are none of her affair, Emily."

"Nor my affair either. Is that what you're trying to say?"

"Emily—"

"Don't 'Emily' me. Just answer my question! Are you coming to the dance?"

Myles hesitated; this wasn't how he had wanted things to go. *I've waited too long,* he told himself. *I should have talked to her last week before Katy got to her. But I was so busy with the harvest, and I dreaded the idea of this encounter so much—*

"Are you coming with the widow? Is that what you're afraid to tell me? Or is it just that you hope she'll be there so you can dance with her all night?"

"Katy was right. I'm not coming to the dance, Emily."

Emily's blue eyes flashed, like a summer sky turned livid with storm.

"How could you? What shall I do? Everyone will expect us to be there together! How can you do this to me, Myles?"

"Emily, please calm down a little and let me explain. Please listen to me."

She had risen and stood facing him, hands on hips.

"I don't have to listen to you, Myles Chadwick. I'm not the least bit interested in anything you have to say!"

"That's not true, Emily. Please give me a chance. You listened to Katy, now listen to me."

She backed away from him, taut with anger and pride. "I know what you're going to say, and I don't want to hear it. In fact, I don't want to ever see you again!"

There were tears in her eyes as she said it, breaking through the cold pride. But before Myles could touch her she turned and ran. He watched her, but she didn't once look back. *I know she expects me to go after her,* he thought to himself. *But I can't do it, I can't play those games any more.*

He bent and picked up the potatoes, and they seemed twice as heavy as they had before. *You've gotten yourself into this, Myles,* he chided himself as he walked along. *And you've got to think of something better than what just happened to get yourself out.*

The night could not have been more perfect if Sarah had ordered it herself. September had forgotten that summer was over and had stepped into her lightest, loveliest gown, trailing the scents of late roses and hollyhocks in her wake. Every star in the sky had decided to shine, and a light breeze freshened the murky river air and sighed through drowsy trees. Sarah's heart ached with the beauty of it all.

When Jacob took her hand it was as though he had never touched her before, as though his presence were as mystical and magical as the night. She clung to him as they walked, drawing closer and closer to the lights and music, to the murmur of voices and laughter that waited ahead.

Then Jacob turned down a narrow lane that took them away from Johnson's field. The lights and the voices faded, and they could hear again the whisperings of the wind and look up into the lighted heavens where the brilliant stars danced and sparkled.

"I have something to tell you, Sarah, and I wanted you to hear it when we could be alone together, like now."

Sarah's heart began to flutter and her head felt light. There could be only two things Jacob would want to tell her in private, and both seemed equally unlikely to her. She pushed back her hair and looked at him, trying to read his secret in his eyes.

Jacob, watching her, was as sensitive to her beauty as she was to the beauty of the night. There seemed something pure and ethereal about her, her loveliness as golden and elusive as the burning stars and the fragrant, restless breeze.

"Sarah, I've asked Myles to baptize me and he's agreed."

"You mean it! You're really—"

"Yes, I'm really going to be baptized. Myles and I talked with the presiding brethren, it's all arranged. And I know what I'm doing, Sarah. You don't have to be concerned about that."

"Oh, I'm not, I'm not, Jacob. I know you well enough to realize that you know your own mind and where you're going. I just wasn't aware that things had come so close to this."

"I had to do it on my own, and you know why."

"So you're sure now?"

Jacob nodded.

"And are you really happy, Jacob? You've made the decision you know to be right, but are you really happy about it?"

Jacob hadn't yet looked at it that way. "I've never given much thought to being happy," he said at last. "I never felt miserable and cheated by life, even when my father died. Even then I felt strong. There were things to comfort me, reasons why I wanted to conquer and go on."

He paused, for the thoughts were slow in coming and the words were difficult to speak. "So I suppose I've always been happy, without really thinking about it, you know."

"And now?"

"Now—since you've made me take it apart and examine it—now I feel different than I've ever felt before. In spite of how much I've fought it, I've found more peace and purpose here than I thought was possible in life."

"That's good!" Sarah's violet eyes were smiling. "And that's only the bare beginning, Jacob. Just a peek at what lies ahead."

"But there are more reasons than one for my happiness, and I can't separate you from the gospel, Sarah, in my heart. It's all too finely interwoven together."

"That's as it should be, too," she said. She leaned over and brushed his cheek with a light, soft kiss. "I'm so happy, Jacob. I didn't think this kind of happiness waited for me."

"It's only the bare beginning," he repeated, "just a peek at what lies ahead."

——————— 16 ———————

The dance was in full swing when Jacob and Sarah arrived. It seemed everyone in Nauvoo was there, from the young boys and girls who took no interest in dancing to the old men and women who couldn't keep up with the tempo of Brother Jepson's band even if they wanted to.

Sarah spied Emily dancing with some boy she didn't know. She smiled and waved, and was surprised when Emily ignored her. With a toss of her yellow curls Emily turned to the young man. He said something that must have been clever, because Emily giggled outrageously and slipped her arm through his, sidling up so close to him that Sarah was shocked. *She must have had an awful argument with Myles to be behaving like that!* Sarah thought. *Where is Myles, anyway?* Sarah spent several moments searching faces, but she couldn't find him anywhere.

It was wonderful having an entire evening to spend with Jacob. Sarah savored his touch, his conversation, his smile—all different for her than they were for anyone else. She was amused by the many curious glances that came their way, as she strolled about with the strange Gentile from Missouri. Through it all ran the knowledge of her new discovery—like some bright thread of happiness and promise weaving in and out of everything they did.

It happened later in the evening, when the band had paused for refreshments and people were visiting together in little groups. Sarah would never forget the pain of those endless moments when it seemed as though a giant ink spot had smudged the sky, smearing the stars until even the glittering sparks went dead, and the air, so sweet and fragrant, tasted sour and spoiled.

Sarah didn't even see her until she was right beside them and the twinkling voice cried, "Jacob, Jacob darling. I've found you at last!"

Then the girl with the silken black ringlets was in his arms, kissing him boldly there under the lights, for anyone who wanted to see. Sarah couldn't see Jacob's face, only the girl's when at last she unwound herself from him and stepped back, her eyes bright with triumph.

"You don't know how much I've missed you! You wicked boy, to go off like that without telling me a thing!"

She moved close to him again and said softly into his ear, "Didn't you know that I can't survive without you?"

Sarah was getting sick now, with a dizzy feeling in her head. She watched Jacob push the girl firmly back and hold her away from him.

"Behave yourself, Alice, or you'll go right back where you came from as fast as I can send you."

A dark look came into Alice's eyes, but she responded to the note of authority in Jacob's voice and was docile long enough for him to introduce everyone in a civil manner—long enough for the curiosity seekers to become bored and drift away.

The band struck up a tune and Alice turned on her charm again.

"What delightful people you Mormons are," she cooed to Sarah. "I don't know what I would have done without Thomas here. He's been so helpful and understanding, haven't you, Tom?"

She pulled the embarrassed boy toward her, fluttering her thick, dark lashes and flirting in a smooth, delicate manner Sarah had never witnessed before. She was so entrancing that Sarah felt awkward and dull in her presence.

Tom, it seemed, had found her — or rather she had found him — when the ferry deposited her on the Nauvoo side of the river. He hadn't known who Jacob was, but he could tell her that there was a dance going on, and most everyone in town was bound to be there. And he had even been so kind as to borrow his uncle's wagon and drive her out here himself.

"Why, I never dreamed Mormon boys could be so sweet," Alice concluded. But her eyes were all for Jacob, not the uncomfortable Tom. "Tell me, Jacob, are the Mormon girls sweet, too?"

Before Jacob could respond Alice turned and slipped her arm companionably through Sarah's.

"It seems you've taken good care of Jacob for me, honey, and that was certainly a sweet thing to do."

Her laughter was as lilting and enchanting as her voice, but there was no warmth in it, and it sent chills down Sarah's spine. She drew back sharply from Alice's touch, but she was too hurt to be able to retaliate with words.

Jacob turned to Alice with anger in his eyes, but just then the band began a new tune and with a quick, deft movement Alice pulled him out onto the cleared field where the dancers were gathering. People were swarming everywhere, separating them from Sarah's sight. For a moment she lingered, but the tears made everything merge and swim; and at last she turned away.

Jacob was trapped until the dance was over. He had a panicky feeling inside because he couldn't see Sarah through the crowds. Alice had never disgusted him more, and he wanted to shake her until her pretty little teeth rattled in her head.

"You're disgraceful, Alice," he told her, with a scorn in his voice she had never heard there before, "and too selfish to understand what a fool you made of yourself back there."

"Why, Jacob, I never dreamed you'd be so happy to see me," Alice purred.

But it didn't work. She hadn't expected to find things this bad. She may have to resort to emergency measures, and emergency measures were not always strictly above board.

By the time the dance was finished Alice had laid her plans

and adopted a sweet, innocent manner; her most difficult to assume. And it was fortunate for her that she didn't know then how long she would be compelled to keep up the act.

Jacob deposited her at the edge of the field and went looking for Sarah. Time and again he passed over the same ground, asked the same people, called her name, while Alice stood fuming and waiting alone. She was angry at his neglect and angry at herself for not dropping the guise and flirting with the moon-faced boys who stole glances her way; it would have served Jacob right.

But when he returned to her side she managed to look troubled and concerned.

"I'm sorry you didn't find her, Jacob. How awful! I didn't know she was so sensitive."

"I'll have to go after her—"

"Oh, Jacob, please!" She rubbed her hand up and down his arm in a helpless little gesture. "It's late and I'm so tired. Can't it wait till tomorrow? She's probably gone to bed and won't talk to you tonight, anyway. And it's been so long since I've seen you . . ."

He hesitated, and she leaned her head against him and ran her finger lightly along the back of his neck and through his thick, soft hair. "Don't you want to hear the news of home?"

"Yes." He was suddenly interested. "What word did my mother send?"

"Sit down by me here and I'll tell you. That is, if you'll stop scowling that awful way!"

He sat and tried to smile, though his heart was heavy and he was fighting a feeling of doom that had settled upon him. She took his big hand in her own, caressing the skin and playing with the fingers as she spoke.

"Your mother's healthy and well. The crops were good, especially in that far south field you planted. She said to tell you she has the harvest well in hand . . ." Alice paused and knit her brow as if in concentration.

"Was that all?" Jacob prompted. "What about me? How is she taking my absence? And why did she tell you I had come here? She did tell you, didn't she?"

"One question at a time, Jacob." Alice took a deep breath; everything depended on what happened next. "Especially . . ." her voice faltered, "since those will be difficult questions to answer."

"What do you mean?"

"Well, Jacob . . . " she hesitated, gazing at him with the most woebegone expression she could muster, allowing the tiniest tremble to appear in her voice. "I hate to tell you . . . I mean . . . well, I don't even know if she'd want me to tell. . . . And yet, I think — I really think you ought to know."

"I'm listening," he said. The cold, hopeless tone of his voice frightened Alice, so that her faltering was sincere as she went on.

"Your mother's been next to distraction since you've been gone, Jacob. I came over the day after you left and found her in bed. It scared me to death to see her that way! She said she had been determined to hold up until you left. But then . . . well . . . she just sort of fell to pieces."

"That isn't like her."

"Of course it isn't like her, Jacob. But what do you expect? Her pride and joy, the son of her heart, her only strength — and you walk out on her suddenly. How do you expect her to react?"

"I didn't exactly walk out on her, Alice, I—"

"It's the same thing to her, Jacob. You've got to realize that. She's afraid to lose you. She doesn't eat well, she never sings, or even smiles. . . ." She paused, touched by the look of pain on Jacob's face. "I think she's afraid she's lost you already."

"And where do you come in?"

It was spoken coldly, dispassionately, and Alice had a hard time contriving the warm, melting smile she wanted right now.

"I've missed you, too. I discovered how hard it was to live without you. I intended to plague your mother until she told me what had happened and where you had gone. But I didn't have to. Once she knew my intentions and my sincerity, well . . . then she nearly begged me to go. She wants me to save you from the Mormons, Jacob. She said if I came here and found you already a Mormon — it would break her heart."

Jacob rose and paced the ground in front of her, staring straight ahead with a stony gaze. Alice felt a chill creep over her. He paused and walked to her, lifting her up from the bench so that she faced him eye to eye.

"Is this true, Alice? Do you swear what you're telling me is true?"

Alice had never come closer to being entirely unnerved. But she held, and gazed back at him without flinching. She thought to herself, *I want you, Jacob Morgan. And I will do anything it takes to get you.*

"Yes, Jacob," she answered him, "What I've told you is true."

She looked into his eyes, sorry she couldn't tell him what had really happened: how proud and patient and trusting his mother had been, how hard Alice had had to work to discover Jacob's whereabouts, and how Laura's eyes had shone when she said, "Bring him back if you can, Alice. I pray every day he'll come home to me again. But tell him that I trust him, Alice."

Jacob dropped his hands from Alice's shoulders in a worn and helpless gesture.

"Come on," he said, "I'll walk you back to town."

She couldn't get him to talk, to respond to her in any way, so they walked through the darkness in silence. By the time they reached the main street of Nauvoo, Alice had decided that she hated the place. It was dirty here and uncivilized, and the people were dull. Too dull to match wits with her. She planned to stick it out until she won; though she hoped to heaven that wouldn't take too long.

"Have you a place to stay?" She started at the sound of Jacob's voice beside her.

"Yes, thank you, though I'd hardly consider it satisfactory."

She bit her tongue, but Jacob hadn't even noticed the sarcastic bitterness in her voice. He walked her to the boarding house and at the door he said, "I'll be here in the morning and arrange for your passage back home. Good night, Alice."

He was gone before she could think of something to keep him there. He had left her at the doorstep, a stranger in a strange town! She was angry, and frightened for perhaps the first time in her life. *What strange power do the Mormons have that they can change Jacob this*

114

way? That girl, Alice thought. *Of course! That innocent-looking girl has something to do with this!* She stomped up the stairs to her room. She had her work cut out for her, that was certain. And she would have to start early in the morning before Jacob returned.

The next morning Jacob could find Sarah nowhere. Every place and any place she was wont to go he checked, and checked again. No one had seen her; not even her mother seemed to have any idea where Sarah had gone. Giving up at last, Jacob rode through town to the boarding house. He dreaded facing Alice; but there was no way to put it off.

She saw him coming, and was down the stairs and out in the street to greet him before he had dismounted his horse. Her ebony curls shone like polished silk in the morning sun and she wore a fresh blue frock — her favorite color — cinched tight at the waist and trimmed with yards of soft, delicate white lace. She flashed a brilliant smile at Jacob and took his arm.

"Good morning, Jacob. I'm so glad you're finally here! You'll never guess all the wonderful things that have been happening to me!"

She sat him down and told him about meeting Sister Paul: how sweet and motherly she was and how, coincidentally, she operated a little millinery shop and had offered Alice a position, as well as room and board with her. Alice squeezed Jacob's hand, her black eyes snapping.

"It's perfect, isn't it, Jacob? I can escape this dreary boarding house, and in no time at all I'll be indispensable to Sister Paul. You know what an excellent seamstress I am."

"Why do you call her 'Sister' Paul?"

"That's what everyone does around here. I think she feels more comfortable that way."

"I'm here to send you back home, Alice."

"Oh, Jacob, please! Don't send me away. I'll behave, I promise. I have to be near you, Jacob." She paused, but he wasn't respond-ing, in spite of her lowered lashes and helpless little sighs.

"I like it here," she continued. "I like the people, Jacob, and I think it would be wise for me to stay."

"Wise? Explain what you mean."

She wanted to pound on Jacob for being so insensitive. Instead she smiled sweetly and said, "If I went back unhappy, with reports of how thoroughly 'Mormon' you've become, what would it do to your mother?" She saw him wince and knew she had finally captured his attention.

"If we *both* stay until spring and go back together, I could help convince her, Jacob."

"Convince her of what?"

"That the Mormons aren't so awful — that the world wouldn't end if you decided to become a Mormon."

He looked up at her and she could see how hard he was thinking behind his eyes.

"My opinion would make some difference with her, you know."

She said it a little proudly, then continued more softly. "Besides, by the time I could make arrangements, it would be too late in the season — too dangerous to travel all the way back."

"I'd go home now myself, but I'm committed here," Jacob said, almost to himself. "The Walkers are depending on me to finish the harvest. There are so many things — I can't just leave everyone hanging. They wouldn't understand . . . they'd think . . ."

"I know that — and so does your mother, Jacob. So don't send me back to upset things even more. Your mother wanted me here to take care of you — for her."

He didn't protest, but she wished she knew what he was thinking. She moved so that she stood close against him and placed her arms loosely about his neck, playing with the thick hair that curled at the back of his head.

"Don't give up hope, Jacob," she whispered soothingly. "If this is what you really want, I'll help you get it. I'd do anything to make you happy."

The last she said into his ear, then turned her face and kissed him, relieved when he responded. She wouldn't release him, but kissed him again, loving the feeling of power it gave her. She was certain that, with a little time, she could win him back again.

17

It was evening now, but Sarah still had not come home. Jacob had toiled in the fields all day and was exhausted physically. But then, he was accustomed to that. It was the cruel play of his emotions which was wearing him down. He questioned Sarah's mother, but her answers seemed evasive. So he stationed himself in the shadows by her front door, and prepared to wait.

He paced back and forth in front of the window, his mind going over and over the places he had searched and the people he had asked. Had he left anyone out? He sought desperately for some clue he could act upon. Was there anyone who might have covered for Sarah, who would have lied to him? It came instantly, a clear picture of the lovely, porcelain features: the fair skin and the high-boned cheeks, piercing blue eyes and fine yellow hair. Emily! Could it be? Could she possibly know where Sarah was?

He covered the distance to the Hutchings's home in long strides, drinking in the cool night air as though it contained some elixir of strength, feeling his weariness fall away from him with each step.

He banged on the door persistently until a light appeared in the window. It was several minutes longer before Emily's father pulled back the latch and opened the door a crack.

"Excuse me for disturbing you," Jacob said hastily, hoping that his ruse would work. "There's trouble at Sarah's house, sir, someone's sick. I think she'd best come home right away."

"Is it that serious, boy? I hate to wake her."

"I'm afraid you'd better. I'm here to take her home."

"Oh, all right, if you insist. I'm sure her mother wouldn't have sent for her if it hadn't been important." He turned and started back into the house. "Do you want to wait inside?"

"No, no thank you. Just hurry, sir!"

Jacob paced up and down by the door, trembling with excitement. He hadn't really lied. Everything he had said was truth, even though it would be wrongly taken. Now, if only Sarah hurried down, without asking too many questions.

She was there! Her shawl flung over her shoulders, her hair tangled and falling loose. Jacob stepped back into the shadows. She paused on the threshold and gazed about. Jacob took her hand, pulling her out beside him.

"Thank you, sir, we appreciate it. Sorry again to disturb you."

Sarah and Jacob were halfway down the walk before she realized what was happening, or whose hand was pulling her in the dark.

"You let us know how things are in the morning, Sarah," Emily's father called.

Sarah began to answer, but Jacob put his hand firmly over her mouth and in one smooth motion picked her up and carried her past the dark houses toward the trees that skirted the water's edge. She struggled in his arms, but her strength was no match for his. When he thought it safe he removed his hand from her mouth.

"Let me down!" she insisted. "Jacob, how dare you! Where do you think you're taking me?"

He didn't answer but widened his stride and laughed out loud in sheer relief. He placed her down beside the big rock by the river, but he held her arm firmly still.

"How did you find me?" she demanded, her voice trembling with angry indignation.

"I finally figured it out for myself," he said, some of his satisfaction seeping into his voice.

"Well, aren't you the clever one?" she replied haughtily. "And you lied! You woke Brother Hutchings in the middle of the night and lied to get me here!"

"I did no such thing. Every word I said to him was true."

"Well, aren't you proud of yourself!" She stomped her foot and glared at him through the darkness.

"Not hardly, Sarah," he said, and his voice grew suddenly soft. "I'm actually very miserable. This has been one of the most difficult days of my life."

"I'm surprised to hear that. I would have expected you to be enjoying yourself with your old sweetheart. I'm sure that's what she had in mind."

"Yes, I'm sure it is."

"Well, don't tell me you didn't see her! I happen to know you did. I happen to know—"

"Ah! So you're not so entirely disinterested."

Sarah paused, frustrated.

"Why didn't you tell me that was the kind of girl you liked? You could have saved us both a lot of trouble, Jacob."

"Sarah, please let me explain!"

"Explain! There's nothing to explain. You apparently were quite serious about . . . what's her name?"

"Alice."

". . . Alice," Sarah continued, "before you came. Now she's here and everything's changed. I assume you'll be going back with her—"

"I'm not going back, Sarah, especially not with her."

"You're not getting baptized, either! Myles told me you had talked to him, and you aren't going to be baptized."

"Alice has nothing to do with my not getting baptized. At least, not directly."

"What do you mean?"

"It's my mother. She didn't want me to come in the first place. Alice tells me it's been harder on her than I knew. My mother said it would kill her if I were to join the Mormon church."

"Do you believe that?"

"I have to believe it! You don't understand, Sarah. I just can't hurt her . . . I promised my father . . ." He stopped, not wanting to have said even that much. "I'll just have to wait, that's all. In the spring I'll go back and talk to her."

Sarah was shaking her head. "It won't work. You can't talk people out of that kind of prejudice."

"It has to work!" he cried, and his hand tightened against her arm.

Sarah laughed; a high, bitter sound in the quiet night. "Well, that's not good enough for me, Jacob. I'm not going to sit here, vying with that creature for your attentions, while you decide what you're going to do."

"You don't have to. I told you I've already decided. I'm going to become a Mormon. And I'm going to marry you, Sarah."

She began to protest, but he pulled her into his arms and kissed her, and it was an angry, demanding kiss.

"I'm sorry Alice came," he said, not letting her go yet, and his voice had grown soft and tender again. "There is really nothing between us; there never was. Her presence here hurts you, and for that alone I could hate her, Sarah."

She turned to him, startled at the intense sincerity in his words.

"I've never loved any woman but you, and I never will. Can't you trust me, Sarah, just a little while?"

She wanted to say yes so very badly. But the fear and pain were like a barrier her love and good intentions could not break down.

"That's all right," he said, holding her gently. "I told you I would earn your love. And I will — whether you want to believe it or not."

They stood together in their own narrow world of silence and pain, both struggling with fears they felt the other could not understand; unable to comfort one another.

Sarah walked briskly. The sky was threatening rain and a gusty wind tugged at her skirts, teasing her hair in long strands across her face. It was nearly two weeks now since Jacob had come in the night to Emily's house and taken her away! She thought, *how different, how dreary life has become since then!* She didn't see him every day as she had managed to do before, and when they did meet there was a strain between them.

She couldn't say she felt hopeless, really, but she was certainly unhappy; and all the light and magic seemed to have vanished from her life. "This, too, shall pass" — how often her mother had quoted that to the family in days of persecution and despair! But why did it have to apply to happiness, as well? Why could nothing remain beautiful and happy and safe?

She was surprised to hear laughter when she entered the house: her little sisters' voices and someone else she couldn't identify. The sounds were muffled; they must be in the back yard, perhaps out by the garden where the pumpkins and squashes and her mother's late asters and marigolds were still in bloom.

She walked back, curious at what could be causing the little girls to squeal in apparent delight. She pushed open the door and looked out, not wanting to believe the evidence of her own eyes. It was Alice—Jacob's Alice—sitting in her mother's chair with Rebeccah on her lap! Louisa was curled at her feet and Ann stood beside her, her hand on Alice's arm. Sarah went cold inside and a hard knot began to form in her stomach. Alice was telling them a story, and the girls were enthralled—sighing and protesting, giggling and screaming at all the right places. Alice's bright, lilting voice seemed to bubble over the air, like the happy sounds of the meadow streams in springtime; light and happy and without a care.

Sarah began backing toward the door, but Alice caught sight of her and called out, "Come over, Sarah. We're just about finished with the story and then you and I can talk."

Sarah came reluctantly, the smile on her face feeling stiff and unnatural.

"Your little sisters are darlings. I've fallen in love with them all," she said, winking at Louisa and tossling Ann's hair.

"Have you any sisters of your own?" Sarah asked, keeping her voice impersonal and polite.

"Heavens, no. Four older brothers, nuisances every one," she laughed.

"Well, I can't see that you'd object to that arrangement. How easy it must have been to become spoiled and pampered, being the only girl."

Alice raised her eyebrows, but said nothing.

The story over, the little girls scattered, leaving Sarah alone with the visitor. Alice didn't seem to notice Sarah's discomfort, but chatted gaily.

"I met your sisters next door just now while I was delivering a dress."

"One you made yourself?"

"Yes, and it was a beauty, too, though my mother would say it was wrong to praise my own handwork. If you ask me, Sarah," she added conspiratorily, "it was much too pretty for the sister who will be wearing it."

She laughed brightly and shrugged her small, elegant shoulders.

Sarah resented the familiar way she used her name, and how easily Alice had taken on the habit of calling everyone "sister" and "brother" — as though she belonged here, as though she were part of the Saints.

"Do you like to sew?" Sarah asked, her voice toneless.

"I've loved it since I was a little girl. And mother, as you would suspect" — she paused and fluttered her thick black lashes at Sarah — "always indulged me. I couldn't resist the beautiful laces, the buttons and ribbons and fabrics she brought home. I've won first prize in the county fair every year since I was ten."

Sarah smiled, or rather she moved her lips in what became only a thin, tight gesture.

"How nice," she said. "Do you think you're going to like it here?"

She tried to ask the question in the same casual tone, but her heart was throbbing in fear of what Alice might reply. Alice considered a moment, pursing her full, red lips and knitting the fine, slender line of eyebrow that arched her beautiful, round eyes.

"Just between you and me, Sarah, I'm going to do my best."

"You don't really like it, do you?" Sarah said, her own voice appraising and hard.

"I didn't say that — and I won't. I've got too much at stake, you know," and the black eyes bored into Sarah so that she felt like shrinking before them.

"So as far as everyone's concerned, I love it here," she said, and her eyes gleamed darkly. "I'm a real little disciple, excited and enthusiastic about absolutely everything!"

"No one will believe you," Sarah said.

The bright smile flashed, showing a row of lovely white teeth.

"That's where you're wrong, my little Sarah," Alice said, gathering her skirts and preparing to go. "Everyone will believe me, honey, just wait and see!"

18

"And I heard the same thing again, just the other day, Jacob."

The look of worry and concern sat well on Alice's face, Jacob thought. He liked the way it softened her features.

"Tell me about it," he said.

"These two women came into Sister Paul's shop. Just looking around, you know. I could tell they weren't buyers from the minute I laid eyes on them."

"And?" Jacob prodded.

"Well, one of them had an extremely loud voice, loud and harsh like a man's, and she said, 'You know that handsome young Gentile?' "

Alice paused and fluttered her eyes at Jacob. "You see, even the homely old ladies notice you, Jacob."

"Go on," he said, smiling at her winsome ways.

"The woman said, 'He was all set to join the Church, you know.' "

" 'Is that right?' the other one gasped, all ears.

" 'Oh, yes,' the lady with the big voice went on, 'but at the last minute he backed out. Just like that. No reason, no explanations.'

"And then she leaned close to the other lady and tried to whisper." Alice screwed up her face in a gruesome expression, imitating the woman. "But I could hear her anyway, you know. 'I've heard he's got mob connections,' she said. Well, her friend was horrified, Jacob, and I almost laughed at the expression on her face. The nasty old lady drew herself up and puffed out her chest and said, so self-righteously, 'I never did trust him. No, in spite of that pretty face, I never did trust him!' "

Jacob laughed, delighted at the vivid picture Alice drew.

"It isn't funny, Jacob," she said indignantly. "I almost tripped her when she walked past me. I could have done it easily, and it would have served her right."

"Stop it, Alice, you know that isn't nice."

"Well, I wish you wouldn't laugh. Doesn't it upset you having people talk about you that way?"

"Not really," he replied thoughtfully. "But it does upset me that I wasn't able to be baptized."

"Does it mean that much to you, Jacob? I mean, is it really, really important?" Alice asked.

"Yes, Alice, I wish I could make you see how important it is. The longer I stay here the more I realize how much I want what the Mormons have."

"And what is that, Jacob?"

"Truth . . . authority . . . answers that make for happiness and peace."

"Happiness and peace! It doesn't seem to me they've had much of either!"

"You have to understand," Jacob said softly. "It's something you have to feel and want before you can understand."

When he left her he kissed her absently on the cheek. As she stood at the window and watched him all her old fears returned. When he got like this she lost her control over him — that influence of her physical powers she counted on. *In spite of my suffering and denial, I'm still losing him!*

The cold fear clutched at her heart and drove her on like a pain. *I shall have to do something more drastic,* she thought, *and I know exactly what! I just don't know if I have enough nerve to carry it out!*

What little nerve Alice lacked was supplied for her in full the next day. It was a Sunday, and the Saints had gathered in the bowery to hear Joseph Smith and Sidney Rigdon speak.

It was a mild day for October, autumn having come gently this year — doing nothing too hurried or too harsh. Jacob had found Sarah and they walked home together, the spell of the autumn day upon them. Alice saw them from her doorway, moving back before they had a chance to discover her. She watched them with a cold appraising eye. *It's the easiest thing in the world to see how much in love with her he is,* she thought. Her heart was pounding, but she waited until they were past, then went out in search of Sister Paul. She would have to speed up her plans, and she knew Sister Paul would unwittingly tell her what she needed to know.

Sarah walked beside Jacob, more aware of him as a man than she had been for a long time. She glanced over at him, and the realization of how much she loved him swept over her. Suddenly nothing else seemed important but his happiness.

"Isn't that Emily up ahead?" he asked, pointing to show her where. Sarah nodded. "Well, who's that boy she's walking with? What's going on? I never see her with Myles anymore."

"I'm not sure what's going on, but I think you and I ought to leave it alone."

"You do?"

She laughed and touched his arm lightly. "I think we have enough problems of our own."

"I suppose. Though I'd like to be able to forget them for a while."

"Why don't we, then."

Jacob looked up, surprised at the enthusiasm in Sarah's voice.

"I mean it," she insisted, the smile in her violet-blue eyes touching Jacob like a caress. "I'll pack a picnic lunch. I've discovered some lovely woods—off to the east there, see?" She turned his head and motioned eagerly. "They'll be beautiful with the autumn colors, Jacob."

"They're some distance off. Would you like to take the Walkers' buggy?"

"Oh, do you think we could?"

"I ought to be able to arrange it."

Sarah hugged his arm in excitement. Suddenly there was no need for words; the magic was between them, and Sarah vowed to herself she would keep it there, at least for today.

"You're getting baptized!" Jacob sputtered. "I don't believe it!"

"And why not?" Alice replied haughtily. "Do you think you're the only one who can become converted to the Mormons?"

"Converted—don't tell me you're really converted, Alice."

"I've been studying the Book of Mormon and the revelations, Jacob," she explained sweetly. "Believe me, I know what I'm doing, and I want to do it, my darling, very much."

She moved close to him and kissed him just once. It was still within her powers, she assured herself, to arouse his desire for her. But now wasn't the time for that. She mustn't cloud the issue, mustn't give him any possible reason for doubt. This was costing her too much—and she was determined to gain the highest possible use from it.

Sarah refused to go to the baptism. For her it would be hypocrisy, though she couldn't explain that to anyone else. She could scarcely believe Alice would go this far. It frightened her to think of the intensity of the girl's ambition. She felt a little lost and betrayed all through the day, especially so since everyone else was making such a fuss. Even her own family had accepted Alice on face value, and the little girls adored her still.

Jacob is a man, Sarah thought uneasily. *He will be so easy to fool! Now that Alice has worked her way into the Church, what plans does she have?* Sarah refused to be frightened, but the fear was there inside her just the same. It wasn't an equal contest; she felt she wasn't equipped to fight Alice on Alice's terms.

She moved about the quiet house from task to task, restless; unable to face the misery of her own solitary company. She had never felt more like a woman than she did today; with a woman's desires and a woman's needs. And she was struggling with a woman's knowledge of what love and hatred, virtue and evil, were really about.

After the baptism and the congratulations, and the festivities, with apple cider and Sister Paul's blueberry pie, Jacob walked Alice home. The autumn day was dissolving into dusk, and the air that rose from the river was damp and chill. But Alice pulled her warm cashmere shawl with the long, knotted silk fringe around her and ignored the cold.

"Oh, Jacob, I'm so happy," she cried.

"Are you, Alice?" he asked gently, and he sounded pensive, almost sad. *The dullard*, Alice thought angrily, *to be pensive at a time like this!*

"Smile, Jacob, your mouth is going to freeze into that horrid expression!" Alice donned her most charming, flirtatious manner and mimicked him until he laughed. She danced along beside him, determined to make him forget himself tonight; determined that he should forget all else but her.

The night was misty and wild and the wind spoke through the trees in a thousand weird, unnatural voices, and whimpered in swirls about their feet. Alice clung to him, desperate to awaken the response she desired.

"I love you, Jacob," she whispered fiercely against his hair. "Please don't fight it, Jacob, love me, too. I told you before how happy I can make you."

She turned in his arms and kissed him, but he wasn't there. She could feel how distant he was, as his eyes looked through her to something she couldn't see. And the spell of the wild night and her own turbulent beauty and desire were unable to call him back.

The morning was too early for the weak October sunlight to hold much warmth. Emily wished she had brought a heavier shawl as she pulled her old one more closely about her shoulders and herded the little ones ahead of her. She was anxious to deposit them safely in the school, see to her few errands, and hurry back to the warmth of her mother's cheery kitchen.

Myles saw her from a distance and waited until she was past the noisy schoolhouse and alone, before walking up swiftly from behind and slipping his arm through hers. She started, then pulled away when she saw who it was.

"Emily, this is ridiculous," Myles said, easily matching his stride to hers. "Do you know how long I've been trying to see you?"

"I don't know and I don't care. There's no reason for us to be seeing each other, Myles. Not as long as you've got an infatuation for a married woman."

"What are you intimating—that when I come to my senses you may be gracious and take me back again?"

"Something like that." She stopped and regarded him haughtily. "I'm getting along just fine without you," she said. But it was more accusation than even defense.

"I've noticed. Well, I won't detain you then any longer." He looked into the blue eyes, and he couldn't see beyond the haughtiness and pride. "I was going to try to explain some things, but I don't think it would do any good. Some time, perhaps, I don't know . . ." He lifted a strand of her flaxen hair, absently running it between his fingers. "Good-bye, Emily."

He walked past her and on down the hill. She watched him: his broad shoulders, the easy movement of his body, the way his hair shone tawny and gold even under a pale sun. She felt suddenly weak and wished there was a place to sit down, or better still a dark corner where she could cry with no one to hear.

Why hadn't she told him she was miserable and lonely? Why hadn't she told him that the eager boys who courted her, all heaped together, couldn't compare with him? She loved him and he had hurt her; and she had been determined to punish him. She had never seriously entertained the possibility that she could lose him. What if she did? What if she lost him to the widow because of her own foolishness and pride?

Alice melted into Jacob's arms, but he pulled away, stiff and unresponsive. *What is happening?* she wondered, panicking. *Why am I losing my hold over him?* She had joined the Church for him — for his sake alone, yet he seemed less impressed than anyone else. *How can he continue to resist me? I'm far more beautiful and alluring than that simple Mormon girl he thinks he's in love with! Besides,* Alice admitted to herself, *I still want him!* She couldn't bear his rejection. Through everything that happened, through the losses and the triumphs, ran the one consistent thread of her desire for him.

Jacob looked across the room at Alice. She was angry with him, he knew. Her black eyes smouldered, and the lines in her face were hard and uncompromising. There was no real talking with Alice; he couldn't begin to explain the feelings inside him, the changes he was experiencing. And how was he to tell her that he didn't love her? That even his desire for her was growing more and more secondary to his love for Sarah?

There was a shout somewhere in the street below, then other voices, loud and excited. Jacob went to the window and pushed it open wide, leaning far out and calling to the people now gathering into a little knot beneath him. Alice couldn't hear what was

128

shouted up in response to Jacob's call, but when he turned from the window his face was drawn tight, so that she noticed the fine, strong line of his cheekbones and jaw.

"There's a fire somewhere at the east end of Parley," he told her, and she couldn't understand the excited look in his eyes.

"So," she answered bluntly. "I'm sure there will be someone to take care of it. It doesn't concern you, Jacob. Not now, when you promised—"

He was pulling on his coat with brief, anxious movements.

"It does concern me," he said, not even looking at her. "That's close to where Sarah lives. Too close. I think I'd better go in case I'm needed."

He was so much the fool that he didn't even try to mask his eagerness.

"You're needed here," she said. Something in her voice made Jacob pause and look at her. She was standing tall and straight, but her face was inscrutable. He could feel her anger reach out and touch him like the hot edge of a blade.

"This is different, Alice, and you know it. I don't have time to argue or explain. I'm going; and you'll just have to accept it."

"And if I don't?"

"If you don't, then you'll have your own decisions to make. I can't make them for you, Alice."

She didn't speak to him, not even to say good-bye, but she stood so straight her back ached, glaring directly ahead until the door closed behind him. She wasn't so sure she didn't hate Jacob Morgan at this minute. When she did move it was to pace the confines of the narrow room, back and forth, her rage needing some active outlet else it would consume her in its power.

Well, now she would have to do what she had hoped she could avoid. She recalled that conversation back in Missouri and the arrangement by which two of Luke Morgan's men had accompanied her to the Mississippi River. Too bad Jacob hadn't responded. Now she had no choice but to use the other method.

Next morning Alice rose and dressed, long before the quiet city around her was awake. At this hour it was neither light nor dark, but some murky shade in between; dull as unpolished pewter, shallow and dead of promise. It fitted Alice's mood as she urged her reluctant horse through the cold mud that marked where last year's trail had been. She hadn't thought it would come to this, and she smiled bitterly at the memory of how she had first scorned the idea. She was not quite certain of the directions and hoped she would recognize the landmarks: a thick copse of cottonwood trees skirted on the west by a narrow stream and off to the south three large evergreens, full-branched and tall, in an even line together.

She bent her head to avoid a cold, wet branch that just caught her sleeve, sprinkling her with pin-pricks of dew. The trail rose and she urged the horse on, hoping he wouldn't slip. At last she reached a wide, grassy meadow, and there ahead was the stand of trees and the sentinel firs, blue-black in the half-light.

It was yet a longer distance than she had thought, and when she reached the firs and pulled up both she and the horse were trembling. She twisted in the saddle and looked in all directions around, but the world seemed as dead as the sky; devoid of movement or sound, devoid of life. She sat a moment longer, listening to her own deep breathing and the breathing of the horse, whose warm, heaving sides against her legs seemed her only contact with life and reality.

Then out of the cluster of trees a horseman came riding. He moved slowly into the clearing, then stopped; a grey shadow against the brown tangle of trees. Alice turned her horse and rode across the meadow toward him. As she approached he pulled in beside her, and together they disappeared among the dark trees and were lost to view. The meadow stretched empty and undisturbed as the first rays of morning broke through the thinning sky.

19

It was dark, more with the storm than with the night. Rain blew in fitful gusts and the air had the breath of winter in it. Jacob didn't hear the men approaching and was surprised when Brother Walker called him into the room. There were three men standing together, their hats stained and dripping from the rain, their cheeks and noses red from the sting of the numbing November wind.

They were all men Jacob recognized; but they wouldn't meet his eyes. Brother Billings, whom Jacob had worked side by side with the day fire broke out on Parley Street, cleared his throat and kept his eyes on the tip of his boot which dug worriedly into the rag rug as he spoke.

"We'll come direct to the point, Jacob. We're here to find out about those reports we've heard."

Brother Walker lifted his eyebrows in question as he and Jacob exchanged a quick glance.

"What reports, Brother Billings? I don't know what you're talking about."

"Come on, now, upriver from here, four nights ago. Group of Missourians crossed the Mississippi and dragged two Mormons back with them. Kept 'em in an old abandoned cabin without food."

"They tied them to a tree and whipped them before they let them go," Brother Mason added, and though his voice was quiet there was a definite note of accusation behind it.

"And?"

"And, son, your name was named as one of the mobbers. George here, well . . . one of the men taken was his cousin. That's how we heard. That's how we know for sure."

"Know *what* for sure?" Jacob asked, walking close to the man, who still did not look up.

"Well, know that you were with 'em! They called each other by name, the mobbers did. And one of the names the men remember was Jacob Morgan."

"Jacob Morgan —"

"That's right. That's you, boy, isn't it?"

Jacob didn't answer. He walked over by the fire, his back to the others, and thought a moment. He was angry, but he couldn't let it show.

"Did they describe this supposed Jacob Morgan to you?" He turned, facing the men now, his voice controlled and quiet.

"No . . . no . . . we didn't get an actual description. But it was your uncle's men, we know that from some of the names, and from that big black stallion Luke Morgan always rides. . ."

Then it's true; Luke has really done this wretched thing!

"And you supposed that I had sympathies with my uncle? Supposed I would sneak away from Nauvoo and join in that kind of an outrage?"

The men hesitated; Brother Billings took off his hat and smoothed his thinning hair.

"He named you, son! What else were we to think?"

Jacob didn't reply, but he stared at the man, forcing him to meet his eyes.

"Four nights ago one of my best milk cows was down with fever. Jacob and I worked with her together for half the night." Brother Walker spoke from the shadows without moving, and his voice was so low that the men had to strain to hear him. "Names or no names, brethren, you've got the wrong man."

Brother Billings shuffled his feet, then his boot returned to tracing circles over the patternless rug. "Now, Owen, we —"

"Michael . . . brethren . . . good evening," Brother Walker said, and he moved to the door and opened it wide. The storm was suddenly with them; the only voice in the quiet room. The three men looked at one another, then at Owen Walker's immovable face, then back to each other again — but no one spoke; and no one looked at Jacob. They walked out into the storm, disappearing as though they had never been there at all, and Brother Walker closed the door after them.

The two men looked at each other across the room, then Owen Walker covered the distance between them and laid his hand on the younger man's shoulder.

132

"You've been like a son to me, Jacob. I know your heart. These . . . these rumors will blow over. The Saints' wounds are newly healed, Jacob, and break open again easily. It might make it a little easier for you to remember that."

Jacob nodded and swallowed, trying to get rid of the hard lump in his throat.

"Your support, sir — I can't tell you what it means."

"You've earned it, Jacob, a hundred times over by now."

Alone in his room Jacob thought that the storm gained in fury, with a thousand demon voices mocking him, like the voices of Luke Morgan and Morgan's men mocking his name and cursing his uneasy peace.

There was a difference after that. Perhaps too many people had heard the rumor; perhaps Jacob's presence was too much a reminder of unpleasant things people wanted to forget. Sarah was aware of the difference, and it cast a shade, a cloud over all she did. Alice was aware of it — and she watched it and tried to measure it, and fed it as men feed carefully the hot, licking fire which gives them both warmth and light.

Alone with Jacob, as she so seldom was these days, she tested the strength, the sting of the searing flames.

"When the chips are down it doesn't take long to find out whether you're among friends."

"What do you mean?" Jacob asked, though he could easily read her meaning.

"The Mormons are a back-biting, fault-finding lot, and they know how to hold a grudge. It doesn't matter whether you were with that group of mobbers or not — they'll never forgive you."

"If that's what you believe, why are you one of them?"

"I didn't know they were that way; they deceived me."

"You know the way out, Alice; no one's holding you here."

She threw back her fine head, the black curls shimmering with motion. "I don't understand you, Jacob. What reason do you have to be loyal to them?"

He smiled; a kind, sad smile, which served only to madden her further.

"I'm not loyal to them, Alice, I'm loyal to their principles. I'm not converted to the Mormon people, I'm converted to the things they believe in."

"It's the same thing, Jacob. If people don't reflect their beliefs, then what good are they?"

Jacob arched his eyebrows at that; Alice was always on her toes, that was one thing he could count on.

"I suppose it boils down to the fact that I don't believe they're as bad as you do."

"You're fooling yourself. You refuse to see them as they are."

He turned to her, his eyes burning with some emotion she couldn't identify that made her feel ill at ease.

"Do the Latter-day Saints see you as you really are, Alice?" He asked it quietly, but it seemed to thunder in the air when his words were through. He left the unanswered question hanging there and continued.

"There's too much of value here for me to throw it away for the sake of a few petty people. The Mormons are human, Alice. There are bound to be bad ones among them. But there's a bigger gathering of great men and women among them than I've ever seen anywhere before. I'll take my chances with the Mormons any day."

She sputtered at him, here eyes smouldering and narrow, unable to find an argument that could better his.

"Poor Alice," he murmured. He rose and came over to her and touched her silken hair gently with his hand. But his touch was like a fire tearing through her; touching not only her hair, but every nerve ending on her body.

"You're searching for happiness everywhere but the one place you will find it; within yourself."

He left her with her anger and his pity; and she found pity a stale and hardened substitute for love.

It was a quiet afternoon. Emily knew the widow would be home; Katy was acting as spy for her and had seen Elizabeth return less than an hour before. It was a bold thing Emily was doing, and rash. But it was the last move left her; after that was only defeat.

She walked up the path through the well-kept yard and knocked purposefully on the door. The woman who answered was lovely, and she wore a puzzled look on her face. But at Emily's request she admitted her, closing the door quietly behind her guest.

Sarah was in the barn. She had just finished the milking and was wiping her hands on her apron and pushing the swarming kittens back from the edge of the bucket with her toe until she could find their dish and pour them some of the thick warm milk.

Myles came in, his face dead white, not creamy like the new, frothy milk.

"What's happened?" she asked. Her mind was blank, unable to picture the kind of tragedy he might be carrying in his hands.

"There was a stranger in town today asking for Jacob. Someone directed him to me and together we found Jacob. He was a Missourian, Sarah; one of Luke Morgan's men."

"I don't care if the man was the devil, himself, Myles! What did he want with Jacob?" Sarah brushed at a fly that buzzed fretfully above her head.

"He had a message that Jacob's mother is sick . . ."

"And he's going to her." Sarah's voice had gone toneless and dead.

"Well, Sarah, what choice does he have? Don't be daft, girl, his mother may be dying! He loves her. It's late to be traveling back, I know, but Luke's man will go with him. They ought to—"

"He won't come back, will he, Myles?" Sarah had sunk down onto the low stool she used for milking. She looked like a shrunken heap, with no real substance as she huddled there. Myles grabbed her shoulders and yanked her up roughly beside him.

"Yes, he'll come back! Of course he'll come back. Are you listening, Sarah?"

He gave her a hard little shake; she was frightening him. He didn't like the blank, vacant look in her eyes. "Stop it, Sarah, do you have so little faith as that?"

Her mouth twisted in what ought to have been a smile but

dissolved into a haunting expression of pain. "His mother loves him; she'll keep him there with her love."

"And what of you? What of Jacob's love for you?"

The twisted look on Sarah's face grew harder. She pulled away from Myles and shrank into a corner, crouching there like some frightened, wounded wild thing. He came up beside her and spoke in soothing tones.

"Jacob will leave at noon and he wants to see you. He sent me to tell you, Sarah. At the big rock down by the river, right at noon. He'll be waiting there for you, Sarah. Do you hear me?"

She nodded, but wouldn't answer or look up. At last he lifted the bucket and left her there. She didn't cry but stared into the dusty dimness of the barn, remembering another night in another barn, and another lost love. And she wondered how many times the same heart could break.

The rock felt cold and damp against Jacob's hand. He ran his fingers over the smooth surface, then paced down to the cold river and back again, needing some release for the pent-up tension he carried inside. He was early; he couldn't expect to see Sarah yet. He looked across the wide water to the opposite shore. *At home,* he thought, *my mother lies dying, needing me. Why is it only Sarah I can think of?*

Alone in Sister Paul's rooms she lived in Alice applied the finishing touches to her make-up and tied creamy wine satin ribbons into her hair. The scent she sprinkled lavishly was an expensive one, alluring yet subtle; Jacob had always liked it particularly. She smiled back at her image in the mirror. She held the winning hand now, and that was how she liked it.

She pulled her black merino cape around her and hurried down the stairs. Timing was of vital importance and each step must be carefully executed now. She mounted the lean grey mare that stood waiting for her, then checked the scroll-carved clock pinned daintily on her dress. She clucked her tongue to the horse and moved out — exactly on schedule.

Jacob didn't see her coming; she made certain of that. He looked over when she slid out from the bushes behind the rock, her skirts whispering against the brittle, bent branches.

"Jacob, Jacob darling, how awful of you!" Her voice was as low and whispery as the branches. She was beside him in her quick, sure way, pushing back his hair and smoothing his forehead; crooning to him as a mother would croon to a child.

"Your mother will be all right; your coming will make the difference. Give her my love, Jacob . . . and . . . make her happy. You're the only person left who can make her happy."

Jacob opened his watch; it was nearing noon. Alice understood his concern, and she purred against him, soothing him, lulling him, enjoying his hidden pain.

"How did you know where I was?" he demanded.

"I found Dudley and he said you'd be leaving from here."

"Alice . . . Alice, we've already said good-bye. I'd appreciate it . . . it would be easier for me if you'd leave."

Alice's purr turned to a low laugh, deep in her throat. "But don't you want someone here to say good-bye?"

She slid her arms up his chest and around his neck. He looked over her head, his eyes searching for movement. But it was Alice who saw the flash of calico and heard the light crack of branches underfoot.

"Alice, please —"

"But, Jacob, you haven't even kissed me good-bye." She stood on tiptoe then and pressed her lips against his. It took him only a few moments to push her away. All she could hope was that those moments had been enough.

Sarah had known in the end she would have to go to Jacob. Perhaps it would be easier, would give her something to wait for. Perhaps he would give her his promise to return. *Could she trust his promise?* a cold voice whispered inside her. But she ignored the voice and walked to the river rock.

She paused because she thought she heard voices speaking, a woman's voice — and then she saw them together. Alice was in his arms, close against him. She watched as he kissed her and the coldness inside her spread. She thought she would get sick; she thought she couldn't bear it. There was a high ringing in her head and her stomach was churning.

She jerked around and made her way back up the slope — carefully so they wouldn't hear her or see her. When she was far enough away she fell to her knees, and cried in great dry sobs that wrenched her body. The pain was so awful. *Perhaps I will die of the pain,* she thought. *Oh, merciful heaven, let me die and escape the pain!*

Back by the rock Alice shook free of Jacob's arms as they set her away from him, and smiled; a soft smile, gentle and demure.

"I'll leave now, Jacob, if you want to be alone. Remember, though—remember how much I love you."

She stroked his cheek and moved her warm lips close against his ear. "Go home, Jacob. This place has brought nothing but sorrow. Go home where you belong—where you can be happy."

She touched his fingers gently, then turned and left him. He watched her graceful figure disappear and cursed her for the sorrow she had brought him. What if Sarah had come and seen her here? He walked along the river in both directions. He couldn't see her. What if she didn't come?

It was cold, he realized, and the wind was rising. They were barely into November, though; the trip shouldn't be too bad if the weather held. Walt Dudley would be here to meet him any minute. Where was Sarah? He closed his eyes and prayed that she would come.

Dudley gave him plenty of time to sweat it out in the cold alone before riding up with the pack animals and his big, empty grin.

"See yer girl, Jake? Hope her kisses were warm ones. It's a cold trail waitin' for us, that's fer sure."

He held his stupid grin till it looked unnatural. Jacob shuddered and mounted and turned his horse. He was leaving with all of his promises left unsaid. He hadn't held Sarah and kissed her and told her he loved her. Alone he would have gone off in search of her. But with Dudley beside him he had no choice but to ride for home. His mother was sick; she could very well be dying. But there were other deaths which only the living suffered. Why must he leave Sarah to that kind of purposeless pain? He, who had been so sure of himself, so cocky—who had thought he would save her from suffering and bring her happiness.

What love she might hold for me, his cruel thoughts taunted, *the pain will devour and destroy. There will be only ashes left—and scars that love can't heal.*

138

The Test of Love

20

Perhaps it was meant to be merciful; a kind heaven's way to keep her from going crazy with the pain. But as soon as Jacob left, everything went wrong. The snug-fitting pieces of life jarred apart, became scattered and scrambled; order dissolved into chaos about Sarah's head. She had no time to think or feel. All her powers were concentrated in one blind purpose: to keep going on.

First it was her father who took the sickness. Weak already, he was no match for the rigor of the ague, the tenacity of the fever which brought the hot, burning sweats when his skin seemed to be smouldering from some inner source of fire that nothing could quench; then turned, with capricious cruelty, to the wracking chills when nothing could make the awful shivering stop.

Her strong, practical mother nursed him tirelessly day and night, leaving everything else in the household in Sarah's care. And while her father slowly recovered, the three little girls took sick. Myles moved in with the Walkers, though he came each day to tend to the animals and do the outside chores. The days were long and dark, filled with endless tasks and a deadening sameness. Always there was the grey haze of fear; the hushed voices, a sudden catch of the breath, the questions never spoken but passed furtively eye to eye. There was no room for anything but the moment; and each moment that passed without tragedy was a miracle in itself.

The little girls held their own, like a long, slow breath suspended, and the green-grey hue of dying began to fade from her father's face. Then one morning Ellen Chadwick failed to get out of bed. Sarah couldn't remember the last time that had happened. It frightened her more than anything that had gone before. It was impossible for anything bad to befall her mother! She was the wise one who never quavered or bent. She was the strength that nothing could mar or shatter. But all that day she stayed to her bed, and the next—until finally Sarah faced the unthinkable. Then, with every strength taken from her, she longed for Jacob!

A cold storm struck, and the snows blew over the prairie, shrouding the land in a whiteness as icy as death. The bitter cold worsened the sickness and many died, lashed with the fury of death while the storm's fury roared, leaving only the cold folds of whiteness to cover the scars.

Ellen Chadwick was strong, with a good constitution; the fever's mocking fury would not claim her. But while she lay helpless and unaware, the black sickness tightened its hold on her youngest daughter. Sarah sat by Ann's bed and wouldn't leave her. Somebody cooked the meals and washed the clothing. From somewhere there was fresh bread for the others to eat. Sarah sat by Ann's bed and watched the fever, alone in the darkened room with the enemy.

When the fits got bad and Ann's little fingers turned black, and her tongue, caught tight in her teeth, needed prying loose, Myles and their father administered to the child. The disease bared its teeth and retreated a little distance. But Sarah refused to leave Ann alone. Ann wasn't strong enough to fight the darkness. Sarah and the darkness were long, old friends. She sat by the death-still form, enwrapped in numbness. No thoughts came through, no feelings; pain stilled them all. But her need for Jacob was there, like a parasite gnawing inside her. The need, like the pain, refused to give her peace.

The trip, for Jacob, seemed like something outside himself—unreal. They crossed the wide Mississippi, then rode in silence. Frontier men don't need conversation for company. Jacob rode with his thoughts; Walter Dudley had none. Long hours of lonely riding had a way of blanking out thought, if that's what a man was after. The weather held, and the white November sun shone down with what warmth was in it. Once into Missouri Jacob felt a sense of urgency, and he would have pressed on when Dudley suggested they make camp for the night. The odd grin spread across his face when Jacob protested.

"Now, Jake, don't be difficult," he drawled, with the maddening grin still sprawled there. "You don't want to spoil the party, do you?"

They were off in the cover now, away from the trail. There was something in Dudley's voice Jacob didn't like. It sent goosebumps rising on the skin at the back of his neck. Dudley laughed and spat and turned in the saddle. Jacob followed his gaze to where a line of horsemen rode out from behind a shelter of trees.

Jacob began to recognize the men one by one as they drew nearer: fat, squat Siras Murdoch, with whiskers that bristled out like the ends of a broom and the foulest mouth in the state when he wanted to use it; Clinton Dudley, Walter's little brother, whose left arm had been shot off above the elbow. Whatever the weather Clint always wore a jacket to hide the stump, and he wasn't really a bad sort unless somebody got him drunk. The men rode with their faces down, and the line was bunching, so that Jacob had difficulty recognizing each face.

He could pick out skinny Pete Funk, so tall in the saddle. Pete wouldn't lay a finger on a horse, but he'd gladly whip a man till he slumped, half-dead. And, of course, Luke Morgan rode at the head of the line on the tall, lean horse that was blacker than night; his face from this distance was a mask that said nothing at all.

The group began to separate and circle around them. It was too quiet, with a high, tight strain in the air. In a sudden, blinding flash Jacob knew what Walt Dudley had meant when he talked of a party — and it was Jacob who was intended to provide the entertainment!

He whirled, dug his heels into his horse's flanks, bent low in the saddle and headed for the widest gap in the circle of men. An open meadow spread out like a bronze-gold carpet; he could never hope to outrun the group of them here. But something inside him refused to just stand and be taken.

Suddenly there was no longer a gap before him, but a horse and a rider that bolted close to his own. His beast shied and reared, turning from the threat of impact. The other rider was so close their legs brushed and the boots scraped together, but twisting and turning Jacob couldn't see the man's face.

Then the cold, hard point of a rifle was leveled at him. His hands tightened on the reins as he looked down the length of the fine, slender muzzle. The rifle was a Greener, a British weapon. A lovely piece, lavish with brass ornamentation and exquisitely-scrolled woodwork — the mark of an English-made Greener. It was an old piece, and it had rested over the mantel of his father's house since Jacob could remember, and longer; from before he was even born.

A taste stuck in his throat, dry and bitter, and he swallowed hard. Now he gazed down the grey, oiled muzzle of the Greener, like an outcast on the wrong side of the fence. The face that watched him from the other end of the rifle was the one face he had not expected to find here.

It was a young face, and in many aspects resembled his own: the deep-set eyes, the prominent hawk-like nose. Maybe the chin was weaker, and the mouth — the mouth was altogether different from his. *Perhaps men, like horses,* he thought, *reflected the forces that broke them; the boy's mouth mirrored a meanness, a sarcasm running to cruelty.* The boy shifted his eyes and for a brief moment brother looked at brother. Then the space around exploded with horses and men.

Someone grabbed Jacob's arms and bound them behind him; another lifted his weapons, but he couldn't tell who. The air, so heavy before with the unnatural silence, rang now with crude oaths and laughter and ugly words. A thin trickle of cold sweat ran down Jacob's backbone. He didn't know what to expect, but whatever they had in mind for him wouldn't be pleasant.

Rough hands pulled him down from the saddle. Losing his balance he stumbled and fell, then struggled to stand. The men clustered around him, edging closer. Their eyes glowed hard like the wolves' eyes that haunted the campfires, hungry and mean. Jacob stood as straight as he could and tried to breathe deeply. He searched for his uncle's face apart from the others and found it, forcing the veiled eyes to look into his own. He held them — knowing that was his only safety.

144

"I think somebody owes me an explanation." His voice, though low, carried above the confusion.

"Then that somebody must be me, and I owe you nothin'. You dog of a traitor, you yellow Mormon-lover."

Luke Morgan strode up and spat the words into his face. Jacob felt the force of them like a blow. He turned his eyes deliberately from his uncle, seeking Ira now, but he couldn't find the boy. At last he spoke into the snarl of faces about him.

"Ira?" His strong voice echoed before it stopped. "Is it a lie I was told about mother?" No answer came, so he stood up a little taller and spoke again to the face he couldn't see.

"Answer me, Ira. Are you afraid to answer your brother — bound and disarmed, and you with a gun in your hands?"

The quiet disdain in his voice was unmistakable. Somebody hacked and spat, and another man coughed against the back of his hand.

"I don't have to answer you, and don't call me brother!" *The voice couldn't be a boy's voice,* Jacob shuddered. *It was too cold with hatred for that.*

"You always was a sucker, Jake," someone called out. It was a high, thin voice and it broke the straining tension, so the men were free to laugh and curse again.

"You lied to me." Luke spoke now, close beside him. "That wasn't somebody's cousin I saw last spring. That was a worthless Mormon you was hidin'. You lied to me. I've killed men for less than that — you know I have, Jacob."

"And I'd have killed you before I'd have let you hurt him."

The blow came harder because it was by surprise. Jacob hadn't thought his uncle would hit him; not now, not yet. It staggered him, and he bent over double against the pain in his middle.

"I ain't used to that kind of back-talk, boy. I don't take it. 'Specially not from a low-down Mormon-lover."

"So you've still got nothing better to do with your time than push the Mormons around? It's an old story, Luke. The Mormons are out of Missouri. They're no longer any concern of you and your men."

"The hell, boy! You think we're jest gonna sit here while they get stronger? Those fool Illinoians'll soon find out what a mistake they made takin' the vermin in. Why, Joe Smith's out to make a regular city-state for hisself there in Nauvoo — buildin' a bigger militia than the whole darn state of Illinois!"

"He's no threat to you."

"The hell he isn't! He already sent Port Rockwell and some of the boys back to stir up trouble. They get strong again, they'll be after us, Jake, you'll see."

"Why did you tell me my mother was sick and dying? It doesn't seem you object to lying if it's done by you."

"You got a mean tongue, boy, a mean tongue. I had my reasons, Jake."

"Then give them to me."

"You ain't exactly in a position to be makin' demands."

There was a shuffle, some of the men moved, and then Jacob saw Ira. He walked up toward them with jerky steps. *Is he scared,* Jacob wondered, *or just uneasy at what he carries in his own mind?*

"Get to the point, Uncle Luke. The men are restless and hungry."

"Awright, son, awright, son. Tell Siras to start a fire."

His voice had softened perceptibly, addressing Ira. But he turned with the same hard look to Jacob again.

"These are your choices. I'm fair, Jake — I give you your choices. You can go back to the Mormons — but you go back our man. See, you work for us, like. You tell us what old Joe is plannin'. You send messages. You do what we tell ya to do."

"And if I don't choose that?"

"Then you stay here and live with your mother. That's simple, ain't it? You marry Alice, and you stop causin' trouble, see?"

"Join you and your men?"

"Not really. Ya just don't fight us. I'd expect you to help us now and then when we need it. I'd expect at least that —"

"Either way I would be your man."

"That's right. I guess you could look at it that way."

It was madness, this couldn't be happening to him! Jacob had never thought of himself as a coward. But fear crawled over every inch of his skin like a sickness.

"I don't think I could live being somebody else's man."

"You tellin' me no? You refusin' my offer, Jacob?"

"I guess you could say so — if you have to see it that way."

"You fool!" he spat under his breath, but his eyes had narrowed. "Hell, boy, think about it. I'm givin' you one more chance." He shouted the words, like a challenge, and his men stood listening.

Jacob was tempted; it would buy him a short reprieve. He might think of something; he might even contrive to escape. He didn't want to be hurt as his uncle would hurt him. If only —

"You skeert, Jacob? Skeert to stand up to Luke?" Ira's voice even sounded like Luke Morgan. Jacob couldn't bear the hate in his voice. There was no way out now; Ira had seen to that: for some twisted reason Ira wanted to see him suffer.

He lifted his head and tried to stop the trembling inside him. "I stand, Luke. I stand on what I said before."

The narrow eyes looked him carefully up and down. "You're forcin' me to do this, Jake, you remember that." He spoke low, and no one else heard him, as he intended. "You're a fool, boy, and you ain't gonna make a fool outa me. Not in front of my own boys, yer not."

He threw back his head now and spoke loudly, in scornful derision.

"You don't appreciate my offer, Jacob? I'm bein' generous, boy, and you throw it back in my face!"

There was a murmur that spread among the men.

"You sure of yourself, are you, Jacob? Think we might change your mind? You — Pete and Siras. Come over here."

He didn't even look back as he spoke and the two men came lightly over, balancing on the balls of their feet and flexing their hands.

"You wanna talk some sense into Jacob here?" Jacob looked into their faces, staring them down. But the eagerness in Pete's grey eyes sent a spasm of terror through him.

"You drop that leather! I don't want no whip, you hear me? You work 'im over, but I don't want you to use no whip." Luke was already turning, his back to Jacob. "See if you can't get 'im to change his mind."

Siras held him and Pete began to hit him. The lean fists were hard and sure, and offered no leniency. At the first blow Jacob felt that his jaw would break. He hadn't fought for a long time; he wasn't steeled to the pain as he should be. With the second blow he broke loose, and this time it took Siras and two other men to hold him. For a while he took it, but it seemed Pete would never stop. The pain was a monster roaring inside his head, a burning lake that he sank in, choking, on fire.

The last thing he remembered as he crumbled into oblivion was the hideous grin lopsided on Dudley's face, and a low whimpering sound coming from somewhere — but his eyes were coated with blood and he couldn't see who was making the pitiful sound.

The pain was there again before he even opened his eyes. Because of it he remembered where he was and what had happened. He moved his mouth gingerly; it felt as though his nose might be broken. There were spots where the pain still burned, but mostly there was a dull, aching throb spread over the length of his body. He opened his eyes to grey sun in a lead-grey sky and to a young face bent over his, watching him intently.

"You can thank Uncle Luke that you opened your eyes just now. Pete would 'ave killed ya if Luke had let 'im have his way."

"I'm surprised he didn't. Why did Luke stop him?"

"I don't know — some rubbage about facing mother."

"Is mother all right?"

"Course she's all right, you fool. Least I reckon so. I haven't seen her for weeks."

"You don't take very good care of her, do you, Ira?"

"That ain't my job, Jacob, it's yours. Yer the big man, aren't ya?"

"What do you mean?"

"Hell, what do you think I mean? Her first-born, her pride, her favorite, and all of that. I'm not enough like father for her to love me."

"You've no call to say that, Ira. It isn't true."

"Huh! You always was a fool, Jacob." The boy stood up, as if to leave.

"Does she know?" Jacob asked him, before he could turn away. "About this — about me?"

148

"She'll know when she sees you ride up. If you make it that far." Ira walked off and Jacob rose, moving slowly and gingerly. Every joint in his body ached, and so did the bruised, tightened muscles.

"You're a sight, boy. Yer mother'll have my hide when she sees those bruises."

Luke grinned and pulled his hat down onto his forehead. "You done any thinkin' since me and you last talked?"

Jacob shook his head. "Not the kind you're meanin'."

"We're movin' out, boy. Sy, tie his hands behind 'im." He looked at Jacob and scratched his head the way he always did when he tried to think. "You're a slow learner, Jake. Well—there's more'n one way to skin a cat. You jest watch us and see."

All that day and the next Luke showed Jacob what he had meant. Across the river on the Illinois side they rode, from place to place through the scattered settlements, stirring up all the mischief they could find. The first day they fired a barn and some haystacks, and even a couple of outhouses here and there. They broke down fences, spooking the stock and scattering them out in the open. They stole whatever they could lay their hands on, often turning around and, at great risk, planting the goods in well-known Mormon areas, delighted as schoolboys at the ruckus that would raise. And the risk and the danger only incited them further.

And everywhere they went they sprinkled Jacob's name—like a housewife liberally sprinkling salt into a pot of stew. They called him and cursed him and questioned and laughed, so that wherever one of them went, there went his name; at every farmhouse and ranch and outlying cabin the startled victims who heard the cries of the raiders made out one name distinctly above them all: Jacob Morgan.

When they made camp they cut loose his hands and he served them while they ate, and they took great delight in harassing him as much as they could; tripping him, shoving him, spilling their hot coffee on him. And as bad as any abuse were the filthy oaths, making him sick to his stomach, and stretching his nerves because they never seemed to cease.

His own food was what leftovers he could find, and as long as the fire glowed they plagued him with things to do: black their boots, clean their rifles, haul water for the horses, unpack the bedrolls — every menial task that could be thought of was thrust upon Jacob.

He bore it in silence; there was little else he could do. He kept his thoughts to himself, and they seethed inside him. They were taking the fabric of his life and unraveling it, leaving the ends dangling, loose and frayed.

The third day out Pete and Walt Dudley got a little carried away. At a lonely spot on the Illinois side of the river they happened upon a man with his daughter alone. When he admitted that he was a Mormon they beat him severely, then ravished his daughter while he was forced to look on. And Dudley, the vacant grin crawling over his face, called Pete by the name of Jacob a dozen times.

They told the story with relish around the campfire. Jacob knew that Pete had been itching to have at him again; but Luke, for reasons of his own, wouldn't allow it. So Pete took his twisted pleasure in torturing another in Jacob's name. And the girl — Jacob refused to let himself think of the girl.

"Hell, they'll be havin' nightmares about you, Jake, for the rest of their lives." Pete, chewing on a roasted rabbit leg, wiped the grease along his sleeve and leered at Jacob. "You go anywhere near a Mormon now and you'll get yerself tarred and feathered, boy."

In the play of the fire's shadows the faces around him looked distorted, and ugly with hate and greed.

Jacob clenched his fist in the darkness, but didn't answer.

He heard a sound beside him and opened his eyes to see Luke's scuffed boots planted inches away from his head. Luke smiled, but there was no mirth to the smile, and he said,

"Guess you've got somethin' to think about now, hey, Jacob? You'd better think about it, too, boy — good and hard."

In the pulsing glow of the fire his dim-lit features resembled the gentle face of the father that Jacob had loved. He shuddered and turned his head and gazed into the fire until his eyes smouldered like the crumbling embers and burned in their sockets, and there were no images, no shadows; nothing but the angry, throbbing red.

21

"I want Alice!" Sarah leaned close, for the child's weak voice was scarcely a whisper. "I want Alice to tell me a story."

Ann's blue eyes opened briefly, then fluttered and closed. Sarah sighed and turned to Myles, who stood beside her. He took her hand, afraid at how tired she looked, at how thin she was.

"She's fallen asleep," he said, glancing at the quiet child. "She won't remember when she wakes up."

Sarah drew her hand away and pushed the hair back from her forehead. "She'll remember. It's the fourth time she's asked, Myles. You'd better go get her."

"Alice?"

Sarah nodded.

"Are you sure?"

Sarah gazed at the thin, wasted form on the bed beside her. "I've fought earth and hell to bring her back from the dead, Myles. If she wants Alice, I guess I can bear that, too."

Sarah watched Myles leave and thought vaguely that she ought to run a brush through her hair, splash some water over her face, and change her dress. But Ann stirred and whimpered and called her name, and she sat down on the bed and took the hot little hand in hers, forgetting instantly any thoughts of herself.

It seemed a long time before Myles returned, and Ann grew restless. When at last he did appear he had Alice with him. She pulled off her cape and hat and long, grey gloves and came over and sat beside Ann. She pushed back the thick damp hair and fussed and straightened things, and Ann's pale face lit up at the sight of her.

"Why didn't anyone tell me you were sick, my darling?" She spoke to the child, her bright eyes warm and caressing. But a tone of accusation was unmistakable in her voice.

"Now Alice is here, my sweet. You want me to tell you a story? I know just the one you'll like . . ."

Sarah stood back and watched the two for a moment, then left the room. She pulled her shawl from the hook by the door and slipped outside. It seemed like weeks since she'd had a breath of fresh air. Could it still be November, or had an entire year passed her by while she sat in that hazy region which is neither life nor death, but a dreariness of fear and pain and longing?

A few leaves, brittle and withered, clung to the branches, but the cold had drawn out the colors and left dull the dying leaves and vines and winter grasses. The sky, in compensation, seemed blue today; blue and clean, in contrast to the greyness. And the sun, though thinning with winter, felt warm on her face and along her thin arms where the shawl didn't cover her skin. She leaned back and closed her eyes, concentrating on nothing but the soothing feeling of the sun.

"She's asleep now."

The soft voice startled her out of her doze. Sarah stirred, but Alice put out her hand.

"Sit still. You look like death warmed over yourself. Why didn't you tell me earlier she was sick?"

"I didn't think to," Sarah answered honestly. "There wasn't enough room to think about anything."

"I can imagine. I only wish I could come again, the poor little dear! But at least you caught me; and I'm glad that you did, Sarah, really. I hadn't decided what I would do about saying good-byes — but now the child has decided for me."

Sarah blinked and pushed back her hair. What was Alice saying?

Alice smiled, and everything about her seemed to sparkle. "I'm going to send Ann a book after I get home. It will give her something to look forward to, and I do hope it helps."

"After you get home?" Sarah asked dumbly, her voice sounding dry and shriveled like the old, brittle leaves.

"Yes, my little Sarah, I'm going home."

"But why? I . . . I don't understand."

"My simple Sarah! Good heavens, what else did you think I would do? Jacob's gone. Do you expect me to sit here all alone and wither away?"

"But Jacob's coming . . ." She stopped herself, but too late.

"Coming back?" The bright laugh rang out in the afternoon stillness. "Do you really believe Jacob will come back? To what, pray tell? The self-righteous Mormon hypocrisy? They've judged him now, Sarah, and he doesn't measure up. He's not good enough for the Mormons to accept him."

"How dare you? That's not true—"

"How dare *I*? I've as much right to judge you as you have to judge me. And you do judge me, Sarah—you know you do. You look down upon me as the most miserable of hypocrites."

Sarah lowered her eyes, for what Alice said was true, and how could she deny it, even now?

"You sit in your smugness and judge me a hypocrite, and that's a sure case of the pot, Sarah, calling the kettle black."

"What do you mean?"

"I mean you're a fine little hypocrite yourself."

Sarah looked up, her eyes wide, her mind a churning confusion of anger and shock.

"That's right. Don't blink those cornflower eyes at me! You think there's only one kind of hypocrisy, Sarah, and you refuse to recognize your own. You claim to be loving and forgiving, but what do you do? You withhold yourself from anyone who doesn't fit the mold. And that includes Jacob, you wide-eyed little bird."

"You don't know what you're talking about!"

"Oh, yes I do. You hold back your love from Jacob because he isn't all you expect him to be, all he ought to be—instantly—by your precious standards. And yet you say you love him more than I do!"

"Stop it!"

"Not yet, Sarah. I'm not quite through. I'd do anything if it would make Jacob happy, but you're too worried about your own happiness. Your love is a false love, selfish, and unrealistic. That's why I have won—and you, my dear Sarah, have lost."

Sarah stood up, her blue eyes brilliant with tears. "Get out of here," she commanded, her angry voice trembling. The tinkling laughter rang out like a curse and a haunting.

"I'm leaving, honey, you don't have to hurry me!"

"You'll never make it. It's too late in the year to be starting."

"Are you worried about me, Sarah? I'll make it, honey, and Jacob will appreciate my coming just that much more."

She tied her silken bonnet beneath her curls. "Good-bye, Sarah. What a pity you had to fall in love with a Gentile! Good Mormon girls should never be so foolish, should they, my dear?"

She turned, her full skirts floating across the lawn, the scent of her French cologne still rich in the air.

"I'll kiss him for you, Sarah," the bell-like voice taunted. Sarah clenched her hands, but the tears were already spilling, tears that choked her breath and burned her cheeks.

There were so many reasons to cry, and she cried for them all. But the bitterness in the tears came from her knowing that what Alice had said about her was true! She was a hypocrite and a fool, and Jacob must know it. She ought to have loved him freely and told him so. She ought to . . . But what difference did it make? What good were regrets when the time was forever past?

A deep, heavy weight of loneliness fell on her spirit. She couldn't lighten the burden by blaming fate, or Jacob, or Alice — or anyone but herself. He was gone, he was lost to her, but she couldn't let go! To love him was to live, and if she stopped loving, what swirling chasms of pain would claim her soul?

It was early still, only half-light; but Elizabeth must leave early. There was no one she could trust to see her go. Both of her neighbors would tell if Myles should ask them. It was better this way; if no one knew where she was, then no one could betray her.

She hurried the two small children ahead of her. A fine, light sprinkling of frost glittered everywhere. Elizabeth lingered, hating to leave the sight, her resolve spilling through her hands like the shimmering beads of frost spilled from the trailing branches she brushed against.

She closed the gate, then took each child by the hand — refusing to pause, refusing to look behind. Myles wouldn't come until Friday, and when he came the little house would be silent and deserted, with no voice to tell what it alone had seen.

"Ira, you ride with Bill and Dudley back to my place. Walt and Siras, you go on into town and pick up the supplies."

Luke Morgan surveyed his men like some petty ruler. He reminded Jacob of an ignorant feudal lord, narrow and arrogant, thinking his word was law, and nothing existed that mattered beside himself.

"I want to ride with Pete and the other boys." It was Ira's voice, as demanding and hard as his uncle's.

"No way, son, I can't push your mother as far as that."

"She's not here to stop you. I carry my weight around here. I've a right to go with the boys—"

"I said no, Ira."

"I didn't know you was tied to her apron strings."

The haughty young voice rang out, and then there was silence. Luke Morgan scratched his head and looked at the boy. Then he slapped him across the face as hard as he could. Ira didn't flinch, but his eyes widened in surprise, and he wiped the smear of blood from across his lip.

"You're still a kid that's wet behind the ears, boy. And much as I love you, you don't talk like that to me. Now you doin' what I say, or are you goin' home to your mother?"

Ira didn't even hesitate. "I'm goin' with you. You know that, Uncle Luke."

Jacob turned his head in disgust at the grin that spread over Luke's face.

"Awright, Pete, you're in charge of the boys, but you take it easy. And be back at my place to report in seven . . . eight days."

Pete nodded. His hand rubbed absently over the smooth, tight leather of the bull whip that hung from his saddle. He stared with hard eyes at Jacob and would not look away. He touched his horse and in smooth deliberation moved toward him. Jacob kept his eyes on Pete's eyes, but his jaw muscles tightened and prickles of fear crawled along the back of his neck.

"I ain't done with you yet, Jake. Luke had no cause to stop me." The little cold eyes bored holes into Jacob's skull. "Yer Uncle Luke won't always be there to protect you. Remember that." He tapped the coiled weapon, not taking his eyes away. "Next time, Jake, you don't get off so easy."

Jacob watched him ride off, angered by the weakness that churned in his stomach. Pete and the boys were riding out after more trouble. "Jest to make sure that yer name don't get cold," Luke had said. The frightened people who saw him would take Pete for himself; an animal like Pete Funk wearing his name, and muddying all that was decent within a man.

"You ready to ride?" It was Luke coming up beside him.

"I know the way home, Luke, it's only a few miles from here."

"Well, I'll jest come along to make sure you do what you're told, now. We wouldn't want Laura worrying over you."

They rode in silence, and the four miles stretched out and seemed like twenty. And the closer they drew the more Jacob dreaded the moment when his eyes would meet his mother's and he would lie — worlds stretching between what he was and what he would seem.

Laura saw the two riders and wondered who they might be. She brought Matthew's old Hawken out of the corner and held it while she stood on the porch and watched. As the men approached she laid down the rifle and ran, gathering her skirts high above her ankles, her hair blowing free. Jacob thought she looked like a girl, flushed and lovely, as he slid from the horse and gathered her into his arms. Luke watched, his face guarded and passive, but Laura turned, reached for his hands and drew him toward her.

"How is it, Luke, that you bring my son home to me?"

The joy in her voice was like the thrust of a knife in a wound to Jacob. Luke stared at him hard, expecting him to answer.

"I ran into Luke over the ridge — he was just as surprised as you are."

"That's right. You know, I thought we'd lost him, Laura."

"But why are you here? We agreed you should stay until spring. And Alice —"

"Alice is fine, mother. You can rest your mind as far as she is concerned." Jacob swallowed against the tightness in his throat. "I was worried about you. I wanted to come home, that's all."

He tried to return her smile, to reflect some of her joy. She led them into the house and insisted they eat, plying them both with questions, fussing over Jacob, until he felt as nervous and stifled as he could tell Luke was, fidgeting in the corner where he sat. He wondered if Luke was pleased with his performance.

Luke rose, obviously relieved to escape, anxious to go. Jacob fell back. He didn't want to be alone with his uncle, so he let Laura thank Luke warmly and see him out. When she returned he had a smile all fixed on his face, but her face was thoughtful and pensive. She didn't sit down, but stood above him in that pose of strength and authority which had always so impressed him as a child.

"All right, Jacob, now you can tell me the truth."

"What do you mean, mother? I've already told you—"

"You've told me a lie, and please don't do it again!"

He rose, feeling stiff, with all his sore places hurting. "Mother, it's late, I think we should go to bed—"

"There'll be no sleep in this house till I have the truth. Do you think I've known Luke all these years as well as I do and then don't realize when something foul is going on? He's up to no good, Jacob. Now you tell me what really happened—and all of it, too."

"I promised Luke, and there's no need for you to be knowing—"

"A promise to Luke is a contract made with the devil, and only a fool would want to play out that hand. Besides, Jacob, a man's word forced is no word at all."

He turned, no longer wanting her to see his face. "I can't tell you, mother. So please don't try to force me."

"Are you that afraid of what Luke might do to you?"

He turned, his look so bitter that she recoiled from it.

"He's hurt you already, hasn't he, Jacob?" she said.

"You could say so, mother, but that's no great matter. There's more than myself to consider. If he ever touched you, if he hurt you in any way—"

"He'd never hurt me, Jacob."

"Don't fool yourself, mother. You don't know what he's capable of—"

"I know! Much more than you realize, I know."

The emotion in her voice seemed to fill the room. "Tell me, Jacob! Tell me all that happened."

There was no way for him to get out of it, so he told the story. She listened without interruption until he was through.

157

"Do you know why Luke spared you?" Her eyes looked dark and older.

"Not really," he said, shaking his head at her question.

"It wasn't in deference to me; Luke isn't that kind." She stood up and walked to the window, then turned back.

"Luke's always been arrogant and foolish," she began. "You know his ways. He's always had trouble . . . well . . . hanging onto things. Through the years your father was constantly bailing him out."

"I think I remember some of that," Jacob said.

She smiled then, but the smile was sad and old, like her eyes. "Several times Luke mortgaged his farm with all he owned, and each time your father came to his rescue. Finally it got too much — we couldn't go on that way forever. So your father bought the mortgage and the lands . . ."

"You mean all Luke owns became father's, in father's name?"

"No. The lands were never in Matthew's name. He put them in mine."

"Your name?"

"Yes, from the beginning."

"That's hard to believe."

"I'm sure it is, but your father felt it was the only way. It would safeguard Luke, and serve as protection for me."

"I understand." Jacob stood, feeling suddenly cold. "So there is no kindness in Luke, no kindness at all."

"I wouldn't say that, Jacob. You have to understand Luke."

"I understand that he feels nothing for you, nor me, nor Ira—"

"No, Jacob, he loves the boy in his own way."

"His way!" The words spat out with his pent-up anger, and he wondered how much he hated Luke after all. "He does all he can to destroy us. It's only because you've got him over a barrel that he doesn't do more. Isn't that right?" he demanded.

But she didn't answer. He sighed and sat down, feeling tired as well as cold.

"Whatever else, he's ruined you with the Mormons, Jacob. And I can't pretend I'm sorry of the outcome; you know I'm not. It's what I've prayed for all the while you've been gone."

He looked at his mother, and suddenly she was a stranger. All he felt, all he loved was alien to her. What of himself could she understand and accept now? He had changed, and all that he cared for she despised.

And all that he was rode the black winds of evil and terror, in the hands of a man who was greedy for his destruction. They had laughed at him as they tore his life into pieces, scattering the fragments far on the heedless wind, and leaving him nothing but emptiness in his hands.

——————— 22 ———————

When Myles discovered Elizabeth's disappearance he confided in Sarah. She walked to the little white house, and when no one answered she peered in at the curtained windows, then went around back and jiggled the locked door. *It's too quiet,* she thought, *and much too uncluttered, too tidy—as though no one lived here at all.*

Once the thought came, it teased at the back of her mind and would not go away. Later that evening she lay on her bed, her hands beneath her head, trying to unravel the matter, which was like a yarn basket filled with tangles of colored strands, wound and snarled and knotted around one another. But one string kept winding itself through all the rest, and when she fell asleep Sarah felt she had found an answer.

The next morning, as soon as she could break away, she walked to Emily's. It was later than she had intended, so she breathed a sigh of relief when Sister Hutchings said, "Yes, dear, she's in her room sewing. Why don't you just run along up there and surprise her."

Emily was surprised, because Sarah came right to the point. "Emily, what did you do to Elizabeth Todd?"

All the color left Emily's face and Sarah knew that her guess had been correct. "You tell me right now what you did!" she boldly demanded.

"Will you tell Myles?"

"That doesn't matter. I have to know."

"All I did was go see her and talk to her, Sarah. That's all."

"Well, that must have been enough! Just what did you say?"

The white face flushed then; the blue eyes almost feverish in their brightness. "I shouldn't have said it, but I had to, Sarah — you know! What else could I do to bring Myles back to his senses?"

Something in Sarah tightened and started to ache. "What did you say?" she pressed, but her voice was softer.

Emily looked miserable, stricken, but she started to speak. "I told her that she was making a fool of herself."

Sarah bit her tongue, but Emily didn't look up to see her.

"I said Myles was mine, that he'd always intended to marry me." The hurt in her voice made Sarah feel sick inside. "I said he was just infatuated with her, that he'd never marry a widow with two small children, that it would break his parents' hearts and mine, too, if he did. I told her that people were talking — that everyone knew what a fool she was but herself."

"You told her that? You really said those things?"

"Yes, I did!" Emily was hotly indignant now, defending herself in anger and fear. "No matter what you say, I had every right. I love Myles, and I won't see that woman take him away!"

Sarah didn't reply, but she stood up slowly.

"I don't care if you hate me," Emily cried. "If it meant that Myles would be mine I would do it again. I don't care how much it hurt her, I'd do it again!"

"No one has a right to hurt someone else that much . . . on purpose. That can't be right," Sarah breathed.

"If anyone ought to understand, *you* should," Emily raged. "What would you do to get Jacob back again?"

Sarah sank back down, her knees suddenly weak beneath her. The angry question had taken her by surprise. And the force of her own suffering hit her again, like an unhealed wound broken open and bleeding fresh. Emily was speaking of something she couldn't face, a thing she had pushed into oblivion these past few weeks. She looked into the angry eyes that were glaring at her. She had to do it — and she had to do it now. *Well, perhaps it is only fitting,* Sarah thought, *that I should be the one to tell Emily. In spite of what she has done, she has lost Myles — he will never be hers again.*

When Sarah left Emily she didn't go straight home but walked the few blocks to the Goodmans' house. If anyone could help, Eliza Goodman could. Sarah was pretty sure now that Elizabeth had run away. But where? She hoped Eliza would have some clues.

Later that evening when Myles walked into the house Sarah had a list for him to try: a cousin across the river in Keokuk, a brother in Ramus, some dear friends in Hamilton. Four names on the list — would any one hold the answer? Sarah saw the trembling eagerness on Myles's face and decided not to tell him about the girl who sat huddled on her bed and sobbed for him.

It was a fine day, warm and mellow, diffused with peace. The harvest was over and lethargy lay on the land, as though it were time to pause and enjoy and rest.

Elizabeth, bent over the washing, felt none of that. She was a stranger here, in spite of her brother's love and her sister-in-law's acceptance; she didn't belong. She missed her home and her friends, her own little life; every small detail precious and personal — and denied to her — lumped in with her loss and pain. She wouldn't think about it, for thinking brought on the suffering that was almost more than she could bear. *Will time make the anguish bearable?* she wondered. *I have known one brief, bright season of happiness,* she tried to tell herself. *Perhaps it is selfish to ask more than that from life.*

When Sally tugged at her skirt she didn't look up. "Mommy's working, Sally, run off like a good girl and play."

But the child was persistent, so Elizabeth dropped the wet petticoat back into the suds and stood, arching her tired back and wiping her wet forehead with the back of her hand. And she didn't look at her daughter's small, upturned face, but beyond it to the tall young man who stood watching her.

He didn't move, but he smiled a gentle smile. "Didn't you know I would find you, Elizabeth?"

She moved back a step or two, with a small cry of pain. "Go away, Myles. You shouldn't have come. Please go away."

He came to her instead, in long, purposeful strides. He took her hands, and she couldn't pull them back.

"Didn't I tell you you could never get rid of me? Remember, Elizabeth, remember what I said?"

"Please, Myles, go away while I still can bear it."

He pulled her against him, carefully, tenderly. "It's my fault that you have suffered so much, my love. What a fool I've been! What an ignorant, cowardly fool!"

She looked up into his face, startled by that. "I should have married you months ago," he said, "and saved you all the anguish you're going through. You're coming with me."

"But, Myles, I can't!"

"Oh yes, you can. I'm waiting for nothing now. We'll be in Nauvoo by nightfall, and tomorrow morning I'll find someone to marry us."

"Marry . . . tomorrow?"

"That's right. I'll go all the way to the Prophet if I have to. Tomorrow at this time, Elizabeth, you'll be my wife."

Myles was true to his word. The next day a small group gathered in the Goodmans' home for the ceremony. The ceremony was beautiful; simple and gracious. Elizabeth looked pale, but slender and lovely and feminine, glowing with the happiness that seemed to her still a dream.

It was pain for Sarah to look upon her face. *This is the closest I will ever get to this kind of fulfillment,* she thought, with a little pang of self-pity; *always being part of someone else's happiness.*

It had been a quiet wedding, simple and very private, so Sarah was surprised by how many people knew of it. Everywhere she went someone would stop her. "We're so happy for Myles" . . . "How wonderful! I'm sure they'll be happy" . . . "She's a lovely girl — Elizabeth. Isn't she?" . . . "Now, that was a surprise, your brother marrying the prettiest widow in the city" . . .

And with the congratulations came something else. Invariably the well-meaning person would say, "Sarah, I'm so glad you didn't get mixed up with that Gentile" . . . "I'm happy to know that Missouri fellow's gone. See how he turned out?" . . . "How fortunate for you, Sarah, that you didn't get fooled by the big Missourian. Look what he's done! He's as bad as his uncle — and worse, pretending interest in the gospel" . . .

Again and again Sarah smiled at the well-meant words and bit back the replies of anger in Jacob's defense.

How could she defend him against what she heard? One by one the stories filtered in, the same old stories of torture, destruction, and pillage. But the fiends, the mobbers, wore Jacob's name and face. Even those who had known him began to wonder.

"He didn't seem like that kind of man, did he?" . . . "I wouldn't have thought him capable of such cruelty, and yet there were people who saw him with their own eyes, and heard the others calling him Jacob" . . . "Well, you never can tell what's hidden inside a man" . . .

It went on and on until Sarah's head was ringing; there seemed no way to deny what others knew. *Could it be Jacob?* she wondered when she was alone, when there was nothing between herself and her fears but the darkness. *Jacob could never be capable of such deeds,* her heart cried out. And yet, she had seen him with Alice by the river. *Why didn't he seek me out to say good-bye? Why did he ride away in silence?* she questioned. *How well, how deeply do I know him, after all?*

She closed her eyes to the images in her mind, tossed and turned and punished herself with doubting, and battled against a foe that was partly herself and partly a shadow whistling nameless tunes.

Alice had nearly frozen to death and been wet for days, she had shivered and retched, and chewed mouldy meat for supper. But she was home again — safe, and beyond the suffering.

She was home again . . . but she hadn't seen Jacob yet. She was afraid to face him . . . and she knew well why she was afraid. She put it off with a dozen little excuses, and with each day that passed her uncertainty grew.

Jacob knew she was there, but he didn't seek her out. He was busy repairing the buildings and organizing the place, and rounding up stock before the onslaught of winter. He was glad there was plenty of work to keep him busy. When he ate meals with his mother, or spent the long evenings alone in her company, the joy on her face and the happiness in her voice were a constant grating reminder of his own misery.

By things that his mother had said, by thinking about it, Jacob had pretty well figured out what Alice had done. He knew he should hate her for it, but somehow he couldn't. Instead he felt nothing; a numbness instead of pain. He was grateful for this dulling of his senses, like a sick man doped with liquor and begging for more, terrified that the pain would claim him again.

He knew his mother; he knew what she was doing. She refused to look beyond her happiness. He was here now, and she wouldn't think beyond it—wouldn't admit there was danger of losing him again. Carefully she wove the threads of her net around him: loving him, needing him, trusting in him again.

When Alice did come it was with surprisingly little fanfare. She appeared one quiet day and her manner seemed gentler; even her clothing was softer and more subdued. She visited with Laura for a while, telling the older woman all she thought she ought to know, leaving out what she chose to keep to herself. Laura's good opinion was priceless now. If the mother was won to her, that was half the battle. And Alice needed all the help she could get.

She found Jacob in the barn and felt suddenly awkward. He was more than dirty and streaked with manure. He was withdrawn and distant, and her luscious, romantic ways failed her suddenly. She had plans and alternate plans of how to approach him, but he had never seemed so cold and remote before.

"What do you want?" he asked, scarcely looking up from his work.

"I wanted to see you." She hesitated. "I . . . there's so much I want to tell you, Jacob, so much to explain and . . ."

He turned then and silenced her with his eyes.

"You've done your best to destroy me and ruin my life. You have even joined with my enemies against me." His voice was like a slow, deep-burning fire.

"No!" she cried, "that's not true. I never meant to harm you. And Luke promised!"

"Promised what?" The slow fire burned deeper in his eyes.

"He promised you wouldn't be hurt, and I believed him!"

"How could you believe him?" Jacob's eyes were so searing that Alice turned from before their gaze, clasping her small, white hands in a helpless gesture.

"He said that he wanted you home and that was all. He convinced me that we were both working for the same thing."

"What purpose could possibly unite you with a man like Luke Morgan?"

Jacob's voice was quiet and even; Alice felt herself shudder. She wished he would shout and grow angry—anything but this distant, controlled disdain.

"He wanted you away from the Mormons and so did I. So did your mother—Luke said he was thinking of her. It was just to get you home, Jacob, that was all."

"And what you were in Nauvoo—that was all a lie?"

A panic rose inside her. "No! That's not fair . . ."

He took her arms and turned her to face him again. "There have been so many lies, Alice, so much deception—I don't think you know how to tell the false from the true. You've fooled yourself more than you've ever fooled others, Alice."

"I don't know what you're talking about. All I ever wanted was you. All I wanted was to make you happy, Jacob."

He softened then, and a sadness came into his face. "No, Alice, you wanted your own happiness and convinced yourself that what would make you happy would make me happy, too."

Her pulse quickened; instinctively she leaned closer to him. "And it could! If only you'd stop and give me a chance!"

Jacob loosened his hold on her arms and stepped back from her. "You're deceiving yourself again, Alice," his calm voice said. "You've brought me nothing but pain and unhappiness. I want no part of you or what you can give."

She stood silent a moment before the onslaught of his words, struggling against the finality which they held.

"I mean it, Alice," he said. His voice was like iron, stern and empty of feeling, lacking even the pity she once had felt there.

She turned and left him, struggling to maintain her dignity, haunted by the pain in his burning eyes, the quiet condemnation that stripped away her pretenses, uncovering the secrets she had always refused to face. She fled; but she felt she would never escape those eyes, and never again find a deep enough place to hide in.

The first real storm of winter came down hard, sweeping the land with brittle, icy fingers, filling caverns and dried-up rivers with wet, heavy snow. The storm showed no mercy, but broke everything weak: snapping branches and caving in cabins, and freezing where they stood sheep or cattle left out in the open.

The storm made Jacob feel more a prisoner, confined now to shorter quarters and stricter routine. Ira was home, and the three of them together made a very strained and stilted company. Laura felt it more than Jacob knew. She laid it down to the weaknesses in Ira, to the differences that separated her sons; she wouldn't admit it could go any further than that.

Jacob didn't realize how quiet he had become; it had grown easier to live unto himself. He existed each day at bare survival level, as if the valves were turned to off and rusted there, and just a trickle of life was seeping through. His mother, watching, told herself it would pass. He would come out of it and be himself again. And she studied him carefully, looking for the signs.

The dull routine of the farm was too much for Ira; nothing of what went on there interested him. Reading and singing and quietly talking together, a parlor game or two before turning in — only old women half-dead ought to live that way! He was accustomed to men and gambling, and cussing and bragging, and he chafed at the narrow confinement so cruel to him. He paced the house like an animal, caged and restless; and he grew snarly and short-tempered as the frustration festered in him.

He took to taunting Jacob when they were alone, ridiculing him in every way he could find. It incensed him further that Jacob never responded, so he grew more vicious and mean as the winter days passed. And Jacob stared beyond him and didn't notice.

Christmas arrived and Jacob tried to rally. Luke came — to check on his prisoner, Jacob was sure. The strain was so tight you could almost reach out and touch it. At last the day was over and Luke had gone. But Ira stayed — against his will, Jacob knew. *Someone must watch the prisoner,* Jacob thought, *lest he grow restless. Someone must keep the prisoner in his place. Morbid. I'm growing morbid living this way.*

166

New storms came now, one on top of the other, emptying the angry heavens upon the land. The breath of winter burned in Jacob's throat when he did his chores and cared for the animals. The air was cold and cleansing and settled his fevered brain. But the expanse of startling white, the ice-crusted snow, shimmered before his eyes and made them ache. It was all the same — one prison or another. He walked inside, where the prison was not so cold.

Alone at night, unable to make sleep come, Jacob had picked up the Bible and started to read. It had become a habit now, and the reading grew longer. Laura dipped further into her store of candles. She said nothing to Jacob, but she still watched him carefully.

Sometimes something he read would reach out and touch him; almost with a sense of shock a thought would come . . . a feeling . . . an impression too strong to ignore. One evening he felt more stifled, more trapped than usual, chafing at the fate of his endless days. He picked up the Bible and turned the wilted pages, aimlessly, too restless to sit and read.

Then the small black print before him began to focus into words that seemed to meet his eye half-way; large and bold and life-like in their power.

"Wait on the Lord," the bold words said to Jacob, and he marked them with his fingers as he read. "Wait on the Lord: be of good courage, and he shall strengthen thine heart." That was all; the words were simple and plainly put. But they somehow opened up worlds to Jacob's mind.

All the wild questioning within him fell into order. "Wait on the Lord." He had failed to do that; he had given up when the first adversity struck. Why had he been so cowed by the power of man?

He searched now — there was another verse he remembered, yet he failed to find what he vaguely knew was there. Then he recalled that it was Myles who had shown him the scripture. Perhaps it wasn't in the Bible at all. He got out his Book of Mormon and hunted there, over and over again. At last he found the words that another Jacob had given to his people — long ago in another place and time:

"Look unto God with firmness of mind, and pray unto him with exceeding faith, and he will console you in your

167

afflictions, and he will plead your cause, and send down justice upon those who seek your destruction."

He hadn't believed or prayed; he had just given up. Now, like a great, shaggy bear that shakes the winter from him, Jacob stood and stretched and shook off his lethargy. He opened the window and drank in the breathless cold, filling his lungs with the piercing, vivifying air. The barrier, his own bleak barrier, cracked and shattered—and his only real prison crumbled around his feet.

The next morning Jacob whistled as he dressed. His mother heard him and smiled softly to herself.

Jacob found Ira loitering darkly back by his office.

"What are you doing here, Ira?" His voice was commanding and sure. Ira looked up, blinking, but answered with truculence.

"I ain't doin' nothin', and what's it to you, anyway? I don't answer to you."

"You haven't, Ira, that's true."

"Darn right, I don't, you liver-bellied coward. I'm Luke's man, and you're his fool—a sitting duck just waitin' for Luke and his men."

"If that's what you think of me, Ira, I guess I've earned it."

Ira turned and spat in contempt. Suddenly Jacob's strong hand closed down on his shoulder with the pinch and force of a vise.

"Hey—get yer hands off me. Whatya think you're doin'?"

"Something I should have been doing long ago." He turned his brother to face him, and the narrow eyes surveyed him with angry suspicion.

"To start, this isn't Luke's hovel you're living in. It's your mother's house and you do not spit in here."

Ira began to protest, but Jacob tightened his grip and the angry words became lost in a low snarl instead.

"Now it seems I heard your mother tell you this morning to feed the chickens and clean out the empty roosts."

"That's work for women. I ain't doin' that dirty work."

"I'm sorry it's so beneath you, Ira, but you'll do it, anyway. And after you're done I expect to see that back stall cleaned and new straw brought in for Moll and her spotted foal. I asked you to do that yesterday, didn't I?"

Ira's eyes were dark and his lips a thin, tight line. "I told you I don't have to answer to what you say."

Jacob's hand closed tighter and the hate flooded Ira's eyes. "You do what I say—do you understand me, Ira?" The boy didn't answer, but stared with his hate-filled eyes.

"Don't cross me, Ira, don't give me cause for complaint. All I need is an excuse. I can dish it out just as well as I can take it."

"You wouldn't dare hurt me! You'd have to answer to Luke!"

"It would be too late for you, though, wouldn't it, Ira? And whether you know it or not, I am not afraid of Luke."

He let the boy go, observing his angry departure with a strange sense of detachment, an almost-calm. He realized what he had said to the boy was true; he was no longer afraid of Luke, or of anything. It gave him a sense of freedom he sorely needed; a feeling he'd thought he might never experience again.

He pulled on his heavy sheepskin and thick fur mittens. It was hard walking, dragging his feet through the wet, packed snow. It was further to the knoll than he had remembered, and he slid down the gentle slope to the snow-filled hollow. Once there he had difficulty finding the grave at all. The winter snows had piled and drifted above it, leaving no sign upon the even, unbroken expanse. Jacob remembered the spot, though, and dug through to uncover the marker. He straightened it carefully and brushed back the clinging snow.

He could only vaguely recall the features of the young man who had come to his land to die—and had changed Jacob's life. He remembered the gentle humor, the warm, kind eyes. Then suddenly a picture rose up before him of Myles standing over the empty body, himself looking on. The words Myles had spoken came to him clear and cutting, with so much more pain than when he had heard them said.

"My sister . . . she loved him . . . they loved one another . . ." Myles had told him. "Heaven help me, I'm going to have to break her heart . . ."

"Break her heart . . . break her heart . . . break her heart . . ."

the cruel words echoed. Jacob looked down at the grave and spoke out loud.

"I've failed you, Martin, and I've hurt her all over again."

He stared, gazing blearily through the snow, but saw a thousand images in his brain, and every one of them was tearing him apart.

"Look unto God with firmness of mind." The words came to him clearly, as though someone had spoken them. "Wait on the Lord" . . . "he will console you" . . . "and plead your cause" . . . "pray with exceeding faith" . . .

The memories dimmed; he could not change the memories. But tomorrow lay unwritten in his hands. He could make of tomorrow anything he wanted. He would wait upon the Lord and pray in faith, and in the spring he would return again to Nauvoo. He would not let the obstacles deter him. There would be a way — though he couldn't see it now. He would believe in his tomorrows, and trust in the Lord.

23

In some parts of the river the ice was pocked and rutted. But here, where the end of Main Street sloped down to the shore near Brother Joseph's homestead, the ice was thick and smooth. On the soles of their shoes, carrying their bodies carefully erect, the young boys could skate the sloped street down onto the water. Some of the littler children steered crude wooden sleighs with their feet, and the river was constantly crowded with happy noise.

It was a gentle winter for the Saints living in Nauvoo. In the long, twilight evenings neighbors gathered to read and sing together, or hold Family Blessing Meetings, where perhaps the best part of the night was the refreshment of sweet new-made wine and warm wheat bread. Sarah's family had settled along with the city, and everyone seemed happier than before. Myles and Elizabeth lived in the little house and came with the children often to visit. Sarah's father, well and stronger, taught now in the evenings; Greek and Latin in the school the Prophet began. Every one seemed to be happy and have a place. Sarah moved among them, but she was not of them; she lived in a world of her own that was always apart. A shadowy world where nothing real existed, and there was no hope of the future to beckon her on.

One evening, late, her father came home from teaching looking happier than usual and with a bundle rolled and stuck carefully under his arm. He sat at the long oak table and beckoned to Sarah. She watched him unfold the paper, a current copy of the *Times and Seasons*. She drew in her breath.

"Where did you get hold of this? Who lent it to you?"

Ebenezer Robinson and Don Carlos Smith, the Prophet's younger brother, had begun publication of the monthly paper last November. Sixteen pages a month at a cost of four dollars per annum; totally out of reach for her father's means. How they had coveted even a glance at a copy!

"It's mine," her father announced, obviously pleased.

"How?" Sarah asked.

"It's a gift from one of my students. A year's subscription, Sarah; just think of that!" Her eyes warmed; what unexpected good fortune! She teased herself with anticipation of reading over and over again the precious printed words.

"What student could possibly give you so costly a gift?"

"It's only partly gift; he called it tuition, and insisted I accept it as payment earned."

"Who, father? Do I know him?"

"I don't think so. He's a young fellow, a new convert from the East. Brilliant mind, on fire for reading Homer. He'll do it, too, he's progressing beautifully."

"He's grateful for what you're teaching him, is that it, then?"

"I think so," her father smiled. "And he has the money. He dresses like a gentleman and owns considerable property already. I even heard him say he's having a piano brought in, Sarah."

A piano! She hadn't seen a piano in years! She wondered if she could still play at all. It had been so long since her grandmother had taught her to play. Sarah's fingers itched for the touch of the keys, and she couldn't get the rich student and his piano out of her mind.

Two weeks later, on a dark and bitter evening, when they were sitting about the fire together, listening to her father read aloud from Shakespeare, there was a sudden knock at the door that startled them.

"Who could possibly be out on a night like this?" The knitting needles went still in her mother's lap.

Her father answered the door and came back grinning, followed by a tall stranger with coal black hair and eyes that were deep and green in a startling contrast. Proudly her father introduced him to the family.

"This is Gordon Steele, one of my most promising students. Wonderful mind—wonderful grasp on things."

The young stranger accepted her father's praise with a quiet grace, and when his eyes came to Sarah they lingered there.

"Sarah . . . you're the one your father speaks of so often. I knew you had spirit and intelligence. Now I see you have beauty as well."

She blushed beneath his compliments and dropped her eyes, and when she lifted them again he had looked away.

He stayed the rest of the evening and read with them, reciting long passages of plays he had memorized. He had a rich, baritone voice, vibrant and expressive, yet free of the affectation Sarah disliked. He laughed as he talked, with a resonance deep and lovely, and Sarah noticed the sea-green eyes resting often on her.

After popcorn and cider he left reluctantly. Somehow it was Sarah who walked him to the door. He paused there, prolonging the night on a note of sweetness, holding Sarah's attention with his emerald eyes.

"Your father may have told you, Sarah, that I have just acquired a piano; a beautiful piece. But it sadly needs someone as beautiful to play it—and skilled. All I do, I fear, is just plunk at the thing." A brief smile; only a lightness passing over his features. "I understand from your father that you play."

"I used to." Sarah sighed unconsciously as she answered. "It's been so long now—but I loved it fervently."

"I should like nothing better than to have you come and play my piano."

"Do you mean it?" Sarah couldn't believe her brashness. But she wanted the piano more than anything.

"I mean everything I say," he answered her gently. "And I never make offers I don't intend to keep. Say, tomorrow evening? I'll come for you around six. We can eat together, and then you may play for me."

Terrified, then weak with anticipation, Sarah passed the long hours until the evening. Gordon Steele swept her into another world; a world she had always dreamed of, but never known. The longings of her spirit he understood. She could share with him her love of poetry. They could talk of thought and philosophy together. He was educated and cultured and knew how to speak, and when she played his piano her joy seemed complete.

Gordon was wealthy and intelligent; sure of himself. He knew what he wanted, and he wasn't one to waste time. Things moved too quickly for Sarah to see what was happening. She basked in the rich pleasure of the dream, not realizing that Gordon dominated her days, not feeling the silken bands that bound her to him.

Then one evening she rose from the piano to find him there, too close to her, and kissing her suddenly. His kiss was sweet and smooth, yet demanding. She pulled away from him, trembling and alarmed.

"Come, Sarah, does it really surprise you to know I love you? Surely you must have read it in my eyes?"

She turned from him, struggling against the strange, new feeling. He didn't touch her but held her with his eyes.

"You may not know if you love me . . . I think you do. But that will come. And this . . ." He swept his arm to indicate the room: the draperies and fine pictures, the polished wood tables, the gleaming piano standing silent now. "All this should belong to you, Sarah. You deserve it! Your spirit appreciates these things. Marry me, Sarah, and let me make you happy."

She didn't sleep that night; her crisis had come, and she must face what she had run away from for so long. She knew that Gordon believed he could make her happy; she even knew that probably he was right. *Do I love him, even a little?* she asked herself. *Can I ever love him?* It's true she hungered for the things that he could give her. Was there anything else her spirit hungered for?

The face came into her mind of its own will. The features were not as smooth and polished as Gordon's; the eyes were less startling, the hair a lighter hue. It was the hardened face of a woodsman, seasoned by struggle, yet the eyes in the face were sensitive eyes.

She closed her eyes and blotted out the face. The face was a ghost, a haunting, nothing more. Gordon was warm, real flesh, and Gordon loved her. The cruel face didn't love her anymore. And Gordon offered her peace and comfort and pleasure. The things she had wanted so badly, for so long—Gordon had made them into reality. All she had to do was reach out and take them. All she had to do was open her hands.

Through the long weeks of winter Jacob persisted. He read and reread his scriptures, and he learned how to pray. He could see how his prayers had progressed from their feeble beginnings; there was power now when he pleaded with the Lord; he was doing his part, and he believed that the Lord would do His.

Jacob discovered that his old friend, Doc Hardy, was making a trip to Hannibal. A cousin of the doctor was dying from some unusual malady, and Ethan Hardy was anxious to study the case, hopeful that he might learn and yet be helpful at the same time. Hannibal lay on the banks of the Mississippi; not far to the north on the opposite bank sat the Illinois town of Nauvoo.

Jacob hurriedly composed a letter to Sarah, and Ethan agreed to carry the letter for him, assuring Jacob in his quiet, solemn manner that he would find someone to convey it on to Nauvoo. It was more than Jacob had ever hoped would happen. The letter, if it reached Sarah, might ease her pain, might make the waiting lighter for her to bear. He had left so much unexplained, unanswered, unspoken; his letter might bridge the gap till he saw her again.

Ira had sulked and wheedled and complained until Luke had come and taken the boy with him. In March an early thaw broke up the ice, and water ran along the still-hard earth, swelling streams and filling deep the fields whose soil was too unsoftened to receive it. Men talked of floods and watched the rising waters and cursed the early warmth as enemy.

Luke, out checking bridges, paid a visit, and made sure to say to Jacob before he left, "Looks like spring might just decide to come early. I hope so. My boys are restless—if you know what I mean."

Jacob read full well his uncle's meaning but didn't give him the satisfaction of a reply. He wouldn't let himself worry, it was too early yet; why worry about the thing before it happened?

The warm spell stuck and the snows continued to run, then the skies grew black and rained new moisture onto the saturated land. The fields disappeared; the fence posts drowned and dwindled. Where there wasn't water there was black mud, thick and sucking. The earth was sodden and dripping, and still the rains came. Even the sun was watery in the sky, and everything looked washed away and grey.

Alice came over unexpectedly. Her father was in need of help and had sent her for Jacob. Jacob rode back with her and worked all night beside her father and brothers digging new trenches for the filthy waters, diverting streams, and dragging the stiff, bloated bodies of dead sheep and cattle out of the debris.

Alice was there now and then with something hot to drink and food to eat. Jacob noticed that she looked pretty; she was pale, and her hard eyes glistened, but she looked pretty. For him it was a dead kind of beauty which had lost the power to reach him any more. Alice didn't try to speak to him or touch him, and he couldn't read what was happening behind the cold, lashed eyes.

For the first time in a week Jacob spent the next evening at home. He sat with his mother and listened to the rain. Laura, watching Jacob, felt that something was coming. So she wasn't surprised when he suddenly closed his book and looked at her across the space of the room. She wanted to stop him; if she thought it would work she might have. But she had been watching him long enough to know that nothing could kill what he carried inside of him.

"I don't know how to break this gently, mother—"

175

"You've never had to break things gently with me. Tell me straight, Jacob; give me that consideration."

"In the spring I'm going back to Nauvoo," he said.

"And how do you propose to manage that, Jacob?"

"I've already made arrangements for help for you; everything's taken care of and in order—"

"That's not what I meant!"

"You mean Luke. I don't know quite yet."

"Well, you'd better know; that's one thing you'd best be sure of."

"I can't be sure how. I just know it will all work out."

She couldn't help showing her disdain of that opinion. "I can't understand your love for the Mormon people," she told him. "I struggle against hating them every day of my life."

He had promised his father to love and look after his mother. He wished that he had known his father better. It seemed he would have felt much the same as Jacob did now. Surely his father would want him to be a man; to face life when it came and carve out his share. Surely he had the right to seek out his own love, to know the joy and fulfillment his father had felt!

He looked at his mother, knowing he could never tell her, knowing that she would never understand. He opened his mouth to try, but the moment froze there, for the room suddenly burst with faces and movement and sound. He was on his feet in a moment, moving with the drawn-faced, worried men, catching only broken fragments of what they were saying.

The bridge over Sunday's Creek had collapsed and broken, and men and horses been tossed into the flood. But who he didn't know, nor even how many. Someone said three, and he heard another shout ten—ten men and horses crushed by the crumbling timber, choked by the muddy water and the rain. He grabbed some rope and a pick and another lantern; anything that came to his hand that he thought would help. He pulled his slicker hastily around him.

The quiet rain was deceiving; it came down steady, and could chill a man after minutes under it. He mounted and hastily joined the waiting men. Seth Sheppard, one of Alice's brothers, rode by

176

him. He pushed his horse close beside Jacob's, cupped his hands, and shouted above the storm,

"Luke and your brother, Ira, went down with the men."

Jacob turned and stared at him stupidly. Had he heard the boy right? Seth nodded at Jacob's look.

"Follow me, I know a shorter way to the spot."

Jacob turned off from the others and followed Seth. Seth was moving fast, though the ground was loose and slippery, and soon he was only a darkened shape ahead. But Seth had been right; in moments Jacob spotted the water — a dark mass, churning and tumbling straight ahead, roaring its own dull challenge above the rain. Jacob rode the line of the bank as close to the seeping, slipping mud as he thought he dared. He slowed his horse and motioned for Seth to go on, then listened for some sound other than wind and rain. He rode till his ears seemed to pound with the howl of the water, till his eyes ached from staring into the shapeless dark.

How long could a man survive in this kind of torrent? The strength of the water was a thousand times the strength of a man; how soon would a struggling person weaken and stop? He inched his horse unwillingly closer to the water and leaned out, feeling the cold spray on his face.

It was then that he heard the first faint cry for help. For a moment he thought it was only the whine of the wind. Then it came again, with somehow a different tone — a human sound, though he couldn't make out the words. He felt every muscle along his body tense and tighten. He rode till his horse's forelocks were licked with foam and the frightened animal refused to be driven further. He called till his own throat burned with the tearing sound. Perhaps he had only imagined he heard a voice. Then it came again, faint still, but it sounded closer. He left the horse and crouched by the water's edge, searching, afraid he might miss what he had to see.

The water ran from his hat down his face in rivulets. He brushed it away impatiently, aware that his hand was cold against his skin, aware that his bent knees ached with the cramping dampness. If someone was really out there he must have missed him. Jacob rose clumsily to his feet and stretched his sore muscles.

Suddenly there was a face so close to his own that he started back in terror at seeing it. At first he thought the face must be drowned and dead; it lifted and rose, then dipped under the muddy swirl. The eyes were wide and staring, the jaw muscles set, the wet hair clinging like seaweed about the face. A sudden swell heaved the man much closer to the shore. Jacob flung the rope and screamed to the face, wading into the cold, sucking water as far as he dared.

The face bobbed drunkenly, heaving the body with it. Then the cold eyes, staring, unseeing, moved in the head and looked at Jacob, who screamed and pushed out further — grabbing the trunk of a tree still rooted in place that leaned far into the river and over the flood. He hung there, reaching for the man through the fast-moving current. The eyes that had looked at Jacob were Luke Morgan's eyes! In a moment the water would carry him out and past, and Jacob's chance to save him would be gone.

The eyes were filling slowly with recognition, and the dawning realization of hope again. An arm shot out of the muddy swirl toward him and Jacob grabbed it, but the force of the water tore it out of his hands, leaving only a jagged piece of coat that he clung to, shaking.

Jacob waited and watched for the head to come near again, an eternity through the screaming, drenching dark. Then suddenly, eerily, Luke was there once more, but the hand that flailed and caught his was weak and cold. Jacob closed his fingers around the wrist and held on tight, and pulled the body toward him inch by inch. The weight of the angry water dragged against him, the fingers that held his own wrist slipped and fell. He tightened his grip, but his arm was turning numb. He called out, trying to encourage his uncle to fight, to hang on. But he couldn't even hear the sound of his own voice.

It seemed he had hung here forever, fighting the water; he couldn't tell if he was making progress at all. Then numbly he felt the drag of the water lessen. Luke's shoulders cleared the flood, and then his chest. Jacob grabbed him under the armpits, but he slipped and fell hard against the water, and they started the painful process over again.

At some point Jacob realized he would save Luke — he could do it; the lashing river had lost its prey. As the body rose and the weak arms reached toward him, Jacob paused, and the white, drained face went grey. The bleary, bloodshot eyes stared into his now. He grabbed the tangled hair and pulled the face closer, pushed back the hair and screamed against the ear,

"My freedom, Luke, my freedom for your life."

A spark rose in the drained and deadened eyes. The head moved imperceptibly in assent. "You understand, Luke, my freedom for your life? Tell me! I want to know you understand."

The purple lips moved slowly, but no sound came. Jacob pressed his ear against the breathless mouth. "Freedom" — the word was formed, not even a whisper. The water tore and Jacob's muscles sagged. He hefted Luke and dragged him through the water, and the ground came reeling to meet them as they fell.

Jacob lay there, drawing in breath in great, rasping gulps, then crawled over to Luke and forced the water out of his lungs. He rubbed the soaked skin and massaged it over and over until the clenched, white lips moved and Luke's breath caught, a mere gurgle at the back of his throat. Jacob worked longer, until Luke was breathing more evenly. The drowned eyes blinked and flickered and swept Jacob's face.

"My life for your freedom. Say it, Luke," he demanded. "Swear it to me."

The grey eyes flickered again.

"Now," Jacob hissed, and the flaccid muscles trembled in the cheeks and jaw as Luke attempted to speak.

"My life . . ." the sounds came slowly, but Jacob waited. "For . . . your . . . freedom . . . I swear."

It was only then that Jacob rose to his feet and dragged himself to the road and hailed the invisible riders out in the night. Someone heard him, and soon there were other men, and warm blankets and strong whiskey, and laughter and talk. Three of the men had been rescued; that was all. Ira was one, Seth told him, riding up. The rest were lost.

Luke was lucky to have his life. Yes sir, Jacob and fate had given it back to him. Jacob listened to the talk but moved into the shadows, his numbed mind repeating what he alone knew; from that ugly struggle in the darkness and the greedy water, fate had handed his own life back again.

24

"I thought you were interested in him," Sarah's father was saying. "I was hoping perhaps something might grow between you two."

"It might have, if things were different," she told him slowly. She took a deep breath, then spoke the words out loud. "I can't marry one man when I'm still in love with another."

Her father studied her face, and his eyes were kind. "Do you know what you're doing, Sarah?" he asked her gently.

"Yes, father," she answered. "I know, and I'm all right. I think that Martin's dying made it harder. I clung to a girlish, romantic love I had lost. I didn't know what real love between a man and a woman was like."

He nodded, his deep eyes studying out the matter.

"Gordon's coming has been good for me," she said. "He's forced me to grow up, to face myself. He's . . . he's brought all my illusions out into the open."

"Does Gordon know this?"

"As much as he needs to." She smiled, reflecting upon her last scene with Gordon beside the piano. His green eyes had been deep and shadowed and his voice an instrument used to draw her when he said, "You're making a mistake, Sarah, so be careful. After today I shall never ask you again. Think well before you give me a final no."

But she had told him no right then, before she left him, and it seemed the sea-green eyes held more anger and pride in them than pain.

"Don't you see, father," she attempted, needing at least one person to understand. "Now I know — and it doesn't really matter what happens."

He pulled her over and held her in his thin, kind arms. It was strange, she thought, leaning her head against him. There was no pain when she thought of Gordon, and the pain of Martin had become a sweet, nostalgic thing. All that was left was this consuming love for Jacob. It was with her, waking or sleeping, whatever she did. And she knew it would be with her until she died.

One fine morning only days later Myles ran over, waving a dirty, crumpled envelope in his hand. He had picked it up in town, he explained to Sarah. She took it in wonder, then recognized the writing, or thought she did—but it couldn't possibly be! Myles watched her, his blue eyes brimming with curious delight, but she abandoned him and fled to the barn, where she could read the letter alone.

"Dear Sarah, this is an unexpected opportunity," the letter began, "and I haven't much time or space to express how I feel. I waited for you to come to the river that day. There was so much I had wanted to tell you before I left . . ."

Sarah clutched the letter. Of course! Why hadn't she recognized that scene she had stumbled upon as Alice's doing? Why had she run away like a little fool? She could see Jacob now, wandering beside the frozen river, searching and longing as she had been longing for him!

She pounded the packed, brittle straw in angry frustration, yearning to recall that instant and live it again and make it the way she had wanted it to be. She returned to the letter and read the strong, bold hand, and the words sent a warmth that tingled along her skin; words she had dreamed of during the long and lonely nights —and they had lived inside Jacob's head, just waiting for her.

"I will come in the spring," he wrote, "I am coming back." "I will come . . ." "I will come . . ." on those words hung her very life! Her love wasn't walking blindly any longer. She could see ahead to the promise of the spring. Each grey and sodden day that passed brought the bright promise closer to reality.

It was March and he probably ought to wait until April. But waiting was such an uneasy thing to do. And Sarah, he hoped, would be expecting him. He only had Luke's word, not the word of his men.

181

He'd be pushing his luck to sit around here waiting, reminding the men of how he was cheating them. It stuck in Luke's craw, he knew, to owe anything to Jacob, especially something as total as his life. The sooner Jacob was gone from their sight, the better. Besides, he felt an urgency to go, as though if he waited longer it might be too late.

His mother was more unbending than he had expected.

"When you walk away from here you're no longer my son."

"Only if that's the way you want it, mother."

"I! It is you who is doing the thing, Jacob. You will be too distant, and your ways too removed from mine. We will seldom, if ever, see each other again."

"Mother, you're being gloomy —"

"I'm being realistic." Her face as she talked was passive and safely masked. "Your father meant for this land to be your land, Jacob. You've earned it long since, yet you're willing to give it up?"

It was a question more than a statement, yet what could he answer? She could not even guess the pain it would cost him to turn his back, to walk away from all that had meant life to him for so long.

"How can I leave this to Ira?" she asked, growing angry. "He's got no more sense than his uncle — he'd bring it to ruin. Your father won't sleep in his grave if —"

"Stop it, mother!"

It was a cry as much as anything, and Laura stopped. She had been torturing him, torturing both of them, and she knew it. But she stopped now, gazing at her son with dark, hollow eyes.

"You're right, Jacob. Nothing I say will make any difference."

She left the room and he didn't attempt to stop her. For the pain she was suffering there was nothing he could do.

He was packed and ready before the last stars had faded. He was taking a few things of his own, things he felt he had a right to take. He had said his good-byes and made his peace with the land, and with the graves of the two men who had so greatly influenced his life.

He ate now, one last time in his mother's house, feeling heavily the awkward strangeness of parting; then he rose and walked to the mantel and lifted down the one remaining thing he intended to take. Both his mother and Ira watched him — Ira, who had come home to observe the last rites with a cold, malicious satisfaction.

Jacob turned and said, "I'm taking the gun; the Greener by rights is mine." He caressed the long, smooth barrel, his mind crowding with memories of when he was a boy, when his father taught him to shoot with this very gun.

"Nothing by rights is yours, Jacob, any more."

The ugly hatred still soured the boy's young voice. Half a dozen times Jacob had tried to talk to his brother, but the meanness, the resentment, went deeper than he had thought. He didn't mind parting with Luke as enemies, but to leave his own brother an enemy — that was different.

"Well, I'm taking the gun, rights or no rights, Ira. I'll not see it used for evil as you would do. It's never served that kind of a purpose yet."

"Take it and good riddance," Ira hissed. "Uncle Luke says he's happy to see the back of you, and he hopes you'll be smart enough not to show your face in these parts again."

Laura stood and spoke, her voice full-toned and alive.

"That will do, Ira. I'll hear no more of such talk in my home."

Ira glared, but he didn't protest, and the room fell silent around them. Laura walked over to her son and placed her hands on Jacob's shoulders.

"I can't send you from me empty," the rich voice said. She walked again, this time to the table beside the fire. She moved aside her sewing and picked up the book, the heavy leather volume that rested there. Slowly she returned to where Jacob stood and placed the ancient Bible into his hands.

"This has been in the Morgan family since time began. It goes with the first-born, Jacob, so take it now."

He touched the smooth, cool leather, then found her hand and pressed it, and she responded and closed her thin, strong fingers over his. Their eyes met and held and spoke for the last time.

"Take this . . . and my love . . . and your own sense of who you are. That ought to suffice to keep you, Jacob," she said.

He kissed her and laid his hand on her thin, soft hair, then turned away and left her standing there. His boots sounded loud as they clattered down the steps; an intrusion in the silence of the dawn.

He mounted and rode away, and he didn't look back. He wouldn't have been able to see much, anyway. Hot tears burned his eyes and he cried as a boy would cry. But when he was a boy tears had eased the pain. Now they made no difference—no difference at all.

Jacob camped that night on a lonely stretch of land. The weather was clear and fine, and he was making good progress; two more days ought to see him safe at the Mississippi.

He tethered the animals and fed and watered them first, then gathered wood for a fire to cook his meal. A brilliant sunset was staining the western skies. He stopped to watch the colors melt and blend, subtle shades he couldn't even put a name to. He was lost in the gentle spell that the beauty laid, and he heard nothing, no warning, before the swath of fire caught round his neck and slid down his shoulder blade.

He grabbed for the thing, but it slithered, razor sharp, through his hands, leaving smears of blood where it bit into his flesh. He whirled, but the cock of a pistol stopped him cold. So he stood, breathing heavily, watching the other man move out from the bushes. When he saw the face a hot terror licked at his stomach, burning him more than the graze of the burning whip.

Pete licked his lips and gazed across at Jacob. "Remember what I told you, Jake?" he said. "I ain't bound by no promise yer uncle made." He grinned and flicked at a twig with the tongue of the whip. "I'm here to keep my word, boy; I'm here to kill you."

The words sounded so simple, so sane in the quiet air. The pack horse twitched his tail at an itching fly; a squirrel paused on a tree branch and cocked his head, then continued his jerky passage along the trunk. Simple, ordinary things kept going on around him —yet he faced a bitter death in this lovely place.

Jacob didn't answer, nor move, and Pete took his time, enjoying the thing too much to hurry it. From the corner of his eye

Jacob could see his father's rifle leaning against his pack where he last had set it. Impossible to reach it from where he stood. But if he drew Pete forward to fight him in that direction . . .

Pete moved, replacing the pistol at his side. The mean, narrow eyes became mere slits in the creased, pocked face as he flicked his wrist, and the leather whip twitched and jerked like a living thing. Jacob moved a step or two back, then another, veering in the direction of his gun.

There was a short, high hiss as the whip reached out and caught him, biting savagely through his shirt and across his chest. He winced with the pain as the evil thing drew back, dangling like a crazy extension of Pete's arm; coiling, uncoiling, waiting to strike again. He smiled across at Pete contemptuously.

"You're a coward. Why don't you drop that thing and fight me like a man?"

Pete's lips twitched, compressed into a thin, bloodless line. "I ain't no fool. I ain't here to fight you. I'm here to kill you, Jake, jest like I said."

After that Jacob didn't speak again, but concentrated on the singing whip; trying to outguess it, dodging the blows. But too many of them began to find their mark. Again and again he heard the leather crack, then felt the lash of fire across his skin, tearing deeper, bringing the savage pain. The land beneath him tilted, then it blurred; he fought to keep his footing and not fall. The whine of one stroke barely fell and ended, before another sang above his head. There was a strange, high ringing in his ears. He stumbled, crawling now on hands and knees. But Pete moved with the whip; he had seen Jacob's purpose. The twitching serpent snapped against the wood and sent the rifle sprawling out of reach.

Jacob rose then with a low growl in his throat. The blows that fell were living fire now, flailing against his back remorselessly. He braced himself to ignore the punishing blows, and concentrated everything left in him on the hopeless purpose that would be his only chance.

In one swift jerk he grabbed the whirling leather, snapped it, and it flung from out Pete's hand. Jacob dived then, and his fingers found the rifle, smearing the smooth barrel with his blood. Pete's hand was moving, ripping out his pistol. Jacob twisted, rolled, and pulled the trigger.

He heard the dull scream as the lead bit wood and splintered. Pete's arm swung, aimed; Jacob closed his eyes and jumped and felt the bullet crease along his shoulder. He spun around, but Pete had taken cover. He spied the tossed whip, bent and scooped it up, then heard a movement to his left and fired.

He ducked behind a bush and, when his gun was ready, fired again into the swaying trees in front of him. His nostrils clogged with the smell of blood and powder, and he clenched his teeth against the urge to retch. Then there was a sudden pain inside his arm, exploding with a force that blurred his eyes. He leveled his rifle in the direction of the noise, and heard his weapon shoot before it fell, and he fell with it, swirling in the pain. But somehow his fingers found the Greener again, and he sat upright and held the weapon against him, steadied it as well as he could, then aimed and fired.

Pete wasn't good with guns and Jacob was. He had that small advantage and he must press it. He heard a scuffle in the bushes and shot once more, then listened—straining now for any sign of movement he might see.

But the horse leaped out before him, scattering stones and dirt and soft pine needles and bounding forward before Jacob could reload. Pete was crouched in the saddle and hunched down low; Jacob couldn't tell if he was hit. He leveled his gun and fired at the retreating figure, but the horse kept moving, and Jacob let him go. It was a pretty good bet that a bullet had found its mark. He didn't know; but at least for the moment he was safe. He stumbled to the stream and bathed the caked blood from off him, the icy water numbing some of the pain.

The burning hurt of the beating he could take; that would go away. It was the gunshot in his arm that worried him. It was difficult for him to examine the wound and he couldn't tell how deep, how bad it was. At least the bullet wasn't lodged inside, and he wouldn't be plagued with the fear of infection. He bathed it and bound it and swallowed a piece of dried beef with a little of the river water, then struggled to stand. He couldn't tell how long Pete would stay away. He might be hidden, watching him right now. The thought made the small hairs along the back of his neck start to prickle. He had to do something to shake Pete from his trail. If he wasn't waiting now, he would be back.

Painfully, slowly, he saddled the tired horses. The venture he had in mind was a risky one. It would lose him two days, maybe three — and he wasn't certain he could stand that loss and still make it to the river. But he didn't see how he had much other choice. He would cross the narrow, winter-bleak cottonwood bottoms. It was Myles who had shown him this other way to go; longer, more difficult country, but less traveled. He would take it now in hopes of losing Pete.

Once the hollow shadows settled, the night came quickly. Dark land met dark sky in a velvet expanse, and the stars slithered and shimmered across the blackness. Jacob blinked his eyes and stared until the stars held still. He climbed a high, narrow ridge, hugging the tree line. He rode until the night thinned and retreated and a high sun washed the greyness out of the sky. He rode until his head fell and his bruised shoulders ached, and his knees shook trying to grip the horse's side. Once over the ridge, in a shaded little gully, he allowed himself to slide from the punishing saddle and crawl deep where the bright, searching sunlight couldn't go.

When he awoke the sun was hot on his face and the welts from the whip felt tightened and painfully drawn. He forced himself to eat and then built a fire, cleansed his wound and packed it well with the cooled grey ash, then bound it again with a fresh, clean strip of cloth. He wouldn't risk building a fire when night came on.

He felt stronger now, but his body still craved rest. He slept until the shadows fell again, then rose and mounted and started on his way. Some of the sores were festering on his back. He stared into the blackness, and every sound set the hair on his head bristling like the hackles on a dog. How many days to the river — he dared not think. He closed his eyes against all thinking and wanting, and simply rode.

Sometimes he wondered how he stayed in the saddle. He rode and rode, forcing himself to go on, ignoring the chills and the ringing in his head. His father's rifle rode across his lap, and his eyes flicked from side to side, searching the shadows, his fingers unconsciously playing along his gun.

Tomorrow he would shift and ride with the sun. He had seen no sign yet of anyone following. But he had to be careful, he had to make it now! He couldn't let anything come that close to defeating him again. So he rode with the darkness across the lonely land where no eyes could see his passage nor mark his way.

Sarah couldn't help herself; she watched for Jacob. She walked the river often, anyway. So she took to wandering down where the ferry beached and searching among the people who came ashore. And soon the frequent walks became daily ritual, and nothing could stop her self-appointed charge. It was almost a compulsion and she knew it, but it helped control her eagerness and her fear. A stray whisper somewhere inside still persisted: *What if he doesn't come? What if he can't? What if something prevents him from making it here?* She couldn't believe that happiness could really reach her, while she only sat and waited for it to appear.

So the days of March warmed into early April and the face of winter lifted from the land. People stirred with the warmth in the air and grew restless for action, and the growing city sprang into life again. There was more now for Sarah to watch as she walked the streets, and happy faces to greet her everywhere. Even the ferryman looked for her regular coming, and he smiled and doffed his cap to the graceful girl who hovered about his boat like an anxious moth, flitting and watchful, then melting into thin air.

Dark things have trouble surviving in the spring. The loveliness was wilting Sarah's fears. There was beauty and new life wherever she looked. And she felt that she was part of the wakening, that the promise of this spring was meant for her, and that nothing could stop her bright tomorrows from happening.

When Jacob at last approached the Mississippi he was in a bad way, and he knew he was. His arm was swollen, his head was hot with fever. And the storm that had been threatening all day broke. It came down with force, like a black cloud that fell from the sky. Everything below it bent and cowered and tried to hide.

Jacob hid, too, crawling inside a shelter to wait out the uncontrolled fury of the storm. The fever beat at his temples and under his skin and pushed at the backs of his eyes, making them throb. He could see that it was deserted down by the ferry; no one would cross the river in weather like this. The fingers of the cold rain found him and he crept in deeper, wet through and shivering, crawling with fever and pain.

He clenched his teeth and prayed for patience to outwait the storm. He listened to the high wind whine and flourish, dwindle to gentle flutters, then rise again. The old trees creaked and bent above his head. The wind's will was to snap and break the branches. But the scarred trees bowed and curved and rose with the mighty wind, moving in intricate harmony with the enemy that would destroy them.

As Jacob watched, the branches moved wilder and faster, until they were swirling in dark rings high above him. He knew the convulsing motion was in his own head—for he felt light and formless and swirling like the trees. He closed his eyes against the giddy motion, until the whirlpool carried him away.

25

The storm had been sudden, bringing cold, gusty winds, and rain that would most likely turn into snow before morning. Sarah, watching it stream down the windowpane, felt a restless frustration with the storm. She had had plans of her own for this afternoon. How dare the cold rain thwart her suddenly?

Tomorrow was her mother's birthday, and now was her only chance to purchase her little presents secretly. And she needed more raisins and nutmeg for the cake. Her mother was sitting with Julia Simpson, who was in labor, and she might not be back until hours after dark. Now was her only time. Sarah walked to the window. She would wait an hour or so and see what happened. Then, no matter what, she was going outside.

When Sarah left, the storm had eased a little. She scurried on her errands, enjoying the rain, loving the rich, musky smells that the moisture magically drew out. The fresh air and the fragrances gave her a heady feeling. She turned, almost without thinking, toward the river, where a group of stragglers gathered around the ferry dock.

A stranger with a large leather portmeau stood on the landing. He was richly dressed, from his fine, brushed leather shoes to the tall, beaver hat that rested jauntily on his head. Sarah, drawing closer, heard him say, "Thanks again, captain, for bringing us across in spite of the storm."

He pressed some money into Captain Nelson's hand, and Sarah could see the captain's eyes light with pleasure. She also saw that the passenger wasn't alone. A small, quiet woman had glided against his side. She looked pale, and Sarah could see she was worn and tired. A bright streak of lightning flashed, and the sound of thunder soon followed. The woman edged closer and leaned against the man.

"I don't know what we'd have done in the storm. I had to get my Mary here to a doctor. When these fainting spells come on her it's dangerous, see, and . . ."

"That's all right, sir, happy to do it." The ferryman doffed his cap and grinned widely at his grateful, generous passenger. "I'd hate to see anyone stuck in a storm like this."

The ferryman turned, but the passenger pulled at his sleeve.

"I wonder . . ."

"Yes? . . ." Captain Nelson was losing interest. Sarah was moving away, but she caught the stranger's next words and halted.

"It's probably nothing . . . but I can't get it off my mind. Across there, when we were waiting by the river, I thought I heard someone calling out of the storm."

Sarah felt a cold prickle trail down her backbone. Nelson cocked his head, interested again.

"Like what?" he asked. "What did you think you heard, exactly?"

"I can't be sure . . . it sounded like a man calling."

"Edward walked back a distance and looked, but he saw no one." The woman's voice was sweeter than Sarah had expected.

"It was eerie," the man continued, "like a voice coming out of nowhere."

"Did the voice cry for help?"

"No, it sounded more like . . . 'Home . . . home . . . miles . . . home . . .' Those two words I seemed to distinguish, like someone babbling in fever and out of his head."

"Did you look around real good?"

"I tried to. But the rain was heavy then, and Mary—"

"Well, leave it alone . . ." The captain shuddered, squinted into the storm, then shrugged his shoulders. "It's common to think you hear voices out in a storm. I remember once when I first took over this ferry, we found a man who'd been . . ."

The captain's nasal voice faded. All Sarah heard were the stranger's words in her head: "home . . . miles . . . home." Myles . . . home . . . The voice in the storm was Jacob! She knew it! She didn't know why, but she knew it was true. Jacob was lying somewhere across the river, in the rain that was turning to sleet and might turn to snow!

How long was it—maybe an hour or two until darkness? Less, with the way the storm clouds swallowed the sky. She waited until the man and his wife were leaving, then caught the ferryman just as he turned away.

"Could a man lost out in this storm live through the night?"

He looked at the small, bright face with the clinging hair. This was the girl he had seen at the wharf so often. The pretty girl he smiled at over the crowds.

"That all depends, miss," he answered cautiously. "If the man wasn't hurt I think he would be all right. It's not bitter winter, I don't think he'd freeze this late—"

"But if he was hurt, then? What if the man was hurt?"

"Now, dearie, I can't rightly answer that. I'd have to know where he was hurt and how long, and how badly . . . and then—" The blue eyes glistened like pieces of shining glass, and the pretty mouth began to tremble slightly.

"How much will you charge to take me across the river?"

"I'm sorry, honey, wild horses couldn't drag me back there. See those dark clouds churning off there to the west? Once they hit again—"

"But a man may be dying out there!"

"Now, honey—"

"It's true! I know it! You must believe me!"

He squinted at Sarah, then pulled her out of the downpour under the lean-to protection he had built. The curious feeling he'd had about this girl began to eat at him now like a rat at a rope. There was something strong that had brought her here each day. And now this crazy talk about someone dying! He impatiently shook the arm he held. "Now, girl, you'd better explain what you're talkin' about."

Sarah took a deep breath and tried to steady her shaking. She had to sound sane, she had to make sense when she spoke.

"I heard what the gentleman told you about the voice, sir. And that voice could be someone I know out there in the storm."

"What? You ain't makin' any sense yet, dearie."

"Well, it doesn't make sense, not really," she cried in despair. "Remember what the voice in the storm was calling? 'Miles and home'—that's what the stranger said. I have a brother named Myles, sir, don't you see? Myles—I think the voice was calling for Myles."

The captain paused. "You think it was really a voice, then?"

"Yes, yes—I know it was!"

The captain looked out at the darkened, rain-drenched waters. He thought, and he didn't answer, and Sarah cried, "Please take me over! Please, captain, don't let him die!"

He looked down at the girl. He knew what it meant to be haunted. If he turned her away, he'd never have any peace. And if a man were really found tomorrow morning . . .

He drew out a slicker and handed it to the girl. "Put this on, miss, and you do exactly what I tell you!"

He tugged at the ropes that bound them against the shore. He was taking an awful chance, he knew he was. The ropes pulled loose and the boat shot into the water. The craft shivered under him, swept by the force of the river. He struggled to keep her steady, his tired arms aching, and cursed himself for the fool he knew he was.

Sarah thought they would never get to the other side. Once there she strained at the captain's slow, careful ways as he firmly attached the boat and secured it tightly. Screaming to each other above the sound of the water, they each took a different direction and started to search.

Sarah walked a few paces, calling Jacob's name, then stopped and listened for an answer through the storm. There was nothing, but she refused to become discouraged. She went on, though her steps drew her further away from the shore. She called and called, though her throat was beginning to ache now. Then she heard it. A voice! And she froze still where she stood.

Jacob, dozing, had heard the new voice intruding, mocking him, calling him — only to be swallowed again by the heavy waves of darkness he struggled through. But this voice was somehow different from the other. What was it saying? This voice was calling his name . . . "Jacob . . . Jacob . . . Jacob . . . Are you out there?" This voice did something crazy to him inside. He ought to know the voice . . . He rose on his elbow and called back as loudly as he could. The voice didn't go away as the other had; the new voice answered! He gathered his strength and called to the voice again.

Sarah, sure now that it was Jacob out there calling, fought down an urge to run toward the sound. She knew she must follow the faint voice carefully. Again it replied, and again, till she knew she was nearer. It was coming from there, from those bushes off to her left! "Oh, Jacob," she cried, and ran the last little distance.

Then suddenly there was nothing under her feet, and a white-hot pain leaped from her wrist up into her arm. The man came from nowhere, the man who held her against him and twisted her arm cruelly behind her back. She gasped and cried out, but he twisted her arm up higher and growled something to her that she didn't quite hear through the pain. She couldn't see his face, this man who held her, but his voice, when he spoke, sent shivers along her spine.

"Jacob, I've got her! You know what I'll do with her, Jacob. You come out here, Jake, if you wanta see her alive."

The brute voice cut through the smothering folds of darkness. Something in Jacob shivered, then settled, then cleared. He moved, though movement sent fire throughout his body.

Sarah could hear the sounds of Jacob moving. The man holding her heard them, too, and she felt him tense. He loosened her arm a little and pulled her to face him.

"Listen to me, you'd better not try to be brave. You try anything, and I'll hurt him more, I swear it. And in case you're wonderin', I found the ferryboat captain. He's out cold and tied, so he ain't gonna come and help ya."

Horrified, repulsed, Sarah pulled back from the leering face that breathed against her. Pete slapped her across the cheek with the back of his hand. She cried out; she had never felt that kind of pain. He twisted her arm behind her hard again, and his other hand held the cold point of a pistol against her temple.

Jacob heard the sound of the blow, and the cry that followed. He rose to his feet and stood there uncertainly.

"Jake?"

Jacob moved and walked slowly into the clearing. Sarah cried out, aghast at the sight of him.

"Well, Jake," Pete drawled, "you look like you're almost done for. Guess this won't take me as long as I thought it would."

"How did you find me?" Jacob noticed a dirty rag wound and tied around Pete's leg, and the stains of travel that showed in his tattered clothes.

Pete chuckled, deep in his throat. "I'll have to admit that you ditched me, Jake, you did. But you didn't hurt me much. This is only a flesh wound." He thrust out his leg and spat, then threw back his head, and his ugly eyes were crafty and mean and small. "I knew you'd come to the river eventually. I been waitin' here for you, Jake. I'm a patient man."

194

"Let her go. You can do anything you'd like with me. Just let her go."

"That's big of you, Jake, that offer. But I think I'd rather do what I like with the both of you."

Sarah felt a slow, freezing terror creep through her.

"It wouldn't be worth it to hurt her," Jacob said. Sarah wondered how his voice could sound so calm, when she wanted to scream and struggle and cry at once.

"They'd find you, Pete. Her brother would easily trace you. You couldn't get away with this one at all. Kill me; you'd better be content with that."

"My whip. You give me my whip, then. It's better that way. Much nicer—much slower—" The gun pressed at Sarah's head. "Remember, Jake, you pull anything, she's dead."

Jacob came back slowly and threw something over toward them. It landed at Pete's feet, and he bent to pick it up. When Sarah saw the thick, black whip she started to tremble. She closed her eyes and prayed that she wouldn't scream.

The whip lashed out with a shudder and then a whine. Jacob swayed as the force of it fell on his torn, scarred shoulder. The man with the whip put his lips against Sarah's ear.

"You watch this, honey, it's gonna be a pretty sight." He raised his voice so that Jacob could hear him, too. "I think the little gal ought to see this, Jacob. Watch me cut you to ribbons before her eyes."

He made an ugly sound, deep in his throat. He kissed Sarah on her neck and against her hair, then whispered, "When I'm done with Jake, I've got something else in mind for you."

In spite of her fear, Sarah struggled at the sound of his words. But he laughed at her and pulled her drawn arm higher, and brandished the black whip above him to strike again.

There was a loud crack, and Jacob waited to feel the leather, the agony of pain grinding into pain. It didn't come, and he opened his eyes in wonder to see Pete slide and slither and fall to the ground, limp like the uncoiled whip that lay beside him.

His mind was too dull to recognize the gunshot. Sarah, unbound, was the first to see the man—the man on the big black horse who rode toward them. He scarcely glanced at her, but pushed past till he stood within inches of Jacob, then stopped his horse.

"We're even now, boy. We're even. You hear me, Jacob?" The voice was a mean growl, deep with authority.

"How did you—"

"Hell, it was easy to figure out. Soon as Pete didn't show up I knew what had happened. It wasn't no secret, Pete's feelings about you."

Jacob nodded. "I guess I owe you—"

"Damn, boy, you ain't listenin'. I saved your life, so I don't owe you anymore! I came here to even things, boy—I can't stand owin' nothin'." Luke looked down at the still body at his feet. "Too bad I had to kill Pete—but he'd have been no use to me now."

Jacob smiled very slowly and nodded in understanding.

"We're even now, boy?"

"We're even," Jacob agreed.

The black horse shook his neck and the long mane shimmered. Luke drew up the reins and pulled the horse's head.

"There's jest one more thing I want to tell you, Jacob." The lines in the hard face tightened as he went on. "If I meet you again, we'll be enemies, nothing more. You remember that, boy — you remember that all your life."

The black horse pranced then and gathered his legs beneath him and disappeared easily, blending into the storm.

Jacob stared across at the girl. She must be a vision—a vision grown out of nightmare, as spectral and unreal. But the vision moved and was suddenly there beside him, and the hands that touched him were a gentle woman's hands. He reached out tentative fingers and brushed her cheek. She caught his hand in her own and kissed the bruised fingers.

"Jacob . . ." There seemed no words that would satisfy.

"How did you find me? How did you know I was here?"

She smiled into his eyes, that were deep with wonder. "I don't know . . . I think my spirit heard yours, Jacob . . . Does that make sense? Do you think that could be true?"

"Yes, Sarah, I believe that love could speak that way."

196

The rain had stopped, but Sarah didn't notice. And for the first time in days Jacob no longer felt his pain.

"I love you, Jacob, I know that now for certain. Even if I had never seen your face again—"

"I have come so near to losing you," he whispered. His face was ashen; she smoothed the pained lines gently.

"But sometimes you can't find something until you almost lose it," she responded.

He looked through her shining eyes into her heart, and he knew that life had begun for him with this moment. He had been so near to her love, and yet so far; and he had found her only because he had found himself.

He leaned on her arm as they walked toward the river. Through the clearing rain they saw the fair city before them, curled in the curve of land on the opposite shore. The hand that builds the storms had destroyed the blackness and stretched a magnificent rainbow over their heads. The beauty and brightness seemed to reach down and touch them.

"A rainbow is for promise," Sarah said.

"Yes . . . and there is the city of promise shining ahead."

He took her face in his hands and kissed her gently, and it seemed to him that this woman he kissed he had never kissed before. She felt it, too, and nothing stood between them, and neither had ever tasted this ecstasy.

"Sarah," he said, "already the rainbow is fading. And even a city of promise can't always stand. The real promise is a power we carry inside us—"

"That doesn't need rainbows and music and poetry?"

"That's right, the promise is all those things together." He thought his heart would break with the joy it felt.

"Good," she whispered, brushing his hair back gently. "We don't need anything but each other, Jacob. We both know how to hold on to happiness."